HOW THE GRUMP SAVED CHRISTMAS

A SMALL-TOWN ROMANCE

CLAIRE KINGSLEY

D1513698

Always Have LLC

Published by Always Have, LLC

Edited by Eliza Ames

Cover Design: Lori Jackson

ISBN: 9798361694686

www.clairekingsleybooks.com

❀ Created with Vellum

"I will honor Christmas in my heart and try to keep it all the year."

~A Christmas Carol, Charles Dickens

ABOUT THIS BOOK

Hardworking Isabelle Cook has a serious problem. Her family farm, site of Tilikum's Christmas Village, is in trouble. Big trouble. And worst of all? The man trying to buy it is none other than the grumpiest, grinchiest man of them all —Elias Stoneheart.

That's a big nope. She's not letting *him* get involved. Not with his heart made of coal.

Elias Stoneheart is in the business of making money, not friends. Especially when his boss is promising a long-awaited promotion. All he has to do is convince one struggling family to sell their farm.

The problem? It's Cook Family Farm. And Isabelle Cook is his ex.

He might have history with Isabelle but this is just business. A Christmas-loving farm girl is not going to come between him and his ambition.

And Christmas? He hates it. Christmas Village needs to go.

But as Elias spends time in the small town, holiday sprit

—and Isabelle—get under his skin. And she might be the only one who can melt the ice around his heart.

Author's note: a sassy farm girl takes on a grumpy businessman in this cozy, snowy, small-town Christmas romance. Saucy banter, a guard donkey, plenty of holiday cheer, and a heartwarming happily ever after that will make you believe in the magic of Christmas.

A note about reading order: How the Grump Saved Christmas is a stand-alone holiday romance. It takes place in Tilikum, home of the Bailey Brothers series, and the timeline overlaps with Rewriting the Stars, Bailey Brothers Book 6. You can read How the Grump Saved Christmas before or after the Bailey Brothers. Either way works!

1

ELIAS

*T*he lobby coffee shop looked like the bastard love child of a Hallmark movie and an ugly Christmas sweater. Silver garland decorated the front counter, twinkle lights hung everywhere, and a Christmas tree decorated in coffee-themed ornaments and colorful blinking lights stood in the corner.

I almost turned around and left.

And then, the music. Were they serious? It was the beginning of November. Did they have to play the music, too?

An ominous voice in the back of my mind spoke: *it has begun.*

I'm dreaming of a white Christmas...

No, I wasn't. I was dreaming of a cup of dark roast—the coffee here was exceptional—and the shot of Irish whiskey I was going to add to it that were going to get me through the rest of this nightmare of an afternoon.

Really, if I could be dreaming of anything, it would be a deserted tropical beach with a gorgeous woman dressed in something sheer. But I had too damn much work to do to make that dream a reality.

Yet another reason this day was grating on my nerves. Who scheduled a holiday party for three o'clock in the afternoon at the beginning of November?

My boss, apparently. Or maybe HR had talked him into it. Either way, getting an email with a garish invitation complete with snowmen and candy canes, to a holiday party the first week of November was crap. I didn't care if they thought that meant more people could make it, since December was a busy month. It made it harder—impossible, even—for me to claim I had plans and skip it.

Not that I ever had holiday plans. But in December, I could say I did and no one asked questions. Early November? Harder to make an excuse.

Plus, this year I needed to play the game. That meant I had to come back to the office after my off-site meeting and show my face at this party.

The holiday music made my back tighten and my jaw hitch in annoyance. The lady in line in front of me was having a crisis of indecision. She babbled at the barista, talking a mile a minute. Her laugh grated on my nerves almost as much as the music. It was all I could do not to growl at her so she'd move out of my way.

Finally, she ordered something and paid. I stepped up to the counter. The barista was wearing a headband with blue and white snowflakes that bobbed when she moved.

"Happy holidays!" Her eyes were too wide, like she was slightly insane. Or maybe she was just overly caffeinated. "What can I get started for you?"

"Twelve-ounce dark roast with room."

"Room for cream?"

"No. For whiskey."

"Are you sure you don't want our special holiday blend?"

My jaw hitched again. I hated being questioned. "No."

"Okay, no problem. It's just really good and we only serve it for a limited time."

I had no idea why she thought I cared. She kept looking at me with those wide, crazy eyes, an inexplicable smile on her face.

Since she wasn't ringing up my order, I pulled my card out of my wallet and held it up with a scowl.

"Oh, sorry." She laughed and rang up my coffee.

I paid and the too-big smile never left her face.

My brow furrowed. "Why are you smiling like that?"

She shrugged. "I just love the holidays. Don't you?"

I eyed her with mild disgust. "No."

That finally got rid of the annoying grin. I moved down the counter to wait for my coffee, ignoring the tip jar and her half-hearted, *have a nice day*.

She didn't mean it and I wasn't going to.

It's the most wonderful time of the year...

No, it wasn't.

They couldn't have waited until after Thanksgiving? Not that I cared about that holiday, or any holiday for that matter. But this extra month of Christmas was making my life miserable.

My coffee came out and I got out of there as quickly as possible. In the lobby, a small knot of people were busy decorating a tall tree in the front window. I rolled my eyes and headed for the elevators.

Idiots.

A woman stood in front of the bank of elevators with a large leather bag slung over her shoulder. She was humming something. What was that tune? Jingle Bells? I couldn't help the low growl that rumbled in my throat. I was so over this and I hadn't even been upstairs to the party yet.

Still humming, the woman glanced at me. It looked like she was about to say something—probably some asinine holiday greeting—but as soon as our eyes met, her face fell and she went silent.

Finally.

Ding! An elevator opened but she didn't move. My brow furrowed again—what was wrong with people—and I walked past her to get in. She still didn't move, so I pushed the button for my floor and let the doors close. I didn't know what her problem was—or why she was staring at me like she'd just seen a ghost—and I didn't care.

The elevator went up, arriving at my floor with another ding. Before the doors opened, I could hear the party. Muffled voices and Christmas music drifted through. I took a deep breath and resigned myself to the inevitable.

If the coffee shop had been bad, this was my nightmare come true. My floor had been transformed from office to holiday party with a nauseating display of red and green, silver and gold. Wreaths, garland, and lights had been hung on every available surface and how many Christmas trees did one office party need? Four? No, there was another one in the conference room, so apparently five. The din of raucous conversation did nothing to drown the holiday playlist some dumbass had put together for the occasion.

If that Mariah Carey song came on, I might have to quit.

My coworkers were all dressed for the party, decked out in a mind-numbing array of terrible Christmas sweaters. A few of the software engineers stood together, laughing at the fact that they'd all worn the same red and green monstrosity. Phil from sales had blinking Christmas lights around his neck, Prasad, one of our developers, had silver and gold tassels and a Santa hat, and Janelle from accounting wore a sweater that made one of her boobs look like a reindeer face, complete with a red nose.

Kill me.

Ignoring the celebration, I headed straight for my office. It was just after three in the afternoon, but it was five o'clock somewhere, and there was no way I was doing this without a drink. There was probably spiked eggnog in the conference room, but I didn't do eggnog.

I shut the door, surrounding myself in blissful quiet. I set the coffee on my desk, got a bottle of whiskey from the cabinet, and added a generous pour. I'd contemplated just the whiskey, but I wanted the hit of caffeine along with the burn of alcohol. Plus, sometimes playing the game meant being the one to stay sober.

The door opened, flooding my office with the godforsaken music. My assistant, Alice, poked her head inside.

"Elias?"

"Get in here and shut the door."

She came in and closed it behind her. "Sorry."

Alice was probably in her late twenties with blond hair and—I actually had no idea what color eyes she had. Or much else about her, other than she was good at her job and she only annoyed me about half the time.

Now was one of those times.

Eying her, I took a sip of my coffee. "What are you supposed to be?"

She glanced down at her sweater dress—red with green trim and she had shoes with pointy toes and little balls on the tips. "It's my ugly Christmas sweater. Or dress, I guess. I'm an elf."

"You look stupid."

Her hands went to her hips. I saw that pose a lot. "Well you look like a big old Grinch. Where's your holiday spirit?"

My voice was low and flat. "Have you met me?"

"Yes and I rue the day. Except when I get paid. That almost makes it worth it."

I narrowed my eyes. "If you dress like that again, I'll fire you."

She ignored me, although I wasn't kidding. "Are you coming out to the party?"

"Yes."

"Now?"

"When I'm ready."

"Okay, well, when you do, watch out for Demi Simpson. She's already drunk and trying to sit in people's laps."

A shudder ran down my spine. Sober Demi Simpson was a normal middle-aged woman. Drunk Demi Simpson was a cougar on the prowl. The last thing I needed was her trying to rub her boobs in my face.

Again.

Another shudder.

I took a drink of my coffee, once again contemplating a straight shot of whiskey before I entered the arena.

"I think I'm going to head out, though," Alice said. "I've mingled enough."

"You can't leave."

"Why not?"

"It's three o'clock on a Friday. Where are you going to go?"

"Home? You know, the place where I go when I'm not dealing with your grumpy self at work?"

"We're still working."

She gestured toward the party outside. "No one's working."

"We are."

She huffed, like working on an actual workday was some big inconvenience. It wasn't like I was asking her to come in on a weekend. I ignored her little display of temper and flipped through my messages on my phone. Nothing critical.

"Fine." She opened the door as wide as it would go and left it that way as she walked out.

Maybe I would fire her.

Or not. Hiring someone new would be a pain in the ass and I had enough going on.

I added a little more whiskey to my cup and replaced the lid. Then I wandered out into the party.

Usually, DataStream was a good place to work. We were an IT consulting firm with a solid reputation, specializing in managed services and high-level data security. We'd gone from a handful of employees to a thriving corporation of over two hundred people in a short period of time; and we were still growing.

Growth meant opportunity. Opportunity meant money. Money meant success.

I moved around the small groups of people chatting and laughing with their appetizers and drinks. I seemed to be the only person who'd spurned the ugly sweater. Not like I cared. My only nod to the casual dress code in our company was to keep the top button of my shirt undone and cuff my sleeves. I preferred the more professional look of a gentleman in a suit and tie but that wasn't the culture at DataStream.

I played the game. And it worked.

I'd risen through the ranks fast, proving myself as the financial wizard I was. My next goal was CFO.

From there, the world would be mine for the taking.

"Damien is on it but I heard he's struggling to close the deal."

The snippet of conversation caught my attention and I paused. Damien Barrett struggling with anything was something I needed to know about. Pretending not to eavesdrop, I sipped my coffee and kept listening.

"What's he struggling with?"

"From what I heard, whoever owns the land doesn't want to sell."

"So why not just find a new location?"

"You know how Nigel can be. He wants what he wants. And Damien's a kiss-ass."

"True. He better get it done. My clients are getting impatient."

"Mine, too. The demand is there. We just need the infrastructure."

With a slight turn, I moved on. They were right about that; the demand was there. We'd been planning to build a secure datacenter at a remote location for the last six months. At least half our clients were demanding it and the other half would be when our sales staff pitched it to them. Damien Barrett—bane of my existence and my only real competition for CFO—had been handed the project. All the jackass had to do was find a suitable location and secure the land. How hard could that be?

And yet, here we were, six months later, and apparently no progress.

My mouth twitched in a subtle grin. Suddenly this entire holiday party had been worth it.

I caught sight of my boss, Nigel Ferguson. He was in his sixties, with silver-streaked hair and a strong jaw. Although he could have been nearing retirement, it was hard to fathom him ever leaving the company he'd founded. He wore a slightly more dignified version of an ugly Christmas sweater and drunk Demi had him cornered near his office. Perfect. I could get rid of her for him and solve his land problem.

Leaving my coffee on someone's desk, I made my way through a cackling group of women and headed straight for Demi. She was leaning into Nigel with her hands on his chest. He had his hands up, palms out, as if to make it extremely obvious that he was not harassing her.

I met his eyes as I approached and tipped my chin, then took Demi's arm and moved her a few steps away.

She giggled and sagged against me. "Hi, handsome."

"Demi, I can't imagine why your husband left you."

"What?" She laughed again. "Are you flirting with me, Elias?"

"No. I'm stopping you from making a fool of yourself with our *boss*." I emphasized the word. "Go sober up."

"I'm not drunk." With another giggle she tried to slide her hand between my shirt buttons. "Where's your sweater? Did you take it off? I can take mine off if you want."

"Not even if Nigel offered me his job. You're a disgrace." I gave her a nudge toward the elevators. "Take an Uber home."

With an exaggerated pout, she walked away.

"Thank you." Nigel straightened his sweater.

"Can I see you in your office?"

"It's a party, Elias."

I glanced around at the garish decorations and my back muscles twitched at the music. "I know."

"Five minutes. Then you go enjoy the party."

I did not say that it would be a cold day in hell before I enjoyed a company holiday party. Although I never kissed anyone's ass, I was smart enough to keep my mouth shut when it was necessary.

Instead, I just nodded and followed Nigel into his office.

The literal corner office.

Windows showcased the breathtaking view of Lake Washington and the growing urbanization of downtown Bellevue, a thriving city just across the lake from Seattle. I didn't envy Nigel his office for the scenery, nor the sleek furniture and tasteful decor. It was what this represented.

Money. Success. Power.

Yes, I was after the CFO job. But that was just a stepping stone. This was what I wanted.

And I always got what I wanted.

"What couldn't wait until Monday?" Nigel asked.

"What's going on with the site for the new datacenter?"

The quick breath he let out told me volumes. He was frustrated. "It seems to be at a standstill, unfortunately."

"Do we have any backup options?"

"Maybe, but I'd like to see if we can make this work." He leaned against his desk. "The mountain location is ideal for physical security, the land out there is affordable, and there's an existing town where on-site employees could live. There's even a college. It's not big, but it's a nice place."

Something about his description pricked at me. Small town with a college? Mountain location?

That sounded a lot like—

"Where is it, exactly?"

"It's off highway ninety-seven on the other side of Steven's pass. The town's called Tilikum."

I cleared my throat. "I'm familiar with it."

"Are you?"

This should not have been hard to admit. Who cared if

I'd lived there? It was just a small town. It didn't mean anything to me.

Not anymore.

I pushed aside the vestiges of emotion that tried to well up inside me. "I used to live there. When I was a kid."

"You're kidding. Tilikum is your hometown?"

"It's not my hometown. I just lived there for a while."

"Do you get back there often?"

"No."

He lifted his eyebrows like he was mildly intrigued. But I wasn't here to reminisce about my shitty childhood. It wasn't anyone's business.

Taking down Damien Barrett. That was my business.

"I hear Damien's having a tough time securing the land."

Nigel nodded, a quick burst of frustration coloring his features. "I thought we'd have wrapped it up months ago. It's a farm that's been struggling for years, but Damien can't seem to convince the owners to let it go."

"Who are the owners?"

"Faye and Russell Cook."

If I'd still had a heart in the cold, empty space in my chest, it might have stopped beating at hearing those names. But I didn't, so nothing happened.

"I know the Cooks."

Nigel's eyebrows lifted again. "You do? Family friends or something?"

More like the parents the girl I'd almost married when I was too young to know better. "Something like that." I paused, keeping my posture casual, like this was just an idle suggestion, not a calculated move. "Do you want me to talk to them?"

"That would be great. Damien's been dealing with their daughter." He picked up a folder from his desk and started thumbing through the pages. "Her name is in here somewhere."

"Isabelle." Her name rolled off my tongue like it had no meaning.

Good. Because it didn't.

And that meant I could take care of this. Feelings need not apply.

"Right, Isabelle Cook." He held the folder out to me. "If you could get this moving, I'd really appreciate it."

I took it. "Consider it done."

"Great. Now, enough work. Go have a drink and enjoy the party. You can tackle this on Monday."

I nodded, giving him the impression that I'd do what he said.

Instead, I left his office and went in search of Alice.

I found her in the conference room, chatting with one of the receptionists. I didn't know her name but she straightened as I approached, putting a slight arch in her back so her boobs stuck out.

"Hi, Mr. Stoneheart."

I ignored her and shoved the folder at Alice. "Make copies of these and meet me in my office."

"What? Why?"

"Because we have work to do."

"It's the holiday—"

"Holiday party? Like I give a shit. You can party on your own time."

Alice glared while the receptionist batted her eyelashes at me.

"You're buying me a very expensive Christmas present this year," Alice said. "I hope you realize that."

"I already bought you a present."

"That was last year."

"So?"

"And I'm not staying late. I have to go pick up my daughter."

"Any more demands before you do your job?"

"No, that's it."

"Good. Now make me the copies and put the originals on Nigel's desk."

I didn't wait for her to reply. I already knew she'd do what I told her. And we did have work to do. I needed to find out everything I could about the Cook family farm. Current acreage, ancillary assets, number of employees, debt to income ratio.

If I knew Isabelle—and I did—she was the reason Damien was having such a hard time closing this deal. I'd never encountered a woman more stubborn than Isabelle Cook. If she didn't want to do something, she'd dig in her heels like an obstinate donkey.

Like Horace, the guard donkey.

I wondered if they still had Horace. Mean son of a bitch.

Shutting out the noise of the party, I also shut the door on that memory. Who gave a shit about Horace the guard donkey? What I needed to worry about was ammunition in the upcoming battle. If I could get enough data on my side, I'd have this deal closed with a phone call. Isabelle was stubborn but so was I.

And I was going to win.

2

ISABELLE

*T*he stack of bills was ominously high. I sipped my tea and flipped through the envelopes. The early morning sun peeked through the kitchen window, sending a shaft of light onto the maple cabinets. The counters were lined with an array of mason jars and canisters and a wooden sign with the words *Home Sweet Farm* hung on the wall. I'd always loved that little sign. But the comfort of my parents' kitchen wasn't enough to suppress the knot of worry that had taken up residence in the pit of my stomach.

So many bills.

At least they'd stopped hiding them from me. Now they left them sitting in a basket on the sideboard instead of stuffing them away in a drawer. That was something.

With a resigned breath, I put the newest bill on top of the stack. There was always a certain level of overhead to running a farm but a decade-long drought had meant a string of poor Christmas tree harvests. Add to that a list of equipment that had all needed replacing in the last several seasons—and the debt that went with it—and things were tight.

Cook Family Farm had been the site of Tilikum's Christmas Village for decades. My parents had started it back in the day with their u-cut Christmas trees, adding a few booths with baked goods and Christmas ornaments for sale to entice more people to come cut their own trees at the farm. Over the years, it had grown, with cute little buildings replacing the booths, increasingly elaborate decorations, the addition of our reindeer herd, and the best Santa photos this side of the Cascades.

The village was a Christmas wonderland. Although it wasn't exactly a money maker for the farm—it barely broke even—it did help bring more customers to the tree farm.

Would it be enough to keep us going another year? That was the big question.

The back door opened and Mom came in, carrying a basket of fresh eggs from her flock of hens. She kept her silvery hair cut short and her only nod to fashion was a pair of diamond stud earrings she never took off—a gift from Dad when I was born. Despite the early November cold—it had gone from unseasonably warm to freezing practically overnight—she wasn't wearing a coat. Just a long-sleeve shirt with a puffer vest and a pair of jeans with patched knees. Faye Cook was tough down to her core—born and raised here in Tilikum and no stranger to hard work.

"Morning." Her eyes flicked to the envelopes as she walked past the kitchen table to set the eggs on the counter. "What are you doing over here so early on a Saturday?"

"I was out of tea."

"Can I make you breakfast?"

"That's okay. I can get something at home."

I still lived here at the farm, just not in the main house. After high school, I'd remodeled an existing cottage on the property and turned it into a rather cute little home, if I did say so myself. Leaving had never really been an option. My parents were in their sixties—they'd had me later in life after years of believing they couldn't have children—and they'd struggle to run the farm without me.

Plus, I loved this place. The rolling fields surrounded by mountain peaks. The carefully tended rows of evergreen trees. Not to mention the sparkling spread of holiday happiness that was Christmas Village.

Mom raised her eyebrows. "Do you have anything to eat at home?"

That was a good question. I hadn't been to the store in a while. "Maybe?"

She shook her head. "Let me make you some eggs. It's not like we don't have enough. The hens are still laying."

"Thanks."

I took the stack of bills and put them back in the basket on the sideboard.

"Stop stressing about it." Mom started cracking eggs into a bowl. "It won't help."

"Who's stressing?" I sat back down at the table and wrapped my hands around the warm mug.

She glanced over her shoulder with a look of skepticism. "I know you, Izz."

"I'm only stressing because I'm sitting here not doing anything about it. You know what, never mind about breakfast. I should really get to work."

"Stop." Her no-nonsense tone kept me from getting up. "There's nothing out there that can't wait half an hour."

With a sigh, I slumped in my chair and took another sip of tea. She was probably right. But I'd never been good at sitting still, especially when there was work to be done or problems to be solved.

I had haystacks of both.

"You work too hard anyway."

Dad appeared in the kitchen dressed in a dark green flannel and denim overalls. "Isn't that the truth."

"Morning, Dad."

He came in and gave me a quick kiss on the top of the head. My dad had long ago lost every bit of hair on his head and grown a thick gray beard to make up for it. His skin was weathered from a lifetime of farm work and he had the biggest hands I'd ever seen.

"Breakfast will be ready in a few minutes." Mom stirred the eggs. "Do either of you want toast?"

"Just eggs for me," I said.

Dad glanced at the back door, twitching with restless energy. "I'll eat something later, I—"

"Don't even think about it." Mom's no-nonsense tone worked just as well on Dad as it always had on me, and he took a seat at the table. "You can eat first."

She dished up our eggs and we sat together and ate. Dad and I chatted about the farm. We had a long list of things to do before we'd be ready to open the village for the holiday season. Decorations to construct and repair, vendor contracts to finalize, seasonal workers to hire, not to mention all the regular farm chores.

Mom set her fork down on her empty plate and picked up her mug. "Do the two of you ever talk about anything but work?"

Dad shoveled another bite of eggs in his mouth, as if to get out of having to answer.

"There's just a lot to do," I said. "It's a busy time of year."

"I know that as well as anyone. But the holiday season has barely begun and you're already working seven days a week."

"Mom, it's fine. I'll sleep in January when everything

calms down and we know we can keep the farm out of bankruptcy."

"At least take a little time off. An afternoon, even. It's the weekend. Go do something fun." She paused and the tiny throat-clear was all the warning I had. "What about a date?"

Not this again. "I don't have time to date."

"That's what I'm talking about. You should have a life outside the farm."

"I do have a life outside the farm. I'm hanging out with Annika and Marigold tomorrow. Mari's cutting my hair."

Annika and Marigold had been my best friends since kindergarten and were the closest thing I had to a social life. By the dissatisfied look on Mom's face, a haircut at Marigold's salon wasn't what she had in mind.

"Your mom's right." Dad pushed his empty plate to the side.

"This from the man who once threatened to lock me in my room if I ever got a boyfriend."

Dad's mouth twitched in a grin. "If I recall, you were fifteen. Things change."

"We just want you to be happy," Mom said.

"I'm perfectly happy the way things are. And like I said, too busy to date."

Mom was quiet for a moment, picking at her eggs. I had a feeling something else was up.

She sighed and shared a quick glance with Dad before breaking the brief silence. "Damien Barrett called again."

My spine snapped straight with a flare of anger. Damien Barrett worked for a company that had been trying to convince my parents to sell the farm. "You talked to him?"

"No, he left a message. But, you know—"

"Don't say it." I held up a finger. "Don't even say it."

"Izz, you can't keep avoiding this conversation."

"Yes, I can. I'd rather talk about dating."

"Russell, can you talk some sense into her?"

I met Dad's eyes and raised my eyebrows.

He looked at me for a few seconds. "Nope."

Mom sighed in exasperation. "I know that selling the farm is a last resort, but we can't keep pretending this isn't a possibility."

"I'm going to pretend you didn't just say the s-word."

"She's right, Izz," Dad said, a hint of sadness in his tone. "This might be the opportunity we need."

"Opportunity? Selling our farm isn't an opportunity, it's quitting."

"If we keep resisting, they're going to go elsewhere," Dad said.

"Good. We want them to go elsewhere. That Damien Barrett jerk-off can get bent."

"He's a little arrogant, I suppose," Mom said. "But he's not that bad."

"Mom, he's a first-class idiot. Do not speak to that man."

Dad chuckled, like this was somehow amusing. "Honey–"

"What? First of all, their offer is insulting. This place is worth way more than that. Second of all, we're not selling the farm."

Something about the glance Mom and Dad shared was infuriating. I hated seeing the sad resignation in their eyes, as if failure were inevitable. I knew they were getting older and starting to slow down. Some people their age were retiring, not faced with having to work harder just to keep their livelihood.

But they didn't have to do it alone. They had me.

I was going to fix this. I didn't know how, but there had to be a way.

Too antsy to sit still, I got up and put my dishes in the sink. "Thanks for breakfast, Mom. I need to get to work."

"You're welcome."

I paused next to the table and met their eyes. "Don't talk to that Damien jerk without me. I don't want him taking advantage of you."

"We won't," Dad said. "But this conversation isn't over."

I didn't argue with him. Not out loud, at least. In my head, I told him that this conversation was completely over and I wasn't going to hear another word about selling. Especially to some dumb jerk. No way.

But if I said all that, Dad would just tell me I was being stubborn—which was so not true—and that I needed to listen to reason—also not true—and we'd be right back where we started.

Talking wasn't going to accomplish anything. Working harder? That might actually help. And that, I could do.

"Love you," I said, managing what I hoped was a convincing smile.

"Love you," they said in reply.

I swept out the back door before either of them had a chance to say more.

My blood was boiling so I was halfway to the barn before I realized I'd forgotten a coat. The cold air cut through my long-sleeve shirt and jeans, although my work boots kept my feet warm. I decided it didn't matter. I'd be sweating up a storm in no time anyway.

I got to the barn and tightened my ponytail. I was about to go inside when my phone buzzed in my back pocket. It wasn't a number I recognized but the area code told me everything I needed to know.

Damien Barrett.

I'd been letting his calls go to voicemail but I was in a

mood. He wanted to offer a pittance for my family's lifelong hard work and home? He was on my last nerve.

"What do you want now?"

"Excuse me?"

Wait. That wasn't Damien Barrett's voice. His was more of a tenor whereas this man was all bass.

And familiar. Why was it so familiar?

"Sorry, I thought you were someone else. This is Isabelle."

The pause was just long enough to feel odd.

"Isabelle Cook?"

"Yes."

"It's Elias. Elias Stoneheart."

The blood in my veins froze and my heart stopped.

3

ISABELLE

*T*he shock of hearing *that* voice say *that* name in my ear left me paralyzed. Speechless. A tornado of emotion whirled through me, leaving my insides flattened and littered with debris.

"Elias?"

It was a dumb question—he'd just said it twice—but I couldn't make sense of it.

"Yeah. Been a while."

That was an understatement. I hadn't talked to him in what, eleven years? "What's wrong? Did something happen to Dale or Hattie?"

"No, there's nothing wrong."

I let out a breath. I had a lot of feelings about Elias Stoneheart—big ones, and mostly bad—but his uncle and aunt, Dale and Hattie Martin, were lovely. They lived in Tilikum and I saw them out and about occasionally. They still smiled and waved at me, and I appreciated that. Made it less awkward.

"Then why are you calling me? Are you in town or something?"

"No, I'm at home." He paused again which was so unlike him. He'd always been straightforward and blunt.

There had been a time when I'd liked that about him.

Now it annoyed me that I remembered, and that I'd once liked anything about this man.

"So what's going on?"

He cleared his throat. "I'm with DataStream. You've been talking to my colleague, Damien Barrett."

"You work with Damien?" That shouldn't have surprised me. A company that would employ one jerk-off would surely employ another.

"For better or worse. I understand he made an offer on your parents' property."

"He did." Where was this going? I was still reeling from the sound of Elias's voice. It was absolutely not making my insides tingle. Not even the slightest bit.

"I'd like to talk to you about that."

"About the offer?"

"Yes. Look, I don't want to be unprofessional, but Damien is kind of an idiot. I have a feeling he didn't come off very well."

"That's true. He came off like a barf bag."

He chuckled, just the slightest laugh. Once upon a time, that sound would have had me dropping my panties in about two seconds. It took a lot to make Elias laugh, but when you did, it was like liquid gold.

Ugh, what was I thinking? I stomped my feet, as if I needed to get mud off my boots.

"I'm sorry about Damien. If I'd known, I would have made sure you never had to deal with him."

I wandered down the gravel path, away from the barn. The tingle in my insides was getting harder to deny. Was he being nice to me? What was that about?

Then again, it had been a long time. Maybe the past was in the past.

"Well, thanks. Does that mean he won't be bugging us anymore?"

"Absolutely."

The prick of temper and swirl of shock began to fade. It was still strange to hear his voice but the tightness in my neck and shoulders eased. "Okay. Thank you."

"Of course. I know things haven't been easy for you. Especially the last few years."

"I've been fine."

"That's good to hear, but the farm's had some challenges."

My spine stiffened with suspicion. "How do you know?"

"Damien had a file. I found out about the whole thing yesterday, so I made sure to do a thorough review. It looks like your dad took out a second mortgage a number of years ago and at quite the interest rate."

"How do you know *that*?"

"It's all public record."

I should have known. That must have been why Damien had started sniffing around. He'd done research on our farm. Done the math. It wouldn't take a genius to figure out we were in trouble.

"Well, despite whatever he had in that file might imply, we're fine."

He paused again and his silence told me nothing. Did he believe me? Was he flipping through our mortgage and property records? Why was he calling me?

"Are you sure about that?" he asked.

"Yes."

"Hmm."

It was so odd. He sounded familiar, yet not. Of course,

the last time we'd spoken, he'd been just shy of nineteen. Still basically a kid. This Elias sounded older, his voice deeper.

The tingle was turning into a whirlpool.

"Obviously, Damien's offer was basically a joke," he said.

"It was an insult."

"I don't know what he was thinking."

"Probably that he could take advantage of a couple of nice, small-town farmers."

"Which is ridiculous."

"Yes. Ridiculous."

"I'm glad we're on the same page."

Wait, were we on the same page? I felt like I was missing something. Like I was letting his deep, velvety voice go to my head.

"Me, too?"

"Good." Another pause. "I have your email here in the file. I'll have a new offer over to you by the end of the day. I'm sure you'll find it more suitable."

I stopped dead. "What?"

"A new offer. The contract Damien wrote up is a mess. You did the right thing in refusing. Don't worry, I'll make this right."

My jaw dropped and the whirlpool dried up in a flash of anger, leaving behind nothing but sizzling steam. "A new offer? I think you misunderstood. We don't want a different offer. We're not selling."

"Come on, Isabelle. I've seen the numbers. I'm sure you've done a heroic job in keeping the place open this long. But it's time. I can make sure your parents are taken care of. Everything is going to be fine."

I could hear the lie in his attempt to soothe me. He

didn't care about me, or my parents. He wanted their farm, just like Damien.

"Did you seriously call me after eleven years thinking you could convince me to sell the farm?"

"I'm trying to help you."

"Is that what you're telling yourself?"

"No, it's what I'm doing. Facts are facts, Isabelle. You can't afford to keep the farm. Anyone can see that. It was only a matter of time before someone like Damien came along and tried to swindle your parents out of their land. If you work with me, I'll see to it that you get a fair price."

"And then what?"

"What do you mean?"

"If you buy it, what happens to the farm?"

"Does it matter?"

"Yes, it matters a lot. Damien wouldn't answer my questions about that either. Reason number three hundred fifty-two I don't trust him."

Elias sighed, like this conversation was starting to annoy him. "My company wants the site to build a secure datacenter."

"So you'll close the farm."

"Anyone who buys the land will close the farm. It's a money pit."

I got a sinking feeling in my stomach. "But where would we have Christmas Village? Where would our reindeer go? What about Horace and my mom's chickens?"

"Horace is still alive?"

"Yes, he's still alive. Donkeys can live to be like forty."

"I had no idea."

"They can. And we can't close the farm. Tilikum needs this place."

"Tilikum needs jobs more than it needs Christmas Village."

The way he said that, his voice dripping with disdain, snapped the last string holding my temper in check. "I don't know who you think you are. We haven't spoken in years and you call me out of the blue acting like you care about my parents but all you want is to get your greedy paws on their land. Well you know what? It's not happening. We're not selling to you or to your assface friend, Damien."

"He's not my friend."

"As if I care!" I realized too late that I was shouting. But I didn't care about that either. "Do yourself a favor and find some other sweet old couple to con out of their family farm. Because you're not getting ours. And while you're at it, lose my number forever."

"Isa—"

I hung up.

Gripping my phone in my hand, I clenched my teeth and yelled in frustration.

"Are you okay?"

I whirled on Cole, our full-time farm hand. He flinched back with his hands up, like I was an enraged animal, prone to attack.

"Sorry." I took a deep breath. "I just got a very frustrating phone call."

"I can tell. Want to talk about it?"

Cole was tall and thickly built—a farm boy, through and through. Sandy blond hair, blue eyes, and skin bronzed from the sun. He was a couple of years older than me and he'd worked for my family for years. We'd dated for a while and he was absolutely the nicest guy. Our breakup had been remarkably amicable; we'd agreed we were better as friends and even more remarkably, we'd been right. I knew my parents had been hoping we'd stay together and get married —inherit the farm together and be a cute little small-town farm couple. And on paper, it made sense. Cole was basically a male me. But in reality, our romantic relationship had been stunted and awkward. It had never felt right to either of us.

But Cole Phillips as my friend? He was awesome and I was so grateful that two years after we'd broken up, we still got along.

"It was Elias Stoneheart."

His eyebrows lifted. "Oh. Shit."

"Yeah. Exactly." I tipped my head in the direction of the field. "I need to walk it off."

"Sure."

I made my way down the gravel path toward the grassy field. Cole fell in step beside me.

"The farm's in trouble," he said, and it wasn't a question.

"It is." I wasn't going to lie to him. "But I'm going to do everything I can to save it."

"What did dickface want?"

"The farm."

Cole glanced at me, his brow furrowed. "Why?"

"His company wants the land for a secure datacenter, whatever that is. All I know is that he's a jerk and it would mean closing the farm. And Christmas Village."

"The fuck? He can't close Christmas Village."

"I know!"

"Are you going to have a choice, though? Be honest."

I kept walking, pondering his question for a long moment before answering. "I don't know."

"I guess now would be a great time for me to find out I have a rich uncle I never knew who died and left me his fortune."

"Or maybe we can team up with Harvey Johnston and find the Montgomery treasure."

He laughed. "Good luck with that."

I smiled and shook my head. Harvey Johnston was a local guy and most people thought he was crazy. He dressed like a miner from the gold rush and wandered around town muttering about the squirrels and the fabled Montgomery treasure. Tilikum was full of tall tales, and the story of a treasure buried in the mountains had been around for generations. I didn't think it existed.

"I'm not sure what to do," I said, "other than work my ass off to make sure this year's Christmas Village is the best it's ever been so we can keep paying the bills for another year."

"That's what I would do."

"Well, then that's what I'm going to do. Elias Stoneheart can eat a dick. We're not selling him the farm."

"That's the spirit." He nudged me with his elbow. "What are you doing wasting time out here with me? Better get to work, slacker."

"You're the one slacking. Those reindeer aren't going to pasture themselves."

"Ain't that the truth."

"Thanks, Cole."

"Anytime."

I turned and headed back toward the barn, already pushing the call with Elias out of my mind with a mental to-do list. Work hard. Keep busy. That was the answer. It was how I coped with stress, adversity, everything.

And somehow, hard work was going to save this farm. Elias Stoneheart thought he could take it? He had no idea who he was dealing with.

I was going to win.

4

ELIAS

*T*he Christmas decorations were still sullying the office Monday morning. I paused long enough to rip down the wreath someone had hung on my door and tossed it onto the floor. I went into my office—no one had the balls to put up any decorations in here at least—took off my coat, and sat at my desk.

The first sip of coffee was pleasantly hot and bitter on my tongue. I'd almost bypassed the lobby coffee shop and the crazy-eyed barista, but their coffee was good and I was too stubborn to change my routine. Fortunately, she hadn't questioned my order or suggested any of the holiday menu selections. She hadn't even smiled, which was an improvement.

Of course, I was in a terrible mood and I'd glared at her like she'd just kicked a puppy or asked me to join her family for Christmas dinner.

Damn Isabelle Cook.

After the frustratingly unsuccessful phone call Saturday morning, I'd given her time to cool down before trying to build a bridge and get her talking to me again. She'd declined my call, sending it straight to voicemail. She did the same when I'd tried again later, except she'd changed her voicemail greeting to, *Hi this is Isabelle, please leave a message. Except Elias. Don't leave a message and never call again.*

Texting had at least gotten me a reply, although all she'd done so far is tell me to get bent, screw off, and leave her alone.

This was going to be harder than I'd thought.

Alice came in, dressed in a white blouse and dark skirt. Hopefully she'd burned the elf outfit.

"Morning."

I grunted a reply.

"The income statements you asked for are in your inbox."

"Good."

"And the company is taking up a collection for one of those Christmas wishes programs. Do you want to contribute?"

My brow furrowed. "What?"

"You know, to buy toys for kids whose families can't afford Christmas presents."

"Why would I contribute to that?"

"Because it's the holidays."

"No."

She sighed. "Bella wants to set up a meeting. Will you be in the office this afternoon?"

"Bella?" The derivative of Isabelle's name crawled up my spine like a spider.

"Yeah, Bella McDaniel, director of marketing?"

I took a drink of coffee to cover my momentary lapse in composure. "What does she want?"

"More money for her department would be my guess. But she didn't say."

"Put her off. Whatever she wants, I'm not approving it."

Alice sighed again. "She's not going to like that."

"I don't like her."

"You don't like anyone."

"That's not true."

"Name one person you like."

I opened my mouth to reply but for a second, nothing came out. "You're wasting my time."

"Fine. I'll tell Bella you'll meet with her next week." She lowered her voice, muttering under her breath. "And leave out the part where you're too cheap to give her a decent budget."

"I heard that."

"I know. Don't forget, I'm taking a long lunch today."

I glanced up. "Again?"

"I take a long lunch every other Monday because of my daughter. You know this."

"Kids are a pain in the ass."

"You're a pain in the ass."

I ignored her attitude. "Don't be too long. I'm going to need your help researching this land deal."

She lowered herself into the seat across from my desk. "How exactly did you worm your way into that project? Did you get Nigel drunk at the Christmas party?"

"Damien can't close the deal. I simply suggested to Nigel that I step in and help."

"And by help, you mean undermine Damien at every opportunity, make him look bad, and hopefully get him fired, all while swooping in as the company hero?"

I leaned back in my chair. "That sounds like my Christmas list."

She laughed. "If taking Damien down is the goal, I'm in."

"Why?"

"He's a jerk in general. And he hit on me at the party on Friday." She shuddered.

I narrowed my eyes. Alice's personal life was her own—I didn't give a shit what she did outside of work—but the idea of Damien hitting on her pissed me off. I wasn't sure why. She was cute and didn't take any of my crap—both points in her favor—but I wasn't attracted to her. I didn't want her for myself. So why did I care if Damien did?

It didn't matter why it bothered me. Damien was an asshole, especially to women, and he needed to stay away from my assistant.

"If he does that again, tell me," I said, my voice flat. "I'll deal with it."

Alice's mouth turned up in a small smile. "Thanks."

"Don't thank me. Help me ruin his career."

"I'll do my best. What's the story on this place?"

"Cook Family Farm, located right outside Tilikum. It's a small town, not a lot out there. The farm has been in financial trouble for years but the family is in denial. Damien made the mistake of low-balling them because he's an idiot. Now they're digging in their heels and claim they won't sell."

"So it's past the point of simply making them a better offer."

"Indeed."

"Have you talked to them yet?"

"I talked to the daughter."

"And?"

"She's — determined."

"Sassy farm girl, huh? Is she cute?"

Beautiful, actually.

I cleared my throat to get that unwelcome thought out of

my head. "I don't care what she looks like. I'm not going to seduce her to convince her to sell."

Alice rolled her eyes. "I know, and I'd never suggest such a thing. I was just wondering. Maybe you need a sassy farm girl in your life."

That was a *hell no*. "Stop wondering and start doing something useful. I need a different angle."

"You're the boss." She got up and went to the door. "And don't angry text me when I'm not here this afternoon. Long lunch. Every other Monday."

"Right." I waved her off, barely listening. Something about Monday, it didn't matter. I was too busy thumbing through the file on the Cooks' farm.

What would it take to convince Isabelle that I was right and she needed to let the farm go?

Not even a minute later, my door flew open. Damien shut it behind him—not quite a slam, but close. He was mid-thirties with dark hair and a weak chin. The sloppy bastard was dressed in a navy polo and cargo pants. It was one thing for the software guys to saunter into work in their video game t-shirts and shorts. That was their thing. Fine. But Damien was a finance guy. He should know better.

"Can I help you?" I asked.

"What the fuck did you do?"

"You'll have to be more specific."

"I just got out of a meeting with Nigel. He said he passed the datacenter project to you."

I leaned back in my chair and pressed my fingertips together. "He did."

"That's my project."

"It was."

"You have a lot of nerve going behind my back like that."

"No one went behind your back. You failed. Nigel brought me in to clean up the mess."

His face flushed and a vein stuck out on his forehead. "I didn't fail. I haven't closed the deal yet, but I was making progress."

"No, you weren't. You were being ignored by the Cooks and hung up on by their daughter."

"How did you know that?"

"Lucky guess."

Impotent rage reddened his face further—emphasis on *impotent*. A guy like Damien was clearly compensating for something. Or a lack of something. "You're an asshole."

The corner of my mouth twitched. "I know."

He pointed a finger at me. "I'm going to take you down, Stoneheart."

I didn't move. Just blinked once.

"Fuck," he said under his breath and turned to storm out.

"Damien." My voice was low but he stopped with his hand on the doorknob and looked at me over his shoulder.

"What?"

"If you ever bother my assistant again, I'll kill you and no one will ever find the body."

The color drained from his face and he swallowed hard. Without another word, he turned and walked out.

Piece of shit.

But I couldn't underestimate him. He was angry which was making him sloppy. Threatening me was an idiot move, but he'd calm down and realize it. Under all that bluster, he was smart. A prick, but smart. He could still make trouble. I'd need to be careful.

Letting out a long breath, I went back to my phone. What was I going to do about Isabelle Cook?

I swiped through our text conversation from the day before.

Me: *We got off on the wrong foot. Can we talk?*
Isabelle: *No.*
Me: *Please?*
Isabelle: *No.*
Me: *Why?*
Isabelle: *Get bent.*
Me: *Still sassy. I like it.*
Isabelle: *Screw off.*
Me: *We both know this would be easier if you'd just talk to me.*
Isabelle: *You're wasting your time. We're not selling.*
Me: *The numbers don't lie. You won't have a choice.*
Isabelle: *Still no.*
Me: *Just talk to me. Let me help you figure this out.*
Isabelle: *It's a Sunday and I'm at the salon. Leave me alone.*

I'd decided to do what she asked. For the time being. I hadn't texted her back, giving her the impression that I'd respect her wishes and give her space. In reality, I was calculating my next move.

And had she really been at the salon? Or was she making up an excuse to get rid of me? A salon seemed odd for her. She'd never been particularly concerned about her hair or appearance. A memory of picking hay out of her ponytail flashed through my mind.

But it had been a long time. Maybe she'd changed.

The corners of my lips lifted as I read over our exchange again. I had to admit, that round had gone to her. One thing hadn't changed. She was still the same vicious kitten with sharp claws. Get too close at your own peril but stroke the right spot, and she'd purr.

Not that I was stroking any of Isabelle Cook's spots.

I knew where they were, but that was irrelevant.

I was a ruthless asshole, but even I had lines I wouldn't cross. Although I had no doubt I could get back in Isabelle's pants if I put my mind to it, that wasn't how I was going to play this.

Besides, I wasn't an idiot. It would take more than prowess in the bedroom—considerable though mine was— to convince Isabelle to sell her family's farm.

What would it take?

I had to face the truth. The answer to that question wasn't in the file or on my computer. It wasn't in a spreadsheet or a set of numbers, clear as those numbers might be.

The answer was in Tilikum.

An unfamiliar twinge swept through me. What was that about? I wasn't afraid to go back. Just because I hadn't been there in over a decade didn't mean it was fear that had kept me away. Indifference was more accurate. I'd moved there when I was eleven and after high school, I'd left. Why would I have stayed? It was a small town with nothing to offer a man like me. Too small for my ambition.

And look how far I'd come. I was this close to an executive position with a net worth that was edging toward respectable. Tilikum had simply never held anything for me.

Until now.

I'd head over tomorrow. Drop in on Isabelle. I'd have her seeing reason soon enough. And let's be honest, if the end result meant the ridiculous Tilikum Christmas Village was no more? I'd have done the world a favor at no extra cost. It was such a waste of resources. I'd be bringing the town more jobs, more money, more prosperity. That was a lot more than the Cooks could say with their antiquated, debt-ridden farm.

Tilikum would thank me.

And so would my boss. Preferably with a promotion, a raise, and more stock options.

My eyes slid over Isabelle's texts again. I'd have this wrapped up in an afternoon.

5

ELIAS

*M*y Tesla cruised around the hairpin turns. The mountains towered on either side of the highway, steep slopes of gray rock peppered with gnarled pine trees. The Wenatchee River meandered its way along one side, the blue-green water swirling and frothing around glacial boulders.

A flash of memory. Inner tubing down another stretch of that same river on hot summer days. The water wide and lazy, blue sky overhead. Dragging a cooler of smuggled beer we were too young to drink.

Focusing on the road, I pushed away the image. That wasn't why I was there.

The Welcome to Tilikum sign as I pulled into town only elicited the slightest twitch in my cool composure. Good. It was just a town, hardly any different than the others I'd passed on the way here.

Granted, no place I'd ever lived had been quite like Tilikum. How many towns had a feud that went back generations? The Haven and Bailey families had been playing elaborate pranks on each other for as long as anyone could remember.

Not that I'd ever cared. In name, I'd been on the Haven side. Mostly because everyone in Tilikum had to be on one side or another, regardless of whether or not they participated in the perpetual pranking.

I hadn't.

It did pique the slightest bit of curiosity, though. Were those guys still pranking each other? Or had they finally outgrown it?

Didn't really matter.

Another memory—this one more unwanted than summer tubing trips or pointless pranks—forced its way to the front of my mind. The first time I'd seen that Welcome to Tilikum sign.

I'd been eleven, fresh off a brush with the law that had sent my parents into a frenzy. Shoplifting didn't exactly mean I was destined for a life of crime, but to my wealthy, image-conscious parents, it wasn't about the implications for my future as much as the stain it left on their reputation. Firing my latest nanny hadn't been enough to appease their anger at their wayward son. They'd shipped me off to live with my aunt and uncle in this random little town in the Cascade mountains.

Why that had seemed like a good solution, I had no idea. Maybe they'd hoped small town living would straighten me out. Or maybe they just hadn't wanted to deal with me anymore.

Considering their general lack of concern for me once I was out of their house, I assumed the latter.

I still remembered what it had felt like to be in the middle of the bench seat of my uncle Dale's truck, wedged in between him and my aunt Hattie, getting my first glimpses of Tilikum. My parents had split their time between Seattle, New York, and L.A.—I'd mostly lived in New York up to that point—but none of the cities I'd been to were anything like this place. No skyscrapers, busy streets, flashing billboards or reader boards. No throngs of people hurrying from place to place.

Instead, there were small businesses and shops, and restaurants with names like Bigfoot Diner, the Copper Kettle, and the Zany Zebra. That one even had black and white stripes all over the building.

It was a place where kids roamed around town by themselves. Where everyone knew your name, and your business. Where squirrels stole your snacks when you weren't looking and gossip moved faster than a summer wildfire.

Not much had changed in the decade or so since I'd been here last—on the outside, at least. But that wasn't a surprise. Towns like this didn't really change. They just got older and people patched them up.

The giant statue of a pinup girl outside the Dame and Dapper barber shop was new, though.

A sign that this town was still weird.

Thinking about that first drive into town forced me to deal with the fact that my aunt and uncle still lived here. Which meant I'd need to make time to see them.

I saw them occasionally, just on my terms. They were both retired, so it was easier for me to put them up in a hotel in Bellevue and treat them to a nice dinner, rather than drive all the way out here from the city.

But since I was here, I'd see them after I dealt with Isabelle. Stop by for dinner or something.

I slowed as I drove through town, my back tightening with irritation at the sense of familiarity. And at the handful of stores already decorated for the holidays.

At least I wouldn't have to be here long.

A squirrel darted across the road in front of me. Instinct made me slam on the brakes to keep from hitting it. Two more ran by, bushy tails streaming behind them. A second later, a scruffy guy in a wide brimmed hat followed, hollering and waving a stick.

Was that Harvey Johnston?

Good thing I'd stopped for the squirrels. I might have hit the crazy old guy.

He didn't seem to notice me or acknowledge that he could have been hit by a car in his quest to chase the squirrels. I found myself shrugging it off, like a random squirrel-chasing man running out into the road was a normal occurrence.

Although in Tilikum, it was.

I didn't like that the quirks of this place were coming back to me so easily. This wasn't home, and I didn't care.

Cook Family Farm was a short drive from downtown. The familiarity of Tilikum had almost poked a hole in my cool composure but it was just a town, easy to brush off, no matter how many memories I had there. But the unwelcome nostalgia that tried to steal over me as I pulled into the lot outside the farm made me grind my teeth.

The gate was closed so I was forced to park in the empty gravel lot. Christmas Village wasn't open yet, but signs of the transformation were everywhere. Lights had been strung on the trees bordering the parking lot and someone had left a ladder near the fence. A pile of extension cords sat near the path leading into the farm and big plastic totes of decorations were stacked nearby.

So much work. And for what?

I got out of my car, the bite of cold air reminding me I was in the mountains. Despite the lack of snow, it was cold. I pulled my wool coat out of the back and put it on over my button-down and slacks. A glance at my shoes made me wonder if I should have dressed differently. But it wasn't like I was going to go wandering around the fields and risk stepping in reindeer shit.

Like the driveway, the footpath was gated, but it wasn't locked. Half-decorated, the village area looked empty and sad. The Peppermint Parlor needed new paint—it was faded and dingy—and the Rustic Noel probably needed a new roof. The path could use fresh gravel and I had no idea how they kept up with maintenance on the public restrooms.

Cash register dings went off in my head as I noted all the work that needed to be done. Rough cost estimates came to me, an instinct I couldn't seem to turn off. There was no way this place earned enough to maintain itself, let alone turn a profit.

And if it couldn't turn a profit, why did it exist?

Isabelle didn't seem to be in the village, so I decided to head toward the farmhouse. It was down another path, away from the public areas of the farm. I went through another gate—also unlocked—and the walkway meandered through pine trees. There were needles everywhere and I wondered how much it cost just to maintain the grounds around the house.

No wonder they were losing money.

I stepped into the clearing outside the house and stopped. The once white paint had faded to a dingy gray and the green shutters were peeling, especially on the upper floor. The stairs to the wrap-around porch looked new but the entire thing needed replacing. I could only assume the roof was old and that was just the outside of the house. Inside was probably just as bad.

Ignoring the warmth of memory that tried to sneak its

way in at the sight of that house, I moved on. I had no idea if she still lived there, but even if she did, she wouldn't be inside. Not this time of day, and especially not in November. She'd probably been working since sunrise.

Her work ethic was admirable. That had never been the problem.

It was too bad she'd dedicated it to this.

I shoved my hands in my pockets against the cold and went around to the back side of the house. The rhythmic sound of a hammer rang out from somewhere inside the big shop. It might have been Russell, but somehow I knew it was her.

The large garage door was open and a hint of sawdust filled the air. The shop looked the same—concrete floor, mismatched shelving along the walls, tools and other equipment lying around. Isabelle had called it organized chaos. To me, it was just inefficient.

At first, I didn't see anyone. The hammering stopped and from behind a pile of reclaimed lumber, she stood.

Her back was to me but the familiarity of that form hit me like a punch to the face. Her hair in a careless ponytail. Sawdust on her clothes. The way her shirt nipped her waist and the flare of her hips in those jeans. She wore a leather tool belt, tan work boots, and no coat. Because of course she didn't have a coat. She was constantly forgetting to put one on.

She'd been a teenager the last time I saw her, with bony arms and a chest that barely filled out her bra. Not that I'd minded. My raging hormones had been on fire for her.

But now? That was no awkward teenager in front of me. This Isabelle was all woman.

My heart tried to do something. Start beating again, maybe. Whatever it was, it hurt and I did not like it.

Straightening my shoulders, I swallowed back the sensation. Forced it behind a wall of ice where it wouldn't get in the way.

When she turned to face me, her eyes widening with surprise, I didn't even flinch.

Despite the fact that she was still the most beautiful woman I'd ever seen.

6

ISABELLE

I slipped the hammer into the loop on my tool belt and stood. Building a new Santa's Workshop sign hadn't been on my to-do list today, but as soon as I'd unpacked the old one, I'd realized it wouldn't cut it. Since I didn't want my dad to argue with me about prioritizing essential tasks—he would have claimed the old sign was good enough for one more year—I gathered some wood we had lying around and took it upon myself to build a new one.

Tilting my head, I admired my handiwork. It wasn't perfect, but paint would help.

An odd tingling sensation raced up my spine and the hairs on my arms stood on end. Maybe it was just the cold. I'd forgotten my coat again but hadn't bothered to trudge back to my house to get it.

Then again, maybe it wasn't the cold. It really felt like I was being watched.

I turned around and almost swallowed my own tongue.

Standing just outside the open garage door was Elias Stoneheart.

Elias.

Here.

At my farm.

He wore a dark wool coat—the nice kind that a man would wear over a suit—with slacks and dress shoes. His dark hair was thick and styled off his forehead and the stubble on his chiseled jaw made him look mature in a way that shouldn't have surprised me. After all, I hadn't seen him in a long time. His bright green eyes were as piercing as ever, boring into me with an intensity that made my breath catch in my throat.

This wasn't the Elias I remembered. This man was thicker, broader, and if it were possible, colder. His eyes weren't blue, but they were frozen. Solid ice.

"What are you doing here?" I asked.

"Hi, Isabelle."

That voice. It was like melted dark chocolate with a hint of peppermint.

And yes, a voice can sound like food. Trust me.

Especially Elias's voice.

"Hi?" I asked. "You didn't answer my question."

"I thought it would be good to talk in person."

"If you came all the way out here to talk to me about selling the farm, you wasted your time."

"How about we go get lunch somewhere?"

Nervous energy thrummed through me. Coming face to face with this man was stirring up a confusing mix of feelings. How could I possibly be happy to see him, considering the way our relationship had ended all those years ago, and the fact that he was trying to swindle my parents out of their farm? And yet a part of me was. There was relief and a weird tingle of excitement, neither of which made any sense.

Pushing those unwelcome sensations out of the way, I

grasped onto the anger and resentment that I'd harbored for years. Those weren't complicated or confusing.

Very straightforward, as a matter of fact.

"No." My voice snapped like a whip.

"No?"

"That's what I said." I grabbed a sawhorse and moved it a few feet closer to the other. "I know, it's amazing that someone could actually say no to you, but let me assure you, it won't be the last time."

"It's just a meal. You must be hungry. I bet you skipped breakfast."

I picked up the sign and hoisted it onto the sawhorses. "Not hungry."

"But you did skip breakfast."

"Don't act like you still know me."

"You're right, I don't. And you're also right that I'm here to talk about the farm."

"Of course I am." I went over to the shelf and started rooting around the half-empty cans of wood stain and paint. "Why else would you be here?"

"You haven't heard from Damien again. I told you I'd take care of that for you."

"Am I supposed to thank you?"

"You could."

"If you told me your company was going away forever and I'd never have to talk to any of you again, then I might thank you. Plus, Damien never showed up here unannounced while I was trying to work."

His frustrated exhale almost made me smile. Riling him up had always been fun.

But this wasn't fun. This was a battle.

"That's because he doesn't care about what happens here."

I snorted, still pawing through the paint cans. What was I even looking for? "And I'm supposed to believe you care about what happens here?"

"Yes."

"I'm not a naïve teenage girl anymore."

"I didn't say you were."

"No, but that's what you're hoping for. You're hoping you can just saunter in here with your expensive coat and fancy shoes and pretend to give a crap about my farm. Meanwhile, you're probably already envisioning what you'll do with the land when you tear everything down."

"That's not true."

His voice was too close. My back prickled and I glanced over my shoulder. He stood behind me, holding a can of red paint.

I swiped it out of his hand. "It is true."

"No, I was thinking about how much it must cost to run this place, particularly with all the maintenance and repairs."

"Our farm is more than a balance sheet." I put the paint down next to the sign and went back to the shelf to look for some green. "Not everything can be reduced to numbers."

"Everything *can* be reduced to numbers."

"Is that really what you think?"

He stepped closer and reached over me to take another can of paint off the top shelf. The scent of him swirled around me, a tantalizing blend of cologne and clean cotton.

"It's what I know." He held out the can of green.

With a scowl, I took it from him. It was heavier than I'd thought it would be and the weight of it dragged my arms down with a jolt.

Elias grabbed the bottom of the can, putting us way too close for comfort.

I straightened and jerked the can away. "I've got it."

The amused glint in his eye and subtle smirk on his lips made me want to smack him.

"And you're wrong," I said. "This farm is a lot more than the numbers. It means something to people and that matters more than money."

He scoffed. "Nothing matters more than money."

Setting the paint down, I raised my eyebrows.

"When it comes to business," he said, as if that made it better.

I gazed at him for a moment. At his styled hair and perfectly tailored clothes. He probably drove an expensive car and lived in a mansion with a view. And I wondered if any of it made him happy.

He didn't seem happy.

But maybe I just didn't know him anymore.

"Well, I guess we'll have to agree to disagree. I think this farm means something regardless of whether it turns a profit."

"Why? Because people come here to spend money they don't have on decorations and junk food they don't need?"

"That's a very Grinchy view of Christmas Village."

"It's a waste of resources. You have acres of property that serves no purpose ten months out of the year. And for what? So you can throw up some lights and cheesy decorations and people can wander around with their snot-nosed kids for an hour? What's the point?"

"Christmas cheer," I said, like it was the most obvious thing in the world. Because it was. "People love Christmas Village. It's cute and fun and makes them happy."

"Not so happy that they pay your bills."

"My bills are none of your business. We're doing fine."

"You keep saying that but we both know it's not true."

Sparks of anger sizzled inside me. I opened my mouth to snap at him when Cole appeared in the open garage door.

"Hey, Izz, are we—" He caught sight of Elias and stopped short.

For the first time ever, I found myself wishing Cole and I had worked out. If only I could have sauntered up to the big, burly farm hand and pressed my body against him. And watched Elias's eyes turn an even brighter shade of green as he seethed with envy.

Then again, that would require Elias to care. Which he didn't.

"Hey, Cole," I said. "Can you give me a minute?"

"You need any help?" he asked, casting a fierce glare at Elias.

"No, I'm good."

He took a step closer. "You sure?"

It was like watching two predators posturing. Elias didn't move but his back was straight and he regarded Cole with cool indifference. I could see the undercurrent of competitiveness, just below the surface of that icy façade.

Cole was more obvious, drawing up to his full height— he was certainly a big guy—and flexing his fists a few times.

"I'm sure." I put up a placating hand toward Cole. "He was just leaving."

Elias's eyes flicked to me, then back to Cole, but he didn't say a word.

He was good, I had to give him that. He didn't argue that he had a right to be there or tell Cole to mind his own business. Just stood his ground, as if completely confident that this interaction was going to go his way, regardless of what the other man did.

Cole wasn't the type to back down, but I gave him a

quick shake of my head. With another hard look at Elias, he turned and left.

Elias shifted so he was facing me. "Where were we?"

"You aren't happy." I closed my mouth, pressing my lips together. I hadn't meant to say that.

His brow furrowed. "What?"

"Never mind." I took a quick breath to steady myself. "I have to go. I have a million things to do."

I left the sign where it was, propped up on the sawhorses, and stormed past him, out of the shop. He didn't follow.

But I was under no illusions that this was over. It had only begun.

7

ISABELLE

*S*weat trickled down my temple and I swiped it with the back of my arm. I'd probably just left a smear of dirt on my face but I didn't care. That was what showers were for.

Horace brayed at me from behind the fence.

"You're not going to die of starvation." I dug my pitchfork into the barley straw and shoveled another heap into his feeding trough.

He brayed at me again. Impatient donkey. If I let him into the enclosure while I was filling his trough, he'd probably knock me over. Not on purpose, he just seemed to have no idea how big he was.

My arms burned and my feet hurt. I'd managed to keep busy since Elias had left—not difficult around here, especially this time of year—but I was running out of energy. I probably needed to stop and eat something now that the animals were fed.

I finished up with Horace's dinner and let him into the enclosure. He was dark brown with a white muzzle and big black eyes. Donkeys were good at keeping predators away from the reindeer and he took his job very seriously. I wasn't sure if he realized he was a donkey or thought he was a farm dog.

With Horace happily munching on his straw, I tightened my ponytail, picked out a few pieces of straw, and headed down the path to my house.

My parents had built the shell of a cottage when I was little, thinking they might rent it out to guests someday, but they hadn't finished the inside. Now it was a cozy house painted a happy shade of yellow. The front porch had a pair of chairs that I'd never used and hanging planters that I needed to take down for the winter.

Inside I had a sectional with a green knit blanket my friend Annika's mom had given me for a housewarming gift draped over the back. A wood stove sat in the corner and windows let in plenty of light. Most of the furniture were things I'd found and refinished, like the table and chairs in the dining area and the bookshelves along the wall.

I loved my little house, although I didn't exactly spend a lot of time here. I was too busy working. But it made life easier to live on the farm instead of in town and I liked having my own space, even if it was mostly just a place for me to sleep.

My phone rang, the ringtone a cheery instrumental rendition of *Let it Snow*. Absently, I wondered if I should get out some Christmas decorations. As much as I loved the holiday season, with all the lights and sparkle, I hadn't gotten around to decorating for myself last year. Too busy.

And I lived just outside the most Christmassy place in town, so that made up for it.

Mostly.

With a sigh, I pulled my phone out of my pocket. If it was Elias again, I was letting it go to voicemail.

It wasn't. It was Marigold.

"Hey, Mari."

"Hi. I'm sorry to bother you. I know you must be crazy busy."

"I actually just got home."

"Forgot to eat again?"

I laughed. "How did you know?"

"It's kind of a pattern."

"That's probably true." I went into the kitchen and started rooting around for something quick to eat. "What's up with you?"

"Nothing exciting. I just had a client cancel so I figured I'd give you a call. See how all the holiday prep is coming along."

"It's coming. There's always more to do than hours in the day, but I'm used to it."

"Just stop forgetting to eat. And get the hay out of your hair."

My hand strayed to my head and I pulled out a piece of straw. "I don't have hay in my hair. It's straw."

"Oh, well that's much better."

With a laugh, I grabbed a string cheese and took it to the couch. "There are worse things."

"True. Is the Grinch still texting you?"

I groaned. "Worse. He showed up at the farm today."

She gasped. "No. Elias was there?"

"Yes and he scared the crap out of me. I was working in the shop and when I turned around, there he was."

"Wow. I'm shocked. Are you okay?"

"I'm fine." Was I, though? "It freaked me out at first but once I got rid of him, it wasn't a big deal."

I was lying to her. Why was I lying?

Because I didn't want to admit how much seeing him had shaken me.

"It had to have been weird to see him, though. Was that the first time? How did he look?"

"The same, but also different. It's hard to explain. Older, obviously. But it was more than that. He was always kind of serious but this guy was downright cold."

"The way you said that totally made me shiver."

A tingle ran up my spine. "Me, too. It's hard to believe I ever— Anyway."

"It was a long time ago and you were both so young."

"I know."

"I'm guessing he didn't apologize for anything."

"Not even close. But that would have surprised me more than seeing him again. I would have had to assume he was either a not-evil clone or an alien."

"I like not-evil clone. That would be nice, wouldn't it? Elias was great when he wasn't being a total jerk."

"Unfortunately, I think the total jerk completely took over."

"Like an alien."

"Exactly."

She sighed. "It's such a bummer. You two were great together back then."

"Don't remind me."

"Sorry. He's horrible and I hope he never speaks to you again."

"Much better, thank you."

"You're welcome. But let me and Annika know if you need help with anything. Like running Elias out of town. I'm sure her brothers would be happy to help."

Our other best friend, Annika, was the youngest of seven, and the only girl. She had more brothers than she knew what to do with. And Mari was right. I'd grown up with the Haven brothers. If I asked them for help, they'd be here in an instant.

But I was terrible at asking for help, even if I needed it.

Which I didn't. Not this time.

"That's okay, I can handle him."

"I have total faith in you."

"Thanks. By the way, I love what you did with my hair. Even though it had straw in it." Marigold was a talented hairstylist and she'd opened her own salon here in town. She'd given me the cutest haircut a few days ago, although because I was me, I'd gone back to my regular ponytail within a day.

"That makes my heart happy. Speaking of pretty hair, and pretty things, are you sure I can't talk you into going to the masquerade ball with me and Annika?"

The Tilikum Historical Society was putting on a masquerade ball at the Grand Peak Hotel next weekend. It was totally Marigold's jam. She was the sweetest, most romantic soul I'd ever met, and a ball with costumes and dancing was probably her dream come true.

Not so much mine.

"I'm sorry, honey, but I just don't have time." Which was true. Even if I'd been dying to go, this time of year I was too busy for much of a social life.

"I'm just making sure. If you change your mind, Annika and I would love to be your dates. And you never know, we might make the acquaintance of some fine gentlemen."

"You're the cutest. But the last thing I need in my life right now is a gentleman. Or any sort of man."

Especially one with coal in place of a heart.

"Okay. I should let you go. Someone just pulled up, so it looks like I might have a walk-in. I'll check up on you later."

"Thanks, Mari."

"Don't forget to eat. And shower."

"I've got both covered. Don't worry about me."

We said goodbye. Like a reflex I couldn't control, I swiped to my messages. I was absolutely not checking to see if Elias had texted again. I was making sure he hadn't. I didn't want to hear from him. Or find out if he was staying in town and where.

I wasn't interested.

Self-delusion was exhausting sometimes.

He was probably staying with his aunt and uncle. I doubted he'd left. A little sass from me wouldn't be enough to dissuade him if he had his mind set on something. Of that I was sure.

Annoyed that he'd invaded my mind, I finished my snack. I thought about a shower, but it was still daylight and I could probably squeeze in a little more work. Why bother getting clean if I was just going to get dirty all over again?

Lively Christmas music rang out again. It was my mom.

"What's up? I was just about to head back to the village to get a few more things done."

"How about you come over to the house instead. I made dinner."

I glanced at the string cheese wrapper—the remnants of my sad meal. "That actually sounds great. I'll be over in a few."

A WREATH with a big red bow hung on the back door of my parents' house and Dad had already strung lights around a few of the trees. One year, he'd asked Mom why she bothered decorating the back where no one could see. She'd replied that she could see it and it made her happy. Every year since, Dad had made sure to put up lights where they could be seen from the kitchen window.

That was love, right there.

I went inside and the smell of homemade chicken soup and fresh rolls filled the air. Dad was busy ladling soup into bowls while Mom set the butter dish on the table.

"Wash up," Mom said.

I was already heading for the sink. It was an iron clad rule in Mom's house that everyone wash their hands before sitting down to eat.

Farm life.

"Dinner smells great." I lathered up with lavender scented soap. "I'm glad you called. I still haven't been to the store."

"I had a feeling," Mom said.

We all sat down with our meal. Mom gave Dad a side-long glance as he added a pile of pepper to his soup. I took a roll and buttered it.

"Are you going to bring it up or do we have to pry it out of you?" Mom asked, breaking the brief silence.

I stopped with my roll halfway to my mouth. "Me?"

"Yes, you."

With a sigh, I set it down. "You must have talked to Cole."

"He stopped by the house before he went home. Was Elias really here?"

"Unfortunately."

"What on earth did he want?"

"He works for DataStream with that jerk-off Damien Barrett. He actually called me over the weekend to try to get me to talk to him about selling the farm. Long story short, I hung up on him and he showed up here earlier today."

Dad's expression was hard. He was not a fan of Elias Stoneheart. "You should have sent him to me. I'd be happy to talk to him."

"It's fine Dad, I have it under control."

"If he comes back, you need to tell me. I don't want him on my property."

"I know, but I got rid of him." I took a sip of soup.

Mom's eyes were warm with sympathy. "Are you okay?"

"Of course I am. Why wouldn't I be?"

She shared a quick glance with Dad. "You haven't seen him in a long time."

"That's why it wasn't a big deal. We dated in high school. It doesn't matter now."

"Honey, if you want to talk about it, we're here for you." She reached over and touched my arm.

Her attempt at comfort was making me edgy. I took a couple mouthfuls of soup and mentally calculated how much daylight I had left. Then again, I could also go out to the shop and put a coat of paint on the sign I'd built this morning. I didn't need sunlight for that.

"There's nothing to talk about. We're not selling to him any more than we were going to sell to Barrett. And sure, he's my ex, but that was a long time ago. The past is in the past."

Thankfully, they didn't press the issue. Mom started eating but Dad only stirred his soup, added more pepper, and stirred it again. He cleared his throat and he and Mom shared another look.

I put my spoon down. "You guys are acting weird. What's going on?"

"We've been talking," Mom said.

Dad stopped stirring. "About the farm. Specifically, about Christmas Village."

"What about it?"

"This is going to be the last year we have it open."

My dad's words seem to hang in the air over the table. I stared at my parents, waiting for the punch line.

"I'm sorry, what did you say? Because I think you just said you're closing Christmas Village and there's no way I heard you correctly."

"We love the village as much as you do," Mom said. "But it takes up so much space, not to mention the time and labor."

"I know it's a lot of work but it's iconic. It's a Tilikum tradition. We can't close it."

"We've tried to figure out a way to make it work," Dad said. "Believe me, we've looked at all our options."

"So that's it? We're giving up? Should I call Elias right now and tell him he can have the farm?"

"No, that's why we have to close the village," Dad said. "It's the only chance we have to keep the farm."

"I'm not following."

Dad took a deep breath. "You already know we're in debt up to our eyeballs. But what you don't know is that a couple of years ago, I borrowed money from a private lender, with the farm and its income potential as collateral. Now, before you tell me that was a terrible idea, I didn't have a choice. The bank wouldn't extend us any more credit and I thought we could pay it off."

"But you couldn't."

He shared another sad look with Mom and shook his head. "No. So now we're stuck. Christmas Village takes up valuable space that could be put to better use."

"What better use?"

"A commercial crop. Once the snow melts in the spring, we can get to work clearing the area and getting it ready for planting. With any luck, we'll have a good enough harvest to pay off at least some of the debt—enough to keep us here, at least."

"Do we have enough space for that?"

"If you add the pasture to the space we use for the village, we have room for a solid crop that will pay well, especially if we qualify for subsidies."

"But if we're using the pasture for crops, where are we going to—" I stopped short, my eyes widening. "You can't be serious. Our herd? You can't get rid of the reindeer. They're part of the family."

"Honey, we love them, too," Mom said. "But they're expensive to maintain."

"And Horace?"

They looked at each other again, foreheads lined with discomfort.

"Horace has to stay with the reindeer. He'll go crazy if you separate them. And who's going to take a herd of reindeer and a guard donkey?"

"Horace will be fine," Dad said.

"No, he won't. Neither will the reindeer. And neither will this town. This can't be the only solution."

"Sometimes there aren't any good answers," Mom said. "And we have to accept the things we can't change."

I pushed my bowl away, my appetite gone. "No. I won't accept that. There has to be a way to keep the farm and Christmas Village. We've talked about making it more permanent or using the buildings for something else in the summer. And what about farm tours? We hardly do any because we don't promote them. But if we did—"

"Who's going to take that on?" Dad asked. "You? You're already too busy. And we can't afford to hire more help."

"Then how are you going to destroy the village in the spring?"

Dad sighed. "Re-purposing the land will require some upfront costs but I've run the numbers and it should work."

I shook my head. "You didn't buy this land to become a part of corporate agriculture. Don't get me wrong, I don't have anything against growing commercial crops. People have to eat. But you built this farm because you wanted to create a place that honored the land and provided something important to the community. And you've done that for years. You can't sell out now."

"We don't like it any more than you do," Mom said. "But either we sell out to DataStream and lose the entire farm or we sell out to corporate agriculture and get to stay. The choice is obvious."

Frustration thrummed in my veins. I wanted to get back to work, as if somehow I could build or fix something that would make a difference. But this was bigger than a new Santa's Workshop sign. Bigger than any farm chore I could complete tonight.

Still, there had to be a way. My parents were tired. They'd been struggling to keep our farm open for years. I didn't blame them for thinking they had to give in.

But I wasn't ready to throw in the towel. Not by a long shot. I was going to find a way to keep the farm and keep Christmas Village. I had to.

And I was not letting Elias get involved.

8

ELIAS

*T*his day had too many thresholds. First the town, then the Cooks' farm. Now this.

I stood on the doorstep of my aunt and uncle's house for the first time in years. The last time I'd been here, I'd been nothing but a dumb kid. Fresh out of high school and itching to leave my life behind. Get out of Tilikum and make my mark.

Get away from the pain.

There wasn't pain anymore. I'd buried it a long time ago, encased it in ice.

Which meant knocking on this door didn't hold any special significance. It didn't have meaning. I was just stopping by since I was in town.

The familiar chill spread through me as I pushed away the emotions that tried to leak through.

Better.

I knocked.

Aunt Hattie opened the door and her eyes widened. Her gray hair was in a low ponytail and she was dressed in a hooded sweatshirt and jeans. She was my mother's older sister, but whereas my mother was tall and lean, Hattie was on the shorter side with a softer frame. She'd spent her life working as an elementary school teacher until she'd retired a few years ago.

"Elias." Her voice was almost a whisper. She blinked. "Is everything all right? Come inside."

"Everything is fine." I let her lead me into the house. A hint of wood smoke from the fireplace mingled with the scent of her laundry soap. It was uncomfortably familiar.

"Are you sure? Did something happen to your father?"

My brow furrowed. I rarely thought about my father and spoke to him even less. "Not that I'm aware of."

"Are you okay?"

"Yes."

"Then what are you doing here?"

"I was in town."

She shut the door. "In town? Why?"

"Business."

"Oh. Well, then. I wish you would have called, I'd have had something on hand for dinner. But never mind. You're here."

I didn't know why she was making such a big deal out of my presence. I'd seen her six months ago.

Or maybe it had been eight.

More?

I didn't know.

"It was last minute. I didn't think I'd have to come all the way out here."

She smiled, revealing more lines around her eyes than I remembered. "I'm so glad you did."

"Is Dale home?"

"He's around here somewhere. Probably out back." She

gestured for me to follow her into the living room. "Have a seat. I'll go find him. He'll be so glad to see you."

I mumbled a reply but didn't sit down. I didn't want to get too comfortable. Hattie hurried through the kitchen and out the back door.

They hadn't changed a thing since I'd lived here. Same worn chocolate brown couch with a distinct depression in Uncle Dale's spot. Same coffee table cluttered with books— Aunt Hattie liked thrillers—and a few of the snow globes she collected. She had more on the mantle and a few others on the bookshelves flanking the fireplace.

I wandered over to the mantle. Next to a snow globe with a pair of ice-skating penguins was my senior picture. I scowled at the young man in the frame, at his subtle smile and careless hair. I barely recognized him.

"Well, I'll be." Uncle Dale came in through the kitchen. He was tall and lanky—all long arms and skinny legs. He still had a full head of hair, although it had gone gray. "I thought Hattie was pulling my leg."

She nudged him with her elbow. "I told you he was here."

"Uncle Dale." I offered my hand.

He took it and shook with a firm grip, his expression hard to read. "Good to see you. What brings you to Tilikum?"

"I'm here on business."

"What kind of business would you have here?"

My first instinct was to keep it vague. Not mention the Cooks' farm. But why? It was just a real estate transaction. I didn't have anything to hide.

"My company wants to acquire Cook Family Farm. I came to speak to the family about the deal."

Dale's eyebrows lifted. "What does your company want with a farm?"

"They want the land it's on."

"But what would happen to the farm?" Hattie asked.

"Obviously everything has to be demolished to make room for the datacenter complex we're going to build."

She gasped. "But where will they have Christmas Village?"

I let out a frustrated breath. What was with people's obsession with the village? "That's not my problem. I'm just here to iron out the details of the deal."

"I'm surprised the Cooks are willing to sell," Dale said.

"They aren't exactly amenable to our offer," I admitted.

Hattie crossed her arms. "I see. So you're here to convince Isabelle. That should be interesting."

Interesting wasn't what I would have called it. "I have to take a second look at the numbers. The cost to acquire the property combined with improvements might be more than we're willing to spend."

And the hassle of dealing with Isabelle might not be worth my sanity.

There were other tracts of land. Working out a deal with the Cooks on this trip would have been ideal, but after my encounter with Isabelle, it clearly wasn't going to happen in an afternoon. I wasn't admitting defeat. I was simply factoring in efficiency. Damien had already spent six months on this deal. I could spend the next six months trying to coax Isabelle into selling, or I could focus my efforts on finding a suitable replacement.

Preferably land that wasn't currently owned by a stubborn woman with sawdust on her ass and straw in her ponytail.

If I delivered an equally desirable piece of land, I'd still show up Damien and prove myself to Nigel.

"Well, it's almost dinner time," Hattie said. "Enough business talk. I think I have some pork tenderloin in the fridge that'll feed all of us."

Without waiting for a response, she went to the kitchen. A moment later, Christmas music filled the air, along with the clatter of cupboard doors, pots, and pans.

"Can I get you a drink?" Dale asked.

"Absolutely."

I resisted the urge to tell Hattie it was too damn early for that music while Dale poured us each a glass of Scotch.

He handed one to me and I took a healthy swallow.

"Have you heard from your father recently?" he asked.

"No. But that's not unusual."

"Hattie called your mother a few weeks back. Seems like she's doing well."

"I wouldn't know." I spoke to my mother about as often as my father, which was almost never. They'd divorced years ago and my mom had remarried soon after. My father had chosen the trade-in method of relationships. He got older but the women were always the same age.

Not that I cared. They both had enough money to do whatever they wanted and I didn't have to waste my time dealing with them.

"How have you been?" Dale asked.

"Fine."

"Fine? That's all?"

I took another drink and wandered over to the window. "I'm busy. Business is going well. I have a jackass in my way but he won't be a problem for long. That's part of why I'm here."

"Always the competitor."

I shrugged. "I'm ambitious. Nothing wrong with that."

"No. As long as your ambition is focused in the right direction."

"There's one direction. Up."

"Up the corporate ladder." There was something in his tone I couldn't quite place. Resentment? Disappointment? "I heard about Jake Marlon. Shame. He was too young."

Jake Marlon had given me my first job out of business school, but more importantly, he'd been my mentor. My rise through the ranks at DataStream had largely been due to what I'd learned from him.

Unfortunately for Jake, he'd dropped dead of a heart attack on the seventeenth green. He'd only just turned fifty.

"Yeah, that was unexpected."

"Was he married? Leave anyone behind?"

"No." I almost chuckled. Jake had not been the marrying kind. "He probably had a girlfriend, but he went through women too fast for me to keep track."

"Well, I was sorry to hear the news."

"Me, too."

"What about you, Elias?" Hattie called from the kitchen. "Are you bringing anyone special home for Christmas this year?"

My brow furrowed. I never came home for Christmas, so what did she—

Right, she was just asking if I was dating anyone.

"No. I'm too busy."

Hattie leaned out the kitchen doorway. "Too busy to date?"

"Yes." I hoped my tone would end this discussion.

It didn't. "Wasn't there a young woman you were seeing? Dale, what was her name?"

"I don't know," Dale answered. "I don't think we ever met her."

They hadn't. I never dated anyone seriously enough to introduce them to my family.

"I guess he just hasn't met the right girl," Hattie said. "Yet."

There wasn't a right girl. Not in the way Hattie was implying. Relationships were complicated and distracting. I loved women as much as the next man, but I didn't need the baggage—or expense—that went along with dating one seriously.

My phone saved me from having to reply. A spark of hope that it was Isabelle momentarily flared to life before I could squash it. She wasn't going to miraculously change her mind about selling the farm and I had no other reason to speak to her.

And it wasn't Isabelle. It was Nigel.

I set down my Scotch and went outside to take the call.

"Stoneheart," I answered.

"Any updates?"

"Not yet. I spoke with Isabelle Cook briefly, but she was — busy."

"Hmm." He didn't sound pleased. "Elias, I'm going to level with you. It's no secret that you're a possible candidate for CFO. So is Damien. In fact, I was ready to hand him the promotion until he got tangled up in this land deal. It should have been fairly straightforward but he's been dicking around for months. I'm impressed that you took the initiative to step in."

"Thank you."

"But initiative and success are two different things. I need you to close this deal. If you do, the promotion is yours. Are we clear?"

"Absolutely. Consider it done."

"Good. Keep me updated."

"Will do."

He ended the call.

The fire of ambition burned in my veins. The fact that he'd considered Damien over me, even briefly, was infuriating. But now the ball was in my court.

Close the deal. Get the promotion. And everything that entailed.

Gone were any thoughts of finding another tract of land. This was my shot. I was going to take it.

But I'd underestimated Isabelle. That was a mistake I wouldn't make again.

Although I didn't relish the idea of spending more time in Tilikum, I didn't have a choice. Isabelle could ignore my calls and texts. In order to wear her down, I'd have to be here in person.

I brought up Alice's number.

"This is Alice."

"I need you in Tilikum by tomorrow."

"Excuse me?"

"Nigel wants me to close this deal but it's going to be tricky. I'm going to need to stay here in town."

"What does that have to do with me?"

"You're my assistant."

"I know my job title. Why can't I just work from the office?"

"Because I need you to work from here."

"There's no logic to that."

I clenched my teeth. "There is logic to it, but that's beside the point. Be here by noon tomorrow."

"I can't just up and leave. I have my daughter, remember?"

"Bring her."

She sputtered before answering. "I can't just bring her."

"Why not? How old is she?"

"She's five."

"Then how much space could she occupy? Get a room with two beds."

"It's not about space. She goes to preschool."

I scoffed. "I'm sure she'll still get into Harvard if she misses a few days of preschool."

"Who's going to watch her while I work?"

That one made me pause until the faint sound of Christmas music reminded me of where I was. "My aunt."

"Your aunt? You have an aunt in Tilikum?"

"Yes and she was a school teacher. Problem solved."

"How do you know she's not busy?"

"She's retired."

"Elias, my daughter has some special needs. She can't be with just anyone."

"My aunt was a special education teacher. She'll be fine."

"Was she really or are you making that up?"

"Why would I make that up?"

"To get what you want."

"I wouldn't lie to get what I want."

She paused, as if she didn't believe me. "Then give me her name and number."

"Why?"

"So I can talk to her myself. If I decide she'd be okay with Maddie, then I'll be there tomorrow."

"Who's Maddie?"

"My daughter," she practically shouted into the phone. "Why are you so clueless?"

Ignoring her insult, I put her on speaker and looked up Hattie's number in my contacts.

"Happy now?" I asked.

"Not at all."

"Stop by my house first and bring me some clothes. I didn't plan to stay."

"Anything else I can get you, your highness?"

"Cute. Look, this benefits you as much as me. If I get promoted, you do, too."

"Does that mean I get a raise?"

I hesitated.

"Elias, don't be a Scrooge. You're going to get a big raise. You can make sure I get one, too."

"Fine, I'll get you a raise. After I get the promotion."

"And you're paying my travel expenses."

I coughed. "Excuse me?"

"You're making me drive over there and stay for however long. I'm not paying for that."

"Fine," I said through clenched teeth.

"And don't put me in some crappy roadside motel. I'm staying wherever you are."

The cash register noises were going off in my head again. "Fine. For fuck's sake, just get here."

I ended the call before she could throw any more demands at me.

The cold air bit my skin but I paused before going back inside. The scent of pine trees and wet earth surrounded me. It smelled like Tilikum.

With an annoyed growl, I went back inside.

Determination filled me. I was going to get that promotion, and I was going to get rid of Damien, all with one little small-town farm. Poor Isabelle. She had no idea who was coming for her.

9

ELIAS

*T*he coffee at the Copper Kettle Diner was mediocre at best. It made me miss the shop in my building, even with the too-early Christmas crap and the crazy-eyed barista. Whitewashed wood, landscape paintings, and an antique quilt on the wall gave the place a farmhouse vibe and the scent of fried potatoes and toast hung in the air.

And of course, it was decorated for Christmas.

Although my aunt and uncle had offered my old room—no way that was happening—I'd set myself up at the Grand Peak Hotel. It would do for now.

I'd done some work this morning from the hotel and decided to find a place to eat while I waited for Alice. I glanced at my watch. She wasn't late, but I was still annoyed. I pushed aside my mostly-empty plate and signaled for the waitress to refill my coffee.

She did. Still no Alice.

Finally, the door opened and she came in. She slipped onto the booth seat across from me. "I'm here. Happy now?"

I looked at my watch. "You're late."

"It's twelve-oh-seven and I had to stop by your aunt and uncle's first, so don't give me crap about it. Speaking of, is Hattie really your aunt?"

"Yes."

"And you grew up with them?"

"For a while."

"Unreal."

"What?"

"I don't know how you could have been raised by such a lovely woman and turned into—" She waved her hand, gesturing at me. "This."

"What is that supposed to mean?"

"I expected her to be mean or grouchy or something. But even on the phone yesterday, I could tell she's a total sweetheart."

"So?"

"I just don't know how you're related to such a nice woman. And she's amazing with Maddie."

"Who's Maddie?"

She glared at me.

"Right, your kid."

"They invited us to stay with them while we're in town and I think I might take them up on it. I don't want to impose, but I think Maddie would be more comfortable there. She already loves your aunt and uncle and they're so sweet."

"Good. Saves me the cost of your hotel."

"Why are you so cheap?"

"I'm not cheap. I'm practical."

"No, you're cheap. You could probably afford their biggest suite but you only got a regular room for yourself, right?"

"I don't need their biggest suite."

"Thank you for proving my point."

"That's not being cheap and why do you care what kind of room I have?"

"I don't. Although if you want to be cheap, I don't know why you brought me out here. I still say I could do my job from the office."

"If I have to be here, you have to be here."

She sighed. "Elias logic at its finest. So what's going on with this farm?"

"I tried talking to Isabelle Cook yesterday but she's being stubborn. Doesn't want to talk numbers, just insists that the farm is special and therefore it doesn't have to do things like cover its costs or pay its bills."

"I take it the farm has been in her family for a while?"

"Her parents bought it before she was born. She grew up there."

"I'd say that makes her attachment to it pretty understandable."

"Her attachment is sentimental and unrealistic. The farm is losing money."

"Okay, but you can't dismiss her feelings like they don't matter."

"They don't."

She rolled her eyes. "Not to you. But how she feels about the farm is a huge part of why she's being stubborn about selling. You can't blow that off."

"Then how do I go around her feelings?"

"Maybe you don't go around them. Maybe you have to work with them."

This conversation was grating on me more than the Christmas decorations. "How the hell am I supposed to do that?"

"Considering your general lack of emotion, you might be out of luck."

"You're not helping."

"I think you should start by acknowledging that for this family, it's not just a business. It's their home and livelihood and obviously they're going to have a certain attachment to it. Plus, it sounds like this town really loves the Christmas Village they do there."

I groaned. "Who told you that?"

"Your aunt."

"We're not talking about Christmas Village."

She tilted her head, regarding me through narrowed eyes. "Why do you hate Christmas so much?"

"Who said I hated Christmas?"

"No one, but you clearly do. You complain about it every year."

"It's a waste of resources. People spend money they don't have buying gifts and throwing parties, not to mention the incessant pressure to spend time with people you don't care about. It's all fake. The decorations, the music, the so-called traditions. None of it actually means anything."

"Such a Grinch."

"Focus. My opinions on Christmas have nothing to do with the Cooks' farm."

"Fine, your hatred of the happiest season of the year can remain a mystery. But I still say you ignore Isabelle Cook's feelings at your peril."

I glanced out the window. I hated feelings. They were messy and irrational. Unfortunately for me, Alice was right. I couldn't pretend Isabelle's feelings didn't exist, unreasonable as they were. I needed to find a way to work with her emotions, not against them.

"Okay, you might have a point. I'll talk to Isabelle about her— feelings."

"Don't worry, it won't hurt you."

No, it wouldn't. Isabelle couldn't hurt me. No one could.

Alice stood. "As much as I'd love to have lunch while we talk about the sassy farm girl, I have other work to do. There's a coffee shop up the street, I'll probably go set up there until I need to get back to Maddie."

I nodded. "I'll text you if I need anything."

"Let me know when you're going back to the farm."

"Why?"

"Because I want to see it."

I didn't know why she wanted to see the farm but I didn't bother asking. "Probably tomorrow. I want to give Isabelle more time to cool off."

Alice's eyebrows drew in and she shouldered her bag. "You really riled her up, didn't you."

"No."

"Okay, sure. I'll talk to you later."

She left and I checked my messages. Nigel had cc'd me on a reply to Damien. It looked like Damien was trying to get the project back by sending Nigel alternative real estate listings. Nigel's reply—*Elias is handling it*—made me crack a smile.

You're going to have to work harder than that to beat me, Damien.

Out of nowhere, Harvey Johnston walked over to my booth and sat down. He had a scruffy beard and wore a wide-brimmed hat and a leather vest over his worn flannel shirt and jeans.

"Are you in the right place?" I asked.

"Sure, sure," he said, his voice gruff. "New in town?"

"Not exactly."

"Don't remember seeing you."

"I lived here when I was a kid."

"Oh." He rubbed his beard like I'd given him something to ponder. "Not much changes `round here, does it?"

My thoughts strayed to Isabelle. To the girl who'd become a woman while I was away. "Some things do."

"Watch out for the squirrels. They're organized."

"Are they?"

"Oh, you betcha. They'll steal the shirt off your back. Gotta be careful."

"I'll keep that in mind."

"How long you staying?"

I wasn't sure why he'd sat down at my table, or why I was letting him engage me in conversation. But I was just curious enough to keep talking.

"Hopefully not long. I'm here to take care of some business."

"Business? Good, good. Business is good."

"Indeed."

"Gotta watch out for the past, though."

That was an odd thing to say. "The past?"

"Yes, yes." He patted his vest as if trying to find something he'd left in a pocket. "The past always catches up with you. Can't hide from it."

"I don't need to hide from the past. It's over."

"That's what we all think. But it haunts us."

This was turning into one of the strangest conversations I'd ever had. "I'm not sure I know what you're talking about."

He met my gaze and the sudden clarity in his eyes was startling. "Can't hide. It always finds you. Better to face it on your terms."

I had no idea what to say to that.

"You grew up here?" he asked, although I wasn't sure if the question was directed at me or if he was clarifying for himself. "Then you'll know. You'll know."

"I'll know what?"

"Past will haunt you," he muttered as he got up and turned in a circle, patting his vest again like he'd lost something. "Look out for those damn squirrels."

Bewildered, I watched him wander to the front and out the door.

What the hell had that been about?

But I didn't have the time—or the inclination—to ponder an odd encounter with Tilikum's resident crazy old man. I needed to stay focused. The sooner I closed this deal, the sooner I could get back to my life. I didn't want to spend more time in this town than was absolutely necessary. Especially with the holidays coming up. I needed to be safely in my condo, insulated from the annoyances of the holiday season.

To do that, I had to figure out how to navigate Isabelle's feelings, a task I was not looking forward to in the least.

10

ISABELLE

I could feel the droplets of paint on my cheek, but I'd clean up later. There was still one more candy cane outside the Peppermint Parlor—the candy shop in Christmas Village—that needed to be repainted. The rest of the building looked quite a bit better. Cole and I had gotten a lot done this morning and because of that, I was in a good mood.

But the sight of Elias walking toward me sucked all the happiness out of the air in an instant.

I groaned. "Great. Scrooge is back."

Cole turned and for a second I wondered how he managed to paint without getting any on himself. Not even on his hands.

"Do you want me to get rid of him?"

Elias wasn't alone. A woman walked with him. She was cute—layered blond hair that even Mari would approve of and dressed in a navy winter coat and slacks.

A twinge of jealousy snaked its way through me. Was she his girlfriend? Why would he bring a woman with him?

Of course, I couldn't possibly be jealous. Elias and I had ended a long time ago. I didn't care who he was with now.

I clung to that lie as he stopped in front of me. His eyes swept up and down and I wondered if he was judging my overalls. His gaze darted to Cole, then back again.

"Isabelle."

"Oh good, you're still in town."

The woman leaned closer to him and whispered. "I like her already."

He shot her a slight glare, then turned his attention back to me. "Morning."

Really? He wanted to exchange pleasantries? "Morning, I guess? Did you bring reinforcements?"

"This is my assistant, Alice."

Alice stepped forward and offered her hand. "Hi, I'm Alice Moore. Nice to meet you."

"Isabelle Cook." I shook Alice's hand. "I don't want to be rude but if you're here to talk me into selling the farm to him, you're wasting your time."

"Actually, I just wanted to see the place."

She seemed awfully friendly. My first instinct was to like her but maybe that was Elias's game. Some kind of good cop, bad cop thing.

"We're pretty busy, trying to get ready for the holiday season and everything."

"I can give her a tour," Cole said.

I looked at him and raised my eyebrows.

His eyes weren't on me. They were on Alice.

That was interesting.

"I'd be happy to show you around," he said.

"This is Cole Phillips," I said, although neither of them seemed to remember I was here. "He knows the farm as well as anyone. I suppose he can show you around if you'd like."

She gave Cole a shy smile. "That sounds great. Thank you."

"My pleasure." Cole grinned. He held out his arm and she slipped her hand into the crook of his elbow. "This way."

Elias stepped closer to me and we watched them walk away.

"Who is he?" he asked.

"Cole works for the farm. And he's my ex."

I wasn't sure why I threw that last part in. It wasn't really relevant. Maybe I just wanted to see how Elias would react.

He didn't disappoint.

"Excuse me?" he growled. "That guy?"

"Yeah, that guy. He's really nice."

"Good for him."

"If she's your girlfriend, you don't have to worry. Cole won't do anything."

"Alice is *not* my girlfriend."

The rumbling intensity in his voice made a tingle race up my spine. And I was not at all relieved to find out he wasn't dating her. It didn't matter, and I didn't care.

I was such a liar.

"Oh. Well, never mind."

He glanced at me, but his expression was so hard to read. I didn't know what he was thinking.

"Back for round two?" I asked.

"I'm not here to argue with you."

"That's too bad. I enjoyed winning the other day."

"What makes you think you won?"

I shrugged. "You left. Then again, that's typical."

He scowled. "I left because you asked me to. But I think we should talk. How about we go get some coffee?"

"Did you bring a PowerPoint this time? Or maybe copies of our financial statements?"

"No. I realize the farm means something to you."

"It does. Which is why we won't sell."

"You keep trying to shut me down, but you can't get rid of me that easily. The farm means a lot to you, and I understand that. It's your home. You grew up here. So it's hard to imagine letting it go."

I dipped the brush into the paint and wiped off the excess before going back to painting a white stripe. "Exactly."

"I'm not trying to belittle your feelings when I say I want to talk about the financial situation you're facing."

"Interesting, because the other day, you distinctly said that money is all that matters."

"I meant it in the context of making business decisions."

"And I still disagree. Some things do matter more than money, even when it comes to running a business."

"Let's agree to disagree on that point. You have your priorities and I have mine."

"We really do have different priorities." I tried, and failed, to keep the hint of sadness out of my voice. "We always did."

He regarded me with those cold, green eyes for a long moment. "What are your priorities?"

I moved the brush back and forth across the stripe, although at this point, I was just moving paint around. "I guess my priorities include making the farm the best it can be for us and for the community and helping my parents so they can eventually retire."

"What about for yourself?"

"Those are my priorities for myself."

"No, those are your priorities for the farm and your parents. What about you? What do you want?"

I dipped the brush. A drop of white paint slid down the

surface and dangled, not quite falling to the ground.

"I don't know. I'm focused on the farm. It's what I do."

"Sure, but don't you want more for yourself?"

"More what?" The drop of white paint splashed on the ground. "More money? More nice things? This is what you don't understand. I love the farm and I love hosting Christmas Village. It makes people happy and spreads joy and that's a bigger priority for me than being able to buy a fancy car or whatever. And don't say spreading joy doesn't pay the bills."

"Well, it doesn't. Clearly."

"You really don't get it." I picked up the paint can and wiped the brush on the lip. "When you look at a balance sheet with just the numbers, sure, it might look like this farm is expendable. But that's not taking into account what it does for the community. And I know we have to pay our bills. I'm not stupid."

"I never meant to imply you were. And that's kind of my point. Don't you think you were meant for something bigger?"

"And by that you mean a bigger bank account."

He hesitated. "Not necessarily."

"Maybe the things I do are small but they can still have an impact."

"Candy cane stripes. Vital to the health of the community."

I heard the humor in his voice. It was so rare—and so disarming. It almost made me smile.

"Ha ha, Mr. Grinch. And you know what, I'd argue candy cane stripes are vital to the health of the community, at least in what they represent."

"And what's that?"

"The spirit of Christmas."

He rolled his eyes. "Don't give me that greeting card crap."

"It's not. Christmas cheer is a real thing and it brings out the best in people. That's what we do here."

"You make Christmas cheer?"

"Yes."

"And that's good for the community."

"Exactly."

"Better than new jobs and an influx of money?"

"Maybe, yeah."

He just stared at me, skepticism written all over his face.

"Don't give me that look. I can prove it."

"No, you can't."

The fire of defiance lit me up from the inside. His smug confidence was maddening. I'd show him. "Wanna bet?"

"You want to bet me that Christmas cheer matters?"

I stepped closer. "I bet I can convince you that not only does Christmas cheer matter, but this farm matters, too."

"How are we going to bet on that?"

"We're hosting a toy drive this weekend. You come help and if you still don't think what I do here has an impact on the community, I'll sit down with you and go over all the financial stuff you have in that folder of yours."

"A real conversation about selling the farm?"

"Yes."

He hesitated, his green eyes locked with mine. This was a terrible idea. I didn't want him here for the toy drive, getting in my way all morning. But now that I'd challenged him, I certainly couldn't back down.

"Deal." He held out his hand.

"But you have to be honest."

"I will."

I put down the paint can and slid my hand into his.

We shook and his grip was firm, his hand surprisingly warm. I would have thought his skin would be as icy cold as his gaze.

It wasn't and that fact was inexplicably tantalizing.

I took my hand back and resisted the urge to wipe it on my overalls. "Sunday. Nine o'clock."

"I'll be there."

My cheeks flushed but it was probably just the cold air. The tip of my nose was starting to feel numb. The urge to move in closer and snuggle up against Elias's hard, warm body hit me out of nowhere.

I stepped back. Definitely no touching.

"I'm not sure where Cole took Alice," I said.

"The tour was his idea. He can drive her home."

That did make me laugh a little. So very Elias. He probably hadn't meant to sound like a jerk. To him, that was just logical. "I'm sure he won't mind."

He nodded once and took a step back. If I hadn't known better, I would have said it looked like he was having a hard time walking away from me.

But that was just silly. I'd watched too many romantic movies with Marigold. He wasn't going to walk backward, eyes on me, inwardly struggling with the urge to rush over and kiss me.

Kiss me? I really had been watching too many movies with Mari. I didn't want him to kiss me. If he tried, I'd—

Anyway.

He didn't. There was no slow-motion retreat filled with angst. His cold eyes left mine and he turned around and walked away.

That was that. Apparently I'd see him on Sunday.

I grabbed the paint can and went back to work, wondering what I'd gotten myself into.

11

ELIAS

*T*he farm bustled with activity. People loaded down with shopping bags hauled their donations from the parking lot into the village. The Cooks had set up a temporary booth with bins and tables and a toy drive sign out front.

It was all very humanitarian, but I still wasn't sure what Isabelle thought she was going to accomplish. What good were toys going to do a bunch of kids? Clutter their rooms with stuff they didn't need and wouldn't care about after a few weeks? For what? A momentary thrill at getting to open a brightly colored package?

Was all the wrapping paper being donated, too? Seeing the size of the bins and the people already arriving with their donations, I had to wonder who was going to spend the time and money to wrap all this stuff.

Toys were fine. There wasn't anything inherently bad about them. But Christmas presents didn't do jack shit to heal a kid's wounds.

I'd know.

I didn't see Isabelle but I did see their farm guy, Cole

something. He was dressed in a dark coat and stocking cap, well-worn jeans, and brown boots. Big guy with thick arms, no doubt from hoisting hay bales or whatever he did around here. I narrowed my eyes. Isabelle had dated him? It made sense. Hard working farmer type, not unlike her. Good natured. Seemed to smile a lot.

So unlike me.

Why hadn't it worked out? There didn't appear to be any animosity between them. Did that mean she still had feelings for him? She probably saw him every day. Was she pining to have those hay-slinging arms around her again?

More importantly, why was I so jealous?

I wasn't the jealous type. If I wanted something, I went after it—and got it. Jealousy was a weakness. A distraction. But when I looked at Cole, I felt the insidious pull of envy, just knowing he'd once touched Isabelle.

Clearly Tilikum was getting to me. I had no reason to be envious of some guy who worked on the farm that I was about to shut down.

I needed to close this deal so I could get out of here.

Cole grinned at someone. Not the friendly grin of a guy greeting a local with a bag of toys. There was heat in his expression. Was he smiling at Isabelle?

My eye twitched. But his flirtatious expression wasn't for her.

It was for Alice.

My assistant approached with a little wave and stopped a couple of feet in front of him. My hands curled into fists. He needed to watch himself with her.

But why did I care? Why was this guy even on my radar? It didn't matter if he'd dated Isabelle or if he was flirting with Alice. Isabelle wasn't mine. Alice was just my assistant. She wasn't even my friend, not in any real sense of the word.

A squirrel ran by and raced up a tree. This place had me on edge. I needed to stay focused.

I walked over to Alice to see what she was doing here. I hadn't told her she needed to come.

Her eyebrows lifted when she saw me. "I didn't expect to see you here."

I wasn't about to admit to my bet with Isabelle, so I didn't bother with an explanation. "Why are you here?"

"Cole invited me." She glanced down at a young child standing next to her. "I don't think you've ever met my daughter, Maddie. Maddie, this is Mr. Stoneheart."

The little girl was the spitting image of her mom with blond hair pinned back from her face with pink hair clips and a yellow coat. She looked up at me with a bright-eyed smile and my brow furrowed. I didn't know why she looked so happy or why she was using crutches.

"Did she hurt herself?" I asked.

Alice sighed. "No. She has cerebral palsy."

"My brain has trouble talking to my legs," she said, her voice as cheerful as if she'd just announced she had ice cream for breakfast. "But I can walk. See?"

She demonstrated by taking a few steps with her crutches. Her legs turned inward at the knees and her gait was awkward, but she was right, she could walk.

I found that strangely endearing.

"Good for you," I said, and there was no sarcasm in my voice. I meant it.

Alice looked at me like something had surprised her. Cole wore a similar expression.

"Is there a rock in your chest?" Maddie pointed a finger at me.

"A rock?"

"Stoneheart."

"No, honey, that doesn't mean he has a rock in his chest." Alice brushed a wisp of hair off her forehead. "That's just his last name. He has a regular heart."

Cole snorted.

I ignored him. "Actually, I might have a rock in my chest. I've never looked."

Still wearing that bright smile, she stepped closer to stand right in front of me, then held up her hand. "Can I feel?"

The furrow in my brow deepened but I crouched so she could reach. She pressed her palm to my chest, her smile fading to a look of intense concentration.

"You have a heartbeat," she whispered.

Did I? Obviously I did. I was alive. But in another sense, I was surprised she could feel it beating.

Without replying, I stood and straightened my coat.

"Good morning," Isabelle said behind me. "Thanks for coming to help."

"Thanks for having us," Alice said. "This is my daughter, Maddie."

"Hi, Maddie. Nice to meet you."

"He has a heartbeat." She pointed at me again. "I checked."

Isabelle glanced between us. "Good to know."

"Hey Maddie, do you want to go for a ride on the miniature train?" Cole asked.

"Yes!"

"Manners, Maddie," Alice said.

"Yes, please." She took a few steps toward Cole, then glanced at Isabelle. "I have cerebral palsy."

"I see," Isabelle said.

"She gets asked about her crutches a lot," Alice said. "I

guess her solution is to just tell people before they ask questions."

"Smart kid. This way." Cole smiled down at her, then took slow steps toward the train so she didn't have to struggle to keep up.

"How old is she?" Isabelle asked.

"She's five," Alice said. "With the vocabulary of a twelve-year-old."

"No kidding. That's impressive. She's adorable."

"Thanks. She's definitely the light of my life."

"Cole is really good with kids," Isabelle said.

"Oh." Alice sounded a little flustered. "Yeah, he seems like it."

Isabelle smiled. "You go have fun. The guy with the heartbeat and I have work to do."

Alice followed Cole and Maddie deeper into the village, leaving me with Isabelle.

"I didn't know your assistant had a daughter, let alone a child with special needs."

I gazed at the little girl with her crooked, halting walk. "Neither did I."

"You didn't know she had a daughter?"

"I knew she had a kid. I didn't know she had cerebral palsy."

"Really? How long have you worked together?"

The hint of accusation in her tone riled up my defenses. "A few years but it's not like she brings her kid to work. How the hell would I know anything about her?"

Isabelle shrugged. "I don't know. Anyway, we really do have work to do."

She'd remembered her coat this time. It was sturdy and practical—moss green with a lined hood. But she didn't have a hat and I wondered if her ears were going to get cold in the chill air. And whether she was wearing overalls again.

Why had those been such a turn-on the other day? Paint splattered denim were a far cry from a sexy dress and heels. But Isabelle in overalls had been inexplicably arousing.

I followed her to the donation booth. A couple of kids—probably high school or college—were taking the donations and sorting them in the bins. Russell and Faye were nowhere to be seen, which was something of a relief. I'd have to encounter them eventually, but I didn't mind putting off that reunion.

"Okay, so it's pretty straightforward," Isabelle said. "People bring their stuff and we put it in the right bin. Everything needs to be unwrapped. Most people know that but once in a while, people bring their gifts already wrapped. You don't have to correct them or anything, just say thanks and put them on that table back there."

"People should follow directions."

She rolled her eyes. "Yeah, well, sometimes they don't and we still appreciate their generosity."

"Fine. What else?"

"Food donations go over there. It's supposed to be non-perishable stuff, since we'll distribute most of it for either Thanksgiving or Christmas dinners. If the bin gets too full, just start stacking on that other table."

"And this is all Christmas cheer?"

She put her hands on her hips. "Yes. It's generosity. Like I said, Christmas brings out the best in people."

I made a non-committal noise in my throat.

Isabelle sent the volunteers to go help elsewhere in the village and we started organizing donations. People trickled in, some with grocery bags of canned and boxed food, others with shopping bags filled with toys or clothes. One guy brought in a wagon that he'd refurbished and another didn't have toys but handed Isabelle an envelope filled with cash.

She greeted everyone with a smile and many with a hug. Most people seemed to know her. People exclaimed their excitement over the opening of Christmas Village and complimented her on how great it looked already.

None of it was fooling me. People bringing in donations didn't prove anything.

A woman in a red knit hat approached the booth tentatively, like she wasn't sure she should be there. She clutched a small paper bag close to her chest. If it had a donation inside, it couldn't have been much, unless it was cash or gift cards.

Isabelle turned around and her face broke out in a wide smile. "Hi, Ms. Myers. How have you been? How are the kids?"

"We're doing well. The kids are getting good grades."

"That's awesome. How about you?"

"I finished my classes and found a good job. I've been there since July."

"I'm so happy for you."

"Thanks." She reached into the bag and took out a small toy car. "This isn't a lot, but I wanted to give something this year."

Isabelle took it and held it almost reverently. "Oh, Ms. Myers. This is wonderful. Thank you so much."

"It's nothing." She crumpled up the bag.

"No, it's not nothing," Isabelle said. "This is so generous. Thank you."

The woman's eyes misted with tears. Somehow, she looked simultaneously happy and sad. I had no idea what was going on. It was just a little car. Next to the stacks of toys we'd collected so far, it really was nothing.

Isabelle wrapped her in a tight embrace. They said goodbye and the woman left.

"What was that about?" I asked.

She swiped beneath her eyes, as if something about the exchange had brought her to tears. "A couple of years ago, Ms. Myers and her two kids were on the brink of being homeless. We provided presents and food for Christmas dinner. She was still trying to get on her feet last year, so we did the same. And this year she had enough to give back."

"That?" I gestured to the toy that couldn't have cost more than a few dollars.

"I know it's not much, but that's not the point. She gave what she could and didn't you see how happy that made her? She got to do a little bit of the giving this year."

I eyed the toy with skepticism, keeping my face carefully neutral. I didn't like the way it made me feel. Like there was a tiny crack in the ice around my heart.

"That's a nice story but it doesn't prove you're right. Christmas Village doesn't have to exist to have a toy drive. You could set up anywhere. In fact, you'd probably get more donations if you were downtown. More foot traffic."

"You're exasperating, you know that?"

"I'm just being practical."

She crossed her arms. "Fine. You know what? You win. If that didn't prove to you that Christmas spirit is important, I don't know what will."

"Are you conceding the bet?"

"For now."

"That's not how a bet works."

"I still say Christmas cheer matters, even if you're too

much of a Scrooge to see it. But I'll sit down with you and discuss the farm."

"Over dinner?"

"We never said anything about dinner."

What the hell was I doing? I didn't want to have dinner with her. Why was I pressing this? "We should have made the terms clear in the beginning, but we didn't, so now I'm clarifying. Have dinner with me."

Her eyes stayed locked with mine, her stance defiant. The challenge in her stare made a coal of lust smolder inside me. I liked it when she looked at me like that—when she tried to defy me.

A few more seconds ticked by, but I wasn't going to back down. Isabelle was having dinner with me.

"Fine," she snapped. "But I get to pick the restaurant."

I gave her that inch. "Fair enough. You know the restaurants in this town better than I do."

Her nostrils flared, a piece of her hair stuck out from her ponytail, and her eyes blazed. Damn it, she was beautiful. A mess, but beautiful.

She always had been.

"Go be a Grinch somewhere else." She waved me off. "I have work to do."

My lips curled in a smile but there was an emptiness to the win. I turned and left, walking back toward my car. It wasn't my fault she'd made a bad bet. How could collecting donations for a toy drive prove anything? Of course I'd won; she'd lost before it had even begun.

Still, I didn't feel my usual sense of satisfaction at having gotten my way. I felt unsettled and restless.

Like I didn't want to leave.

A squirrel ran by, heading in the direction of the u-cut Christmas trees. My feet seemed to want to follow, so without letting myself consider why, I veered in the same direction. Something Harvey Johnston had said came back to me. *The past always catches up. Can't hide from it.*

Of course, he'd also said the squirrels were organized. Maybe I should have dismissed everything he said.

But I couldn't. A big part of my past was here, and as much as I didn't want to face it, something compelled me forward. I stood in front of the big wooden Cook Family Farm U-Cut Christmas Trees sign and I could almost hear the roar of saws and smell the sawdust in the air. Just like the first time I'd been there.

12

ELIAS

ge Eleven

SAWDUST TICKLED my nose and the noise of the saws seemed too loud. Not that I was scared. Back in New York, I'd walked past construction sites that were louder than that. Probably more dangerous, too. But it still made my back tense.

Uncle Dale put his hand on my shoulder. "Don't worry. We won't get too close to anyone with a chainsaw."

"I'm not scared of chainsaws."

"Didn't say you were." He patted my back. "Let's go find the perfect tree."

"Isn't it too early for a Christmas tree? It was just Thanksgiving yesterday."

"That's why we're cutting our own. It'll be fresh. As long as we keep it watered, it should be fine."

"And Christmas trees are so pretty," Aunt Hattie said. "This way we get to enjoy it longer."

That seemed to make sense. I didn't know what their

Christmas tree would look like, but my mom put up a huge one every year. She hired a decorator and there was always a theme. The colors had to match. I pretended like I didn't care that she never put up any of the ornaments I'd made at school. I wasn't a baby anymore. I didn't care about stuff like that.

Although maybe if I made an ornament at school this year, Aunt Hattie and Uncle Dale would put it on their tree.

Uncle Dale led the way down a short decline and past a table where someone was handing out hot cocoa. I eyed the white cups with marshmallows floating in them but I wasn't going to ask for any. Not that I didn't think they'd say yes. My aunt and uncle were really nice to me. But I didn't like asking for things, especially from them. It felt weird.

And there was something going on. I could feel it. Aunt Hattie kept casting nervous glances at Uncle Dale as we made our way down to the rows of evergreens. I hadn't lived with them for very long—only a few months—but I knew that worried look grown-ups sometimes gave each other.

It meant bad news.

The handsaw Uncle Dale carried on his shoulder looked rusty.

"Are you sure the saw is sharp enough to cut down a tree?" I asked.

"Well, we might need to use a little extra muscle, but I think we can handle it."

"We?" Did he mean he was going to let me use the saw?

"If you're old enough to steal a dirty magazine from a corner store, you're old enough to use a saw."

Aunt Hattie clicked her tongue. "Dale."

He winked at me.

I tried not to smile back but it was hard to keep my lips from curling up at the corners. I didn't know how to feel about the fact that he could tease me about what I'd done to get in so much trouble. It was like he wasn't even mad about it.

Not like my father.

Thinking about Dad made me wonder if my aunt and uncle had heard from my parents yet. They were supposed to call and set up my visit home for Christmas. The last time I'd seen them, they'd been so angry. Mom hadn't even looked at me, let alone said goodbye. Dad had just told me that I'd better straighten up. I didn't know what else he'd do to me if I didn't. He'd already sent me away. How much worse could it get?

"Okay, Elias." Uncle Dale stopped in the middle of a row of trees. "I'm counting on you. Find us our Christmas tree."

I glanced around, feeling awkward. I didn't know how to pick a tree. Mom's decorator had always done that and they were fake trees. Not real ones. What if I chose wrong?

"I don't know." I crossed my arms. "I don't want to pick one."

"Oh, come on, now." His gentle voice was oddly reassuring. "At least point to a couple that you like. Help me narrow it down."

Aunt Hattie gave me an encouraging nod. Did they really care what I thought? Or were they doing that thing adults sometimes did where they lied to make you feel included, but really they were just going to do whatever they wanted.

I decided to find out.

"That one." I pointed to a scrawny, lopsided tree.

Uncle Dale's eyebrows drew together and he rubbed his chin. "That one? Are you sure?"

My spine straightened as defiance poured through me. "Yeah. I want that one."

Aunt Hattie circled the ugly tree, like she was inspecting it. "It's a little sparse, but that just means more room for ornaments."

"Good point," Dale said. "And plenty of room for a star on top."

"Our tree last year was too tall," she said.

"It was, wasn't it? Good choice, Elias. This one will be perfect."

"Really?"

"Absolutely." He grinned at me and there was no lie in his smile. "Besides, what did the kid in that Christmas movie say? It just needs a little love?"

"Charlie Brown," Hattie said.

He held the saw out. "You want to give it a try, or should I show you how first?"

A part of me wanted to grab the saw out of his hands and pretend I knew what I was doing, just so I didn't have to admit to not knowing the first thing about how to use a handsaw.

Instead, I decided to trust Uncle Dale, just a little bit. Maybe he wouldn't make fun of me for not knowing.

"Can you show me?"

"Sure can."

Although the tree was small, it took us a while to saw through the trunk. Uncle Dale showed me how, then helped me get situated on the ground. I was getting dirty, but they didn't seem to care, so I decided I didn't either. I drew the saw back and forth, over and over, until my arms hurt too much to keep going. Uncle Dale took over and he finished it in a few strokes.

"You got it most of the way," he said.

A worker put a tag on it and I went with Aunt Hattie to go pay while Uncle Dale brought the truck around. We passed the hot cocoa again, closer this time. I could smell the sugar and chocolate.

"Do you want some?" Aunt Hattie asked, gesturing to the table.

I nodded.

"Go ahead. I'll go pay for the tree and meet you back here."

When we'd passed the hot cocoa table earlier, there had been a lady there, but now it was a girl.

Not just a girl. Isabelle Cook, a girl from my class at school. She had blond hair in two braids sticking out beneath her winter hat and even though it was pretty cold, she wasn't wearing a coat. Just a sweatshirt.

Her smile gave me a funny feeling in my stomach. I wasn't sure if I liked it or not.

"Hi, Elias. Did you get a tree?"

"Yeah."

"Did you pick a good one?"

"No. I picked an ugly one but my aunt and uncle liked it anyway."

She laughed, but I didn't understand why. I wasn't kidding.

"Do you want some hot cocoa?" She picked up a cup and held it out.

"Sure." I took it from her. "Do you get to have any, or do you just have to give it out?"

"I can have some if I want." She smiled again and took another cup. "That's a good idea. It's cold."

It made me nervous to talk to her like this. I saw her at school all the time but we'd never talked. No one talked to me at school. Rumors had spread about why I'd moved here, making most of the kids afraid of me.

I took a sip of cocoa to cover up the awkwardness I felt.

She did, too. I wondered if this was what it was like to be on a date.

If it was, I didn't think I wanted to date a girl. Ever.

Or maybe I did.

I was having a lot of confusing feelings.

"Why aren't you wearing a coat?" I asked.

She glanced down at herself, as if only just now realizing what she was wearing. "I guess I forgot it in the house."

"Where do you live?"

"I live here."

"You live at a Christmas tree farm?"

She nodded. "Yep. It's my parents' farm. We own Christmas Village, too."

"No you don't."

"Yeah, we do."

"No one owns Christmas Village."

"We do. It's part of our farm. Our house is sort of behind it." She pointed. "That way, but you can't see it from here."

"Oh." I took another drink of cocoa. "That's weird."

"No, it's weird that you think it's weird."

That almost made me smile. It didn't seem like Isabelle was afraid of me like the other kids were. I kind of liked that.

I wasn't sure what else to say, so I kept drinking my hot cocoa.

"Did you really move here from New York?" she asked.

"Yeah."

"Do you like it here?"

"I guess."

"Do you want to move back?"

I hesitated and drank the last of my cocoa to give myself a second to think. No one had asked me that, and I wasn't sure if I knew the answer. When I'd first arrived, I'd wanted to get out as fast as I could. I'd even packed my stuff so I could run away.

But my aunt and uncle weren't so bad. They listened when I talked and they'd let me pick an ugly Christmas tree.

I swallowed the last bit of sticky marshmallow. "Not really. But I am going to visit my parents at Christmas. They might not send me back."

Her smile vanished. "Oh no. I hope you come back."

"Why?"

I didn't know why her cheeks were suddenly so pink but it made my stomach feel weird again.

"I don't know. But I'm pretty sure Tilikum is a better place to live."

"They probably will send me back."

She smiled again. "Do you want more cocoa?"

"Are you supposed to give out more than one?"

"No. But I won't tell if you don't tell." She grabbed another cup and held it out.

With a small grin, I took it from her.

"Elias," Aunt Hattie called. "Time to go."

"I have to go. Thanks for the hot cocoa."

"Sure. Bye, Elias. See you at school."

I waved to her and went with Aunt Hattie.

"Do you know her?" Hattie asked.

"She's in my class."

"That's nice. How's the cocoa?"

"It's good."

Uncle Dale had the ugly tree in the back of his pickup truck. Aunt Hattie brushed some dirt off his coat.

"Did you get me some cocoa?" he asked.

"No," I said. "Sorry. I didn't know you wanted some."

"That's okay." He glanced at Hattie and there was that

look again. It made my stomach twist uncomfortably. "Listen, kiddo, there's something we need to talk about."

I swallowed hard. What had I done now? Were they going to send me away, too?

"I spoke with your dad earlier," he said. "And it looks like the plan to have you visit at Christmas isn't going to work."

My stomach dropped to my toes. "What do you mean?"

"You're going to stay here with us for Christmas."

I almost asked why but stopped before the question came out. I knew why. My parents didn't want me. They were leaving me here because they didn't want to see me. Not even at Christmas.

"But," Aunt Hattie said, forcing cheerfulness into her tone, "we're going to have a great Christmas. We have our perfect tree and there will be presents and we'll bake cookies and do all kinds of fun things."

"Speaking of fun things," Uncle Dale said. "How about we go over to Christmas Village while we're here. They have reindeer and decorations and I hear some pretty good cookies. Or maybe popcorn. Do you like kettle corn?"

I shrugged.

"I do. I think we should go get some."

"And we can pick a special ornament for our tree," Hattie said. "We like to do that every year. Do you want to choose one?"

My eyes were on my toes, my extra cup of hot cocoa barely staying in my limp hand. "Okay."

I wasn't mad at my aunt and uncle. This was why they'd let me pick the ugly tree and why they were going to buy me cookies or candy or whatever else I asked for at Christmas Village. They were trying to make up for my parents not wanting me.

"Come on, sport," Uncle Dale said. He took my hand

and even though I was too old to hold hands with a grown up, I let him. Aunt Hattie plucked the hot cocoa away and held my other hand.

I glanced over my shoulder. Isabelle was watching. At least I didn't have to worry about my parents keeping me in New York. Maybe she was right and Tilikum was a better place to live.

Plus, I would have missed seeing her at school again.

13

ISABELLE

*T*his was not a date.

It wasn't a date because I didn't want it to be a date. Neither did he, despite the fact that his phrase *have dinner with me*—especially delivered in his low, velvety voice—had sounded like he was asking me out. Still. I was absolutely not going out on a date with Elias Stoneheart.

This was a business meeting.

I wasn't going to admit to anyone—not even Annika and Marigold—that I'd tried on four different outfits. I really wasn't going to admit that three of them had been dresses.

Dresses were for dates or formal events. This was neither.

I'd opted for a cream-colored sweater, jeans—casual but at least they were clean—and a pair of knee-high boots I adored but almost never wore. Usually I stuck with my work boots—because I was always working—or slip-on sneakers—because they were easy. But for a business meeting that was not a date, this outfit had seemed appropriate.

The restaurant was quiet. I'd arrived early and gotten us a table, and although I'd thought about ordering an appetizer, I'd decided to wait. I didn't know what he'd want. We'd dated as teenagers so the fact that I remembered him liking cheese fries didn't mean I knew what he'd order now, especially from a restaurant that didn't have things like cheese fries on the menu.

He walked in and it was as if he sucked all the air out of the room. My breath caught in my throat and I wasn't the only one. The hostess looked like she'd been sprinkled with a Shakespearean love potion and a waitress stopped in her tracks with a fully laden tray of food to stare at him.

He was quite the specimen, even I couldn't deny that. Time had only increased his physical appeal. His piercing green eyes, stubbly jaw, and broad shoulders exuded manliness. I knew his cool confidence would be ruined by arrogance as soon as he opened his mouth, but from a distance, he was stunning.

I wondered if the guy I used to know was still in there, under all that icy detachment.

He came to the table and sat. "Isabelle."

My name on his lips, in that velvety voice, sent a tingle through me that burst between my legs.

Hormones could never be trusted.

"Elias," I said, trying for a cool tone.

"You look nice. Your hair is down."

Almost involuntarily, my hand strayed to a lock of hair lying across my collar bone. I rarely wore it down, but even though this was a business meeting and not a date, I'd opted to take the time to blow dry it instead of putting it up in my usual ponytail.

"Thanks."

The server arrived to take our drink orders, saving me from having to figure out what to say after he'd just complimented my hair. I ordered an iced tea. A glass of wine sounded nice but this was a business meeting.

Elias ordered a glass of cabernet. I decided that didn't mean anything.

"So, no stack of financial estimates and spreadsheets to convince me we should sell the farm?"

He glanced down, almost as if he'd forgotten something, and I saw the tiniest break in his composure. "No."

"Why?"

"Would it matter?"

"Probably not."

"You already know the farm inside and out, including the finances."

"That's true, I do."

He gave me a single nod, acknowledging the point. But there was something in those green eyes of his. If I hadn't known better, I'd have said he looked troubled. Haunted, even.

I almost asked what was wrong, but he picked up the menu. I did the same, although his presence was such a distraction, it was hard to focus, even just to decide what I wanted for dinner. What was his game? How was he going to try to convince me to sell if not by bombarding me with bleak financial truths?

Why did he seem so distracted?

The server came back with our drinks and took our dinner orders. Elias shifted in his seat and took a sip of his wine. The difference in his demeanor was subtle. Someone who didn't know him probably wouldn't have noticed. But I did. He was edgy and restless—and trying to hide it.

"How did the rest of the toy drive turn out?" he asked.

"It went great. I think we got more donations than last year."

"Good."

"How was the rest of your day? Do you actually take days off or did you go back to work?"

His eyes were on the table and he ran a finger over the rim of his glass. "I took the day off."

I resisted an inexplicable urge to soothe him by reaching over and touching his hand.

What was that about?

"Did you do anything fun?" I asked.

"Not especially."

We lapsed into silence. Frustration made my shoulders tense. What were we even doing here?

"Are you going to tell me why you wanted to have dinner or are we supposed to wait for our food first?"

He hesitated. "Honestly? I don't know. I meant to bring the financials so we could review them but I've had a weird day."

"Are you okay?"

"Yes. Fine."

He wasn't okay. But I'd known that since I'd first seen him at the farm. Despite his air of cool confidence, there was something going on beneath the surface. Something he wasn't letting anyone see.

But I could.

"Do you ever talk to Harvey Johnston?" he asked.

That was an odd question. "Sometimes. I say hi when I see him around town. Why?"

"He's crazy, right? Not coherent?"

"I don't know. Sometimes he seems like he doesn't know where he is. But other times he's pretty normal. Maybe it comes and goes."

He still wasn't quite looking at me and he kept fidgeting with his glass.

"Why, did Harvey say something strange?"

"It's nothing." He stilled his hand and straightened. "The guy's afraid of squirrels. He doesn't know anything."

"Do you remember that time Harvey got stuck in a tree?"

He nodded slowly. "What was he doing up there?"

"I think he'd chased a squirrel."

"Didn't the fire department have to come get him down?"

"Yeah. No one could figure out how he got up so high. And he kept insisting the squirrels stole something from him."

"Probably his sanity."

I laughed. "Maybe."

It felt strange to reminisce with him about that day. I hadn't meant to bring up a story that was so closely tied to our past, but we'd discovered Harvey in that tree because we'd skipped school and driven down an old logging road to make out in Elias's car.

Did he remember that? His expression didn't give anything away.

"He was right about one thing," he said. "Not much changes around here."

"Does Tilikum seem the same?"

He met my eyes and I still couldn't tell what he was thinking. "Most of it."

"I guess that's a small town thing."

"Tell me something. Do you really like living here?"

I smiled. "Yes, I really like living here."

"Why?"

It was interesting, but I didn't hear any judgment in his question. Just curiosity.

"What's not to like? It's beautiful and the air is always fresh. There's no traffic and people are friendly. They can be gossipy, but it's not bad. Plus it's home. Haven't you ever felt at home somewhere? Like it was your place?"

"Not really."

"What about when you lived here with your aunt and uncle? It didn't feel like home then?"

He glanced away. "I wasn't here by choice. My parents sent me here to get rid of me."

Just when I'd thought the old Elias had been frozen out, there was a glimmer of the hurt little boy he'd been. It made me ache for him.

"Sorry. I shouldn't have brought that up."

"It's fine. It's in the past."

Our server came with our meals. I smoothed the cloth napkin across my lap and dug in. If I had to have dinner with Elias Stoneheart, at least the food was good.

Although, so far, this hadn't been a terrible evening.

"Is Alice still in town?" I asked.

"She's staying with Dale and Hattie."

"That's nice of them. How are they doing?"

He paused. "They're fine. Both retired. I suppose that agrees with them."

"So, what about you? What's your life like when you're not trying to talk people into selling their farm?"

"It's busy. I work a lot."

That didn't surprise me. He'd always been hyper focused. But that sense that he wasn't happy was so strong. There was something going on—something other than ambition and greed.

Or maybe I just hoped there was.

"Where do you live? I assume you don't live in your office."

"I have a condo in downtown Bellevue."

"That's a nice area, isn't it?"

He shrugged as if that were irrelevant. "I bought it for the equity. I got a good deal and I'll at least double my money when I sell, depending on how long I keep it."

"So it's more like an investment property than a home."

"You could say that."

"What do you do for fun?"

His brow furrowed, like he didn't understand the question. "For fun?"

"Yeah. Do you go hiking or sailing or to concerts or brew your own beer or something?"

"No."

"So you just work and live in an investment property."

He met my eyes and held them for a moment. "Why the sudden interest in my life?"

"I don't know. I haven't seen you in a long time and I'm curious. Do you have any hobbies?"

"How many hobbies do you have? And nothing on the farm counts."

I opened my mouth to answer, but pretty much everything I did had to do with the farm. "That's different."

"How is that different? You're dedicated to your work. You always were. I'm the same way."

I didn't want him to be right. My life wasn't anything like his. "I spend time with my friends. You remember Annika and Marigold."

He took another drink. "Sure, I remember. Do they still live in town?"

"Yes, and that's what I do when I'm not working on the farm. I spend time with them."

He was quiet and I looked at him expectantly.

"If you're waiting for me to reply that I also spend time with friends, don't hold your breath."

"You don't have any friends?"

"Not really."

"And that doesn't bother you?"

"No. Friends are a distraction."

"From what?"

"Everything."

He'd never been the type of guy to have a big circle of friends. In high school, he'd probably spent most of his time either with me, studying, or working. But no friends at all?

And did no friends mean he didn't have a girlfriend?

It didn't seem like he did. And, really, it wasn't any of my business. In fact, it was totally irrelevant and I wasn't going to ask.

Until I opened my mouth and the question popped out like a jack-in-the-box. "Are you dating anyone?"

His green eyes locked with mine, making my insides swirl. "No."

"Me neither."

I went back to my dinner. Why had I said that? This was supposed to be a business meeting. Why was I delving into his personal life or sharing mine?

"Damien Barrett hasn't called you again, has he?" Elias asked.

I almost sighed with relief at his change of subject. Back to business. "No. You made good on your promise to keep him out of the picture, I have to give you that."

"Good."

"You don't like him very much, do you?"

"He's an idiot."

"He really is." I laughed. "Look at us agreeing on something. It's a Christmas miracle."

The corner of his mouth lifted and my insides tingled again.

Was that him? The Elias I remembered?

I had no idea where this left us. He certainly hadn't said his company would stop trying to buy the farm. Had I won this round? Had he?

Were we even doing battle?

Lines were blurring and I didn't know how to feel about that. For a moment, I'd seen through the cold exterior to the man on the inside. The man I remembered.

The man I'd once loved.

He was still in there. I just didn't know if he'd ever come out. Or what I would do if he did.

14

ELIAS

*I*t had been five days since the dinner with Isabelle and I was still angry with myself. She'd been right where I wanted her. Not ready to sign the papers, but she would have listened to reason. And what had I done with that chance?

Not a damn thing.

Instead, I'd let an afternoon wandering around a Christmas tree farm screw up my head.

Monday morning had brought an unrelated crisis at work and instead of wasting the time to drive back to my office in Bellevue, I'd spent the week in Tilikum, putting out fires from my hotel room. It was efficient. That was why I'd stayed. It had nothing to do with Isabelle or the strange magnetic pull she seemed to have on me.

Dinner with her had been too enjoyable. I'd found myself fighting an almost irresistible urge to reach across the table and touch her.

She was messing with my head.

There was a knock on the door and I got up from my makeshift workstation on the hotel bed to answer it. Alice came in. She glanced around the room as she set down her bag and took off her coat.

"You really are cheap."

"This is the nicest hotel in town. How does that make me cheap?"

"You could have gotten a room with a living area and a desk or something but you're working from the bed." She grinned and I knew she was about to toss a sarcastic comment at me. "No wonder you've never been married."

"I almost got married." Damn it. I shouldn't have said that out loud.

"Really? When?"

"Never mind."

"Come on. Tell me." She sat on the corner of the bed. "Don't you think it's weird that we've worked together for almost three years and I know nothing about your personal life?"

"No."

"And you barely know me." She sat up straighter. "How about this. You can ask me about something personal and I'll tell you, and then you tell me about almost getting married."

I was about to snap at her—tell her there wasn't anything I wanted to know about her personal life—when I realized there was. The memory of her daughter's bright smile and the way she'd put her hand on my chest and told me I had a heart beat filled my mind.

"Fine. Tell me about Maddie's father."

"Oh, wow. You really went for the kill there. But that's okay, it's probably a fair equivalent to your almost-married story." She paused to take a deep breath. "Maddie's dad and I had been dating for about six months when I found out I was pregnant. He chose then to tell me he didn't want kids, which would have been a deal breaker if I'd known. I've always wanted kids. Anyway, he was reluctant about being a father to begin with, but when we found out she had cerebral palsy, he couldn't handle it. He fled to the arms of another woman, someone he worked with. When I found out, he claimed it wasn't his fault and he couldn't help how he felt." She rolled her eyes. "It was such crap."

Anger smoldered inside me. "Does he see his daughter?"

"Not really. I tried to make that work for a while but he blew her off one too many times. She was too young to know but I didn't want to put her through that, especially as she got older."

"He better pay child support."

"Mostly. He complains about it a lot and he tries to fight me when there are extras."

"I want to end that asshole."

"You and me both. But it's all right, I've made peace with it. Now it's your turn. Why did you almost get married? Actually, wait, I want to guess first."

This was dumb but I decided to indulge her. "Go ahead."

"Was it a Vegas thing? Like you were down there with a girl and you guys got drunk and almost got married?"

"No."

"You're right, that doesn't seem like you. Was she a gold digger and she left you when she realized you're actually a cheapskate?"

I narrowed my eyes. "No."

She laughed. "I'm kidding. Seriously, what happened?"

"She was my high school girlfriend. We were young and stupid and at one point, I thought we were going to get married after graduation. We didn't. I left."

"Wait, did you go to high school here, in Tilikum?"

I nodded.

Her eyes widened. "Who was she? Does she still live here? Have you seen her?"

"Yes, I've seen her."

"Oh my god. Is that why we're here? Are you using the Cooks' farm as a way to rekindle your relationship with your high school sweetheart?"

"No. Absolutely not."

Her shoulders slumped. "You've got to give me more than that. What's her name? Have I seen her around?"

"You've met her. She's Isabelle."

"Wait, what? Isabelle as in Isabelle Cook?"

"Yes."

"As in Cook Family Farm."

"That's what I said."

She gaped at me. "Isabelle Cook is your ex-girlfriend and I'm just now finding out?"

My brow furrowed. "Why would you have needed to know that?"

"I think it's pretty important information, considering we're trying to buy her family's farm. Against their will, I might add." She looked around as if trying to find answers to her various questions somewhere in my hotel room. "I just can't believe you didn't say anything."

"It's in the past. It doesn't matter now."

"Are you sure about that?"

"Does your ex have anything to do with your life now?"

"Not really. I wouldn't have Maddie if I hadn't dated him, and I'll never regret having her. But no, he doesn't have anything to do with my life now, other than occasionally dicking me around about child support."

"Exactly. My past with Isabelle Cook doesn't have anything to do with the present."

She eyed me with skepticism. "Okay."

I wanted to change the subject. "What's going on with you and the farm guy?"

"Cole?"

"Yeah, him. You know he's Isabelle's ex, too."

"I know. He told me. And I don't know what's going on." Her cheeks colored. "It's none of your business."

"You're the one who wanted to get to know each other better."

She sighed. "I guess I brought this on myself. I like him, okay? He's kind of amazing. But he lives here and I don't and a long-distance thing would be really hard, especially with Maddie. Although the two of them bonded instantly and it's so cute it makes my ovaries ache."

"I don't think I want to know about your ovaries."

"Fair enough. But that kind of brings up my next question. What are we still doing here? Are you dragging this out to try to get Isabelle back? Be honest."

"No. I'm *not* trying to get Isabelle back."

"Why not?"

"Why would I? We obviously ended for a reason."

"I'm sure you did. But knowing she's your ex explains a lot. Particularly the way you look at her. And why you were willing to spend your morning volunteering at a toy drive last Sunday."

"How do I look at her?"

She wiggled her eyebrows. "Like you want to jingle her bells."

I groaned.

"Fine, you want to deck her halls with—"

"Stop. No holiday sex puns."

"You're no fun."

"For the record, I only helped at the toy drive because

she and I had a bet." I had no idea why I felt the need to explain myself to Alice. "A bet that I won."

"You can tell me whatever you want but I think you still have feelings for her."

"I don't have feelings."

"I used to think that but now I'm not so sure." She tilted her head. "Maddie liked you and she's a very good judge of character. Or I thought she was. Now I'm doubting everything I thought I knew about the world."

"Kids don't like me."

"No one likes you but apparently my daughter wants to be the one to break the mold."

"Very funny. Did the dev manager get back to us yet? I need those numbers."

"He did but I have one more thing before we move on from this lovely little share-a-thon."

I groaned.

"I know you hate being nice but I might not get another chance like this. You're in a particularly good mood."

"No, I'm not."

She waved me off. "Sure you are. It's relative. But I have to ask. Are we sure going after the Cooks' farm is worth it? Considering they don't want to sell and you have history with Isabelle."

"My history with Isabelle has nothing to do with the farm."

"I realize you have the emotional range of a turnip but even you can't actually believe that. Your history with Isabelle has everything to do with it. You can't separate the past from the present, no matter how much you want to."

"Yes, I can."

"You can try, but it won't work. The past always catches up with us."

I almost flinched away. "What did you say?"

"The past has a way of catching up, especially if we have things that were never resolved. Trust me, I'm no stranger to unresolved issues."

"Next time you suggest we get to know each other better, the answer is no."

"I figured. But seriously, think about it. I get that Nigel is dangling that promotion and it would be great if you got it. But some things are more important."

"We're done talking," I said. "Make sure the dev department gets me their budget changes so I can review them."

She held up her hands in a gesture of surrender. "I said what I wanted to say. You'll either listen or you won't. But for the record, the Cooks are a really nice family and I don't want to be a part of coercing them to sell."

That just about made my temper snap. "We're not coercing anyone. Their sentimental attachment to their farm is clouding their judgment. They can't afford to keep it. I'm not going to screw them out of their land by low-balling them like Damien did. They'll get a fair price. But they have to sell. It's inevitable."

"Okay." She got up and gathered her things. "I'll be working from your aunt and uncle's house today."

I grunted in reply.

She left and I glared at the door as it shut.

What the hell did Alice know?

Then again, the truth was right there, staring me in the face. Isabelle was turning into a problem.

Having dinner with her had been a mistake. It had felt too familiar; too intimate. I'd been off-kilter anyway and spending time with her had made it worse.

She was making me weak.

Because the truth was, a part of me, deep down, was

starting to wonder if Alice was right. If we should back off and stop trying to convince the Cooks to sell.

But that was weakness talking. I hadn't gotten to where I was in life by giving mental space to sentimental bullshit.

Which meant I needed to get Isabelle out of my head. I wasn't getting anywhere with her anyway.

Wishing it hadn't come to this, I resolved to the inevitable. It was time to get Isabelle out of the picture and go straight to Russell and Faye Cook.

15

ELIAS

*T*he reindeer barn smelled. Even from outside, the scent of animals permeated the air, although I had to admit—reluctantly—that it wasn't a bad smell, although it was strong. Heavy clouds hung in the sky, obscuring the tops of the mountains. There was a stillness that felt familiar, like the world was settling down, getting ready for snow to blanket the ground and put it to sleep for the winter.

I hadn't seen Isabelle among the workers in the village, erecting elaborate decorations and putting finishing touches on the shops. A part of me was disappointed—wanted to see her, to be close to her again. I shoved that down, as deep as it would go, and sealed it off with ice.

This visit wasn't personal. It was business. The last thing I needed was the complication of her.

Pausing in the barn entrance, I caught sight of the man I was here to see. Russell Cook.

His hair was gone, but baldness suited him—made him look distinguished. The graying beard added to his tough appearance, as did his stout frame and large hands. Lines creased his face but he didn't seem old. Weathered with experience, maybe, but not old.

I'd always liked Isabelle's father. More to the point, I'd respected him. He loved his daughter fiercely and worked hard to provide for his family. A man had to recognize the honor in that.

He shoveled a pile of straw with a pitchfork. The reindeer were in their pens, their hooves shuffling on the bare ground. One of them lifted its head to look at me and memories flashed through my mind. Of another time I'd had to face Mr. Cook in this very barn. I'd been nothing but a kid, coming to him plagued with a mix of hard resolve and sheer terror.

That kid didn't exist anymore. And I wasn't afraid of Russell Cook.

"Morning," I said to get his attention and stepped into the barn.

The rest of the reindeer looked up, heads swinging to take stock of the newcomer.

Russell let the tines of the pitchfork rest on the ground and squared his shoulders. "What are you doing here?"

I took a few steps closer and the nearest reindeer snorted and shook his head. "I thought we could talk."

"We don't have anything to talk about."

Isabelle was so much like her father. Which meant it would be a waste of time to try to convince him to have a conversation. Despite his protest, I needed to get straight to the point.

"We both know the farm is losing money and has been for years."

"You try running a farm during a decade-long drought. See how well you handle it."

I put my hands up. "I'm not judging your management.

You've done the best you can with the cards you've been dealt. I respect that."

"But you're here to remind me that it wasn't enough."

"No, I'm here to offer you a way out."

I didn't miss the slight slump of his shoulders. The long exhale. The tiredness in his eyes.

This was where Damien had gone wrong. This, and assuming he could get the farm for the lowest possible price simply because they were struggling financially. He'd never been here—never stood face to face with this family. He hadn't been able to see the subtleties that would have given him a way in.

Russell Cook was a warrior. But he was losing his will to fight.

"What makes you think I'm looking for a way out?" he asked. "I've worked hard for this farm my entire life. I'm not walking away now."

"What if you could? What if you could close this chapter and move on to the next without any guilt or worry."

He didn't reply. Just scowled and went back to shoveling straw.

I moved closer. The reindeer next to me sniffed through the slats in its pen. "Facing reality isn't the same as quitting."

"No, but walking away is."

I felt his words like a slap to the face. Not that they weren't deserved. But I didn't want to get into my past with his daughter. That wasn't why I was here.

"It's only quitting if it isn't the right move. And sometimes the smart move is to walk away and cut your losses."

Once again, he didn't answer. I was getting to him, so I pressed on.

"Forget about Barrett's offer. He was trying to take

advantage of you and I apologize for that. I'm not here to get every last penny out of the deal."

"Doesn't matter. You're still here to talk us into selling."

"Yes, I am. But think about the impact to the community. This land has value and what we're proposing would bring in new jobs and new opportunities."

"I'm not so sure our community needs the kind of opportunities you're talking about." Faye came in through the other barn entrance. Her gray hair was short and she wore a tan coat with jeans and boots.

"Mrs. Cook." I nodded to her.

"Call me Faye, Elias. You know I was never one for that kind of formality."

Russell cast a disapproving glance at his wife. "Why are you being friendly?"

"Because kindness is free."

He grumbled something incoherent.

"It's been a long time," she said. "How are Dale and Hattie?"

"They're fine. Enjoying retirement."

"Good for them. And what about you? Looks like you're doing well for yourself."

Not well enough. Yet. "I suppose."

"It must be an experience to come home to Tilikum after some time away. Have you been enjoying your visit?"

"It's been interesting." How had I lost control of the conversation so quickly? I needed to redirect us back to the topic at hand. "I was just talking to your husband about the future of the farm."

There was something in her eyes. Disappointment, maybe? "I was wondering why you were here."

"Why else would he be here?" Russell asked.

Her eyes met mine and held them for a moment. "I'm

sure I don't know. Have you seen what Isabelle did with the guest house? She turned it into quite the lovely little home."

"No, I haven't." Was that where she lived? At dinner the other night I hadn't even asked. I fought back the sudden surge of curiosity. Isabelle wasn't why I was here.

"To be fair, I don't think she spends much time there. Works too much, that girl." She gave her husband an admiring glance. "So like her father."

"I don't work too much."

"Of course you do. But you were never one to sit still."

"What good would I be if I sat around all day?" He shoveled more straw, as if to prove his point.

Oddly, that struck a chord.

One of the reindeer snorted and Faye walked over to its pen.

"Aw, Buckwheat, are we not paying attention to you?" She spoke in a soft voice and stroked its nose. "There you go, you big baby. So Elias, what were you saying about the future of the farm?"

That was a good question. What had I been saying about the future of the farm? My mind kept wandering to Isabelle. To the way she'd talked to the reindeer as she fed them, cooing and calling them by name. How they'd nuzzled against her, seeking attention, and I'd teased her about them being spoiled.

What was wrong with me? I couldn't seem to set foot on the Cooks' land without the past seeping into my consciousness.

I cleared my throat, trying to maintain composure. "I was trying to say that selling is your best alternative."

"How so?"

I opened my mouth to answer, but before I could say another word, Isabelle came in. She was dressed in a pair of denim overalls again and why the hell did she have to look so sexy in those? But damn it, she was adorable.

She stopped in her tracks and her eyes widened. "Elias. What are you doing here?"

"We were just chatting," Faye said.

"Chatting about what?"

"The farm." Faye's voice was matter-of-fact.

"He wants us to sell," Russell said. "What else is new?"

I tried not to wince and braced for impact as a storm gathered in Isabelle's eyes.

"You're trying to go around me, aren't you?" she asked.

That was absolutely what I was trying to do, but I wasn't about to admit it. Not in those words, at least. "It's a family farm. I thought it would be prudent to speak to the entire family."

"Without me around to get in your way."

Exactly. "Of course not."

"You're such a liar."

Her defiant stance was such a turn-on. I loved how feisty she was. I always had. Her maddeningly cute ponytail was falling out and her overalls hid the curves of her body while still offering a tantalizing hint at what she had underneath. She was a mess but I wanted to mess her up more.

She was also right. I was lying and I had no idea why I felt so bad about it. But a restless dissatisfaction clawed at me.

"Fine, I came over to talk to your parents alone. I thought they might listen to reason."

"You're unbelievable." She whirled around and stalked out of the barn.

I followed, jogging to catch up with her. "No, what's unbelievable is that you refuse to have a rational conversation about this."

She kept walking and I couldn't tell if she had a destination in mind. "That's because there's nothing left to say. You want to buy something that isn't for sale. We said no. End of story."

"We both know that's not the end of the story. What happens when everything comes to a head? You can keep pretending this isn't going to end in bankruptcy for your parents, but that's where this is going if you don't do something now."

"I realize keeping the farm is a risk but it's one we're willing to take. I'm not giving up. And they won't go bankrupt."

"For your sake, I wish it were that easy."

She stopped and met my eyes. "Do you? Do you actually care what happens to us, or is this just a means to an end for you? Because honestly, I can't tell."

I had no idea how to answer that. Did I care? I'd told myself a thousand times that I didn't. That this didn't have anything to do with me and Isabelle, or the past, or any inconvenient feelings that tried to worm their way into me. The Cooks' farm was a means to an end. A means to getting what I wanted.

But when she looked at me like that—

Why was I so fucking confused?

Cold-hearted determination was easy. Familiar. I put it on, armoring myself against the temptation to go soft. To be soothed by the warmth of her inexplicable pull.

"It doesn't matter whether or not I care. That's not the point."

She shook her head, almost sadly. "I can't believe I almost fell for it."

"Fell for what?"

"Your charm. That mask you wear that hides the fact

that your heart is made of coal. The other night, I actually thought—" She stopped and looked away. "Never mind. I was wrong. You're not the same."

"Not the same as what?"

"It doesn't matter." She pointed a finger at me and the defiant fire in her eyes nearly scorched me. "Leave my parents out of this."

"Belle."

As soon as my old nickname for her left my lips, I knew it had been a mistake. Her expression darkened and I almost flinched away.

"Don't call me that."

I put my hands up in a gesture of surrender. "You're right. I'm sorry."

With another fiery glare, she spun around and stalked away.

This time, I didn't follow.

Damn it.

Why did I keep screwing this up? What should have been a simple business transaction had turned into a heaping pile of complications.

I hated complications.

A squirrel ran by and I glowered at it, as if somehow this was its fault. The worst part was, I didn't know what was bothering me more, the fact that I'd made no progress on this land deal or that Isabelle was so angry with me.

Or maybe I did know.

I wasn't supposed to care. Not about her or her farm.

But I did.

And I had no idea what to do about it.

16

ISABELLE

A friendly plume of smoke curled from the farmhouse chimney and the afternoon sun was low in the sky. Marigold and Annika had come to the farm, and because they were the best friends in the history of friendship, they'd happily spent the afternoon helping me check things off my never-ending to-do list. With the new Santa's Workshop sign installed, it was time to call it a day, especially because I didn't want them to feel like they had to work for hours just so we could all hang out.

I led them around the back of my parents' house and through the kitchen door. My hands were a mess, so I headed for the sink to wash up, then reached for the kettle.

"You go sit," Marigold said, pointing to the kitchen table. "You've been working all day. I'll make us some tea."

My tired body longed for the simple relief of sitting. "I'd argue, but my feet are killing me."

I sat and stretched my legs out, pointing and flexing my toes. I'd been up before dawn and instead of letting my brain stew over Elias—the big, Grinchy jerk—I'd hopped out of bed and gone straight to work. I hadn't slowed down since, not even with Marigold and Annika here.

Annika took off her coat and hung it on a hook by the door, then helped Mari get tea going. The pink tips of her blond hair hung just past her collarbone and looked so cute on her. It was fun and flirty, which I had a feeling Annika needed. She was a single mom to the sweetest little two-year-old boy, Thomas, and I knew it was hard for her to keep herself on her priority list.

Mari made tea and served it in three of my mom's mismatched floral teacups while Annika brought a plate of cheese and crackers to the table. They sat with me and we all shared a contented sigh as we took our first sips.

"I almost hate to ask, but I have to," Mari said. "What's going on with Elias?"

"Other than he's a real-life Grinch? Or maybe he's Ebeneezer Scrooge. I can't decide."

"Is he still in town?"

I sighed. "Yes, unfortunately. He's driving me crazy."

"I'm sorry you're dealing with this," Marigold said. "If you need help burying the body, you know we've got you."

That made me smile. Marigold was as sweet as sugar, but you crossed someone she loved at your peril. "Thanks. Hopefully it won't come to that but I'll let you know."

As much as I loved my friends, and generally told them everything, I didn't want to talk about Elias. I had too many conflicting feelings. I wasn't sure what to do with them yet. I needed to change the subject. Hadn't they gone to that masquerade ball recently? That would be a much better topic.

"How was the masquerade?"

Marigold sighed. "It was delightful. Annika was a wonderful date and I danced with several fine gentlemen."

"Why are you so cute?" I asked. "What about you? How many fine gentlemen did you dance with?"

"I don't think she danced," Mari said. "Did you?"

Annika curled her hands around her teacup and shook her head. "I didn't dance with anyone. But you guys, I have something to tell you. It's kind of big."

I sat up straighter. There was a wistfulness to her tone that I'd never heard from her before.

"What happened?" Mari asked. "Is everything okay?"

She took a deep breath and the words came out in a rush. "I've been secretly texting Levi Bailey and I've never told you. And at the ball he pulled me into a closet and kissed me in the dark."

I gaped at her, my eyes widening. Mari gasped and clasped her hands against her chest.

"I'm sorry I never told you," Annika said. "I felt like I couldn't tell anyone."

This was blowing my mind. Annika was a Haven, and the Havens and Baileys were long-standing rivals. She'd kissed a Bailey? This was crazy. "Wait, wait, wait. You've been secretly texting Levi Bailey? Since when?"

"For the last year or so. We actually used to text each other in high school but stopped after I went to college."

"Oh my god." I still couldn't wrap my head around this. To someone who wasn't from Tilikum, a generations-long feud between families would probably seem silly. But the fabric of this town had been woven by the feud. No one crossed it. Ever. "Oh. My. God. You were texting him back then and you never told us?"

"I know, I'm so sorry." Her shoulders slumped. "I thought about telling you but there was something fun about keeping it a secret between the two of us. It felt like if anyone else knew, the magic would be gone."

"It's okay, you don't have to apologize. I'm just surprised, that's all."

Annika went on to explain how her friendship with Levi Bailey had blossomed back in high school. They'd lost touch when Annika had gone away to college, but after she'd moved home, they'd started texting again. And things had only escalated from there.

"Okay, but go back to the part about kissing him at the masquerade," Mari said.

I nodded. I wanted to hear this part.

"He walked past and kind of touched my arm," she said and Mari gasped again. "Our eyes met and it was like, I don't know, like fireworks going off inside me. He gave me this look and I somehow knew he wanted me to follow him. So I did. He ducked into a closet. As soon as I got inside and closed the door he asked me if I was there alone, and when I said I was, he kissed me."

"Wow," Mari said, her voice breathy.

"I know. It really was wow," Annika said. "And then he came up to my house at night and threw pebbles at my window and climbed up to my balcony and kissed me again."

Marigold sighed dramatically and slumped in her chair. "Are you kidding me?"

"No. And that's not all. There was a minor car accident outside Luke's shop the other day and he was one of the responders. We met on the side of the shop and he kissed me again. I'm talking pushed me up against the wall and devoured me."

"Dang, that's hot," I said. And I was not jealous of my friend for being kissed like that. Not at all.

Okay, I was. But not in a mean way. I was happy for her,

just the tiniest bit sad for me. I couldn't remember the last time a guy had devoured me.

Or maybe I could. And I really didn't want to think about that.

Mari draped her arm over her forehead. "I'm going to die of swooning."

"And then..." Annika hesitated, her cheeks flushing pink.

Marigold and I leaned forward. This story actually got better?

"I was alone last night after Thomas went to bed so I asked if he could talk. He called and we kind of—"

"What?" I was dying to know where this was going.

"We kind of maybe had phone sex."

My eyes widened. "No. Way."

Her cheeks turned an even deeper shade of red. "I know, I almost can't believe I did that."

"That is the most romantic thing I've ever heard in my life," Mari said.

"Phone sex is romantic?" I asked.

"Obviously. I'm a romantic, not a prude. They're secret lovers. This is amazing."

"I don't know if we're secret lovers," Annika said.

"What else would you call it?" Mari asked.

I nodded. "That definitely sounds like secret lovers."

Annika looked down at her tea. "What am I going to do? He's a Bailey. My brothers will murder him."

She was right about that. She had the most overprotective brothers ever. "Don't tell them."

Mari pointed. "That."

"That's fine for now," Annika said. "But how long can a secret lovers thing last if it has to stay secret?"

"Uh-oh," I said and exchanged a knowing look with Marigold.

"What?" Annika asked.

"You really like him."

"Yes, I really do. That's the problem. He's not some random hot guy I met who's just a warm alternative to my bullet vibe. He's..."

"Go on," Mari said.

"He's sweet and surprisingly funny and also kind of intense."

"And hot, let's be honest," I said. Which was true. All the Bailey brothers were brutally hot, but because of the feud, I'd never gotten to know any of them.

"So hot," Annika said on a sigh. "But we all know the reality of the situation. With the feud the way it is, we can't be together."

"I've always wished someone would end the feud," Mari said, her voice wistful. "I hate it when people are mean to each other."

I glanced at her. "That's because your heart is made of pure gold and sunshine."

"I don't think anyone could end the feud," Annika said. "Especially now. I told Josiah he shouldn't get involved with Gram Bailey's land but did he listen? No, of course he didn't. He never listens to me."

"Why does he want it so badly?" I shifted in my seat, suddenly uncomfortable. The Havens were trying to buy out Gram Bailey's land—she was the matriarch of the Bailey clan—and the rest of the Baileys were pissed. "Maybe I'm overly sensitive because I have the prince of darkness trying to get my parents' farm, but isn't it kind of crappy that he's trying to buy her out?"

"I know it looks bad. But he's just trying to help our

parents. The logging industry has been dying for decades and Haven Timber is dying, too. Josiah thinks we need to transition to something else. Maybe something in tourism or recreation. He wants to develop a resort or cabins or maybe both, but all the land Haven Timber owns is so hard to reach. Gram Bailey's land shares a border with some of ours on the far side. He figured if she has to sell it anyway, why not sell it to us? It's not like he'd put her out in the cold, but I told him the Baileys would never agree."

"And it's not like Josiah has the best people skills," I said, which was so true. Josiah was about as charming as a tree trunk. "He should have sent in Luke. Or even Zachary."

"He shouldn't have done it in the first place," Annika said. "There has to be another way to save Haven Timber without turning the stupid feud into a war."

"But don't you see?" Marigold sat up straighter, her eyes brightening. "If this is true love, it'll have the power to end the feud."

Annika laughed. "No pressure or anything."

"No, I just mean there's hope," Mari said. "If this turns out to be true love, there's nothing more powerful in the entire world. And if it's not, well, it wasn't meant to be anyway."

"How do I know if it's true love?" Annika asked.

"Oh, you'll know." Mari nodded sagely.

"Bringing this back down out of the clouds of romanticism," I said. "If you ever need an alibi, just ask. I'll be happy to cover for you."

"Me, too." Mari pressed the tips of her fingers together and raised her eyebrows. "You know, Levi lives right around the corner from me. I've seen him and his brothers coming and going a million times."

Annika's attempt at a casual shrug was totally transparent. She knew exactly where Levi Bailey lived. "Yeah."

"No one would question it if your car was in my driveway."

"That's perfect," I said with a grin, and Annika's cheeks flushed again. "You're blushing."

She touched her face. "Am I?"

"You're definitely blushing," Marigold said. "And it's adorable."

It was completely adorable. I wanted this so badly for Annika. Even though he was a Bailey, and that made things stupidly complicated, I could see it in her eyes. She really liked this guy.

She took a deep breath. "Can we just pause for a moment to appreciate how wonderful you two are? You're the best."

I winked. "We've got you."

"So you don't think I'm crazy for letting this happen?"

"No," I said. "It's complicated, but not necessarily crazy. If it's just a secret fling, then by all means, have some fun. You deserve it. But if it goes beyond that, I won't lie, you have a mountain to climb."

"But it'll be worth it," Mari said.

Annika smiled and something inside me knew it would be worth it. Although I cast a quick glance at Mari and we wordlessly agreed to do something terrible to Levi Bailey if he hurt our girl.

We kept chatting as we sipped our tea and nibbled our snacks. Mari got up to make more and for once, I accepted help without complaint, rather than insisting I do it myself. I knew I was bad at relying on other people—that sometimes I needed to let go a little. It wasn't easy for me, but with my two best friends, I could relax.

I was so excited for Annika. But her story brought feelings to the surface that I couldn't ignore.

Maybe I did need to talk to them about Elias.

"Since we're confessing things," I said as Mari poured more tea. "I had dinner with Elias last Sunday."

"Dinner, like you ate a meal together?" Annika asked. "Or like he took you out on a date?"

"That's a very good question. It was supposed to be all business. But we barely talked about the farm and by the end it started to feel a little more like a date."

Mari's eyebrows drew together with concern as she took her seat. "Oh, honey. Are you sure that's a good idea?"

"No. It was absolutely not a good idea. Especially because he turned around and tried to go behind my back to convince my parents to sell the farm."

"That jerk," Annika said.

"He is a jerk. And yet..."

"What?" Mari asked.

"I don't know." I put my head down on the table. "I'm so confused. And that's the thing, I shouldn't be. What do I have to be confused about? We dated in high school and we crashed and burned. Hard. Then he left and I was so mad at him but I told myself it was for the best. If he'd stayed in Tilikum, I would have had to see him all the time. This way, I could just move on."

"But if you are feeling confused, there must be a reason," Mari said.

"Like you still have feelings for him," Annika added.

I lifted my head. "But that's crazier than Annika being with a Bailey, right? I can't have feelings for him. He's a greedy, self-absorbed asshole."

"Is he?" Mari asked.

The skepticism on Annika's face matched mine. "What do you mean?"

"Is he really a greedy, self-absorbed asshole, or does he just seem like one because of the situation?" Mari asked. "I'm not saying I know the answer. And trust me, I have no reason to like him. He hurt you and that put him on my meanie-head list. But you really loved him back then, which means there was something in him to love. So maybe you're confused now because that part of him is still there."

"I don't know if that part of him exists anymore. At dinner, it seemed like I could see it. But then he tried to go around me to get to my parents, which was such a jerk thing to do. I don't know what to think."

"It could also be that being back in Tilikum is throwing him off," Annika said. "There's something about this town that has a way of getting under your skin. When I moved back it was kind of disconcerting for a while. Like I had to get used to the weirdness again."

"Could be," I said. "He definitely seemed off at dinner. Like something had happened."

"His childhood wasn't exactly smooth," Mari said. "I bet he has a lot of bittersweet memories here."

"That's so true. His parents dumped him like an unwanted pet. It was terrible. Not that any of that is an excuse for him being an ass."

"Of course not," Mari said. "But people are complicated. So are feelings."

"Isn't that the truth," Annika said.

I raised my teacup. "To big feelings, complications, and the friends who help you find your way through them."

We clinked our teacups and took a sip.

"Just be careful," Marigold said. "He did a number on your heart. I don't want you to get hurt again."

"That's the last thing I need," I said. "I'll be careful. Honestly, I can't even believe I'm having this conversation about Elias Stoneheart. I swore I'd never speak to him again and here I am, wondering why I'm getting butterflies alongside burning rage whenever I see him."

"Butterflies and burning rage are a potent combination," Annika said.

She was right about that. Very potent. I was so angry and yet I couldn't stop thinking about him. About his intense green eyes and the hard lines of his body. His hypnotic voice.

And the wounded look I sometimes saw on his face.

He was irresistible. And dangerous. As much as I wanted him to be a cozy fire on a snowy winter day, he could just as easily be an out of control blaze, and burn my heart to a crisp.

17

ELIAS

*T*he numbers on the screen blurred. I pinched the bridge of my nose as if that would ward off the oncoming headache. I had a meeting in an hour and I needed to be sharp. Focused. Damien had been sniffing around while I'd been working from Tilikum, spreading rumors, trying to find a weakness. Under normal circumstances, I wouldn't have been concerned. He wouldn't have found one, no matter how hard he looked. I didn't have weaknesses.

Or I kept them buried deep enough that they might as well not exist.

But now? I had a weakness. A big one. And her name was Isabelle Cook.

Coming home should have solved that problem. After my ill-fated attempt to talk to her parents, I'd decided to regroup. I couldn't be out of the office indefinitely and staying in Tilikum wasn't doing any good. It was too distracting.

She was too distracting.

But even here, in my office, I was brooding over her.

She was still mad at me. The question was, why did I care so damn much? Why did the distance of both time and space seem to do nothing to stop me from obsessing over her? It had been more than a week and I should have been over it. She was. After she'd walked away, she'd probably gone back to work and put me out of her mind. With Christmas Village opening, she'd have plenty to keep her busy.

How had the opening weekend gone?

Frustrated, I stood, slid my hands in my pockets, and looked out the window. Why did I care about that? Christmas Village was childish and pointless. A bunch of sentimental nonsense. But I'd spent the weekend wondering whether there had been a good turnout. Whether the crowds were spending enough to cover the costs. Whether there were enough trees in the harvest this year to keep up with demand or if the growing popularity of artificial trees was hurting sales. I'd almost started to research the numbers—were more people opting for convenience and cleanliness over the nostalgia of a real tree—but stopped myself.

Because I wasn't supposed to care.

I really wasn't supposed to hope that their opening weekend had gone well. It was better for me if it didn't. Easier to get them to agree to sell.

And yet...

There was a knock at the door and Alice came in. She paused, looking at me curiously. "Is everything all right?"

"Yes. Why?"

"You're just..." She held up a stack of envelopes. "Never mind. Mail. It was mostly Christmas cards and before you say anything, I kept most of them. But there are a few things in there that I figured you needed to open."

"Leave them on my desk."

She set them down.

"How's Maddie?"

Her mouth opened and closed a few times, and when she finally answered, her voice sounded bewildered. "She's fine."

I glanced out the window again. "Long lunch today?"

"Um, yeah. Maddie has physical therapy. I should be back by two."

"Does it help?"

"Help what?"

"Maddie. Does the physical therapy help?"

"Yeah, a lot. I don't think she'd be walking without it."

I kept my gaze out the window, wondering why the thought of that little girl not walking tugged at something in my chest.

"Uh..." She trailed off and I looked over my shoulder. "Sorry. I had something else to ask you and now I can't remember what it was. No, I do. Bella from marketing still needs a meeting. I don't think I can keep putting her off but—"

"I can see her at three this afternoon."

"Oh. Okay. Good, I'll let her know. Are you sure you're okay?"

No. "Yes." *Liar.*

"All right. If you need anything else, just text me and I'll take care of it this afternoon."

"Fine."

She turned to go.

"Are you still seeing the farm guy?"

"Cole Phillips."

"What?"

"He has a name and it's Cole Phillips. And yeah, I am. I

think. It's complicated." She paused for a moment. "That's not the right word. He's great. The only thing that's complicated is the distance."

I was going to lose her to the farm guy. Why did that piss me off so much? Assistants were replaceable.

"Just do me a favor and don't quit before I get this land deal secured."

"Elias, I'm not—"

"Maybe you will, maybe you won't. It's not my business. Don't be late getting back this afternoon." I pushed up my sleeves and took my seat.

"I won't."

With another bewildered look at me she left, closing the door behind her.

I had no idea why I'd asked her about the farm guy. It had just come out. Another item to add to the *why do I care* column. I'd never paid attention to who—or whether— Alice dated. I'd learned early in my career that it was better to keep personal lives out of the office.

Business and friendship didn't mix.

I grabbed the mail she'd left. There were a couple of things that would need my attention. I set those aside. On the bottom was a red envelope with a holiday stamp. I frowned at it. She knew I hated Christmas cards. I always tossed them without opening, so she'd taken to opening them for me and displaying them on the shelf behind her desk.

My eyes slid over the return address. Vincent Stoneheart.

That was why. It was from my father.

Blowing out a breath, I popped the seal and slid the thick card out of the crisp envelope.

The front was red with silver and gold foil. It read, W*arm*

Holiday Wishes. Trite. I opened it. The inside was decorated with more silver and gold and the script font had another generic greeting: *Happy holidays from our family to yours.*

The signature was a stamp.

Our family? That was a load of shit. He didn't have a family.

With a shake of my head, I tossed it in the garbage. For half a second, I'd wondered if he'd actually sent me a card. But I was just another name on his assistant's list. He probably had no idea who got them.

And I found myself asking the same question again. Why did I care?

I'd seen my father twice in recent years, both times at family funerals. I'd even spoken to him, although the conversations had been brief and impersonal. Enough to make it clear that he wasn't the least bit impressed with me.

He never had been. I'd convinced myself that I'd let go of the wish that my father would ever give a shit. He didn't care about anyone, except himself.

Certainly not the son he'd shipped off to Tilikum all those years ago.

And now I couldn't stop thinking about that damn ugly Christmas tree my aunt and uncle had let me choose. The way the star had been too heavy for the spindly top branch, making it droop to one side. Uncle Dale had put a little hook in the ceiling and rigged it with fishing wire so it would stand up straight. They'd placed the ornament I'd made at school right below it, as if displaying some art project would make up for the fact that I wasn't going home for Christmas.

It had been almost twenty years. Why was I even thinking about that first Christmas in Tilikum? I'd put the past behind me a long time ago. I wasn't that angry kid anymore.

A chill ran through me as I froze out the memories, the emotions. The burn of cold tightened my chest but I ignored that pain. It was better than the alternative.

I had to focus. My job, my office, my salary, my wealth —it was good. I'd done well, but there was still so far to go. So much left to accomplish, to acquire. I wasn't going to let a bunch of sentimental bullshit distract me, make me weak.

So when my eyes slid over my phone again and the urge to text Isabelle tried to overtake me—to apologize, of all things—I firmly ignored it. Froze it in ice and moved on.

I NEEDED to start taking a different route home. My condo was only a few blocks from the office, so unless the weather was terrible, I walked. The walk home always gave me time to process the day, think things over, plan for tomorrow. I liked routine and this was part of it.

But downtown Bellevue was lit up with so many Christmas lights, it could probably be seen from space. How had I forgotten the parade that clogged Northeast Eighth every night? The crowds packed shoulder to shoulder on the sidewalks, the flurries of artificial snow. The floats and drummers dressed like toy soldiers. Didn't these people have any dignity?

Instead of trying to push my way through the throngs of people waiting for the show to begin, I detoured around Bellevue Square. It meant a longer walk and there were still too many people laden with shopping bags. Christmas music filled the air, piped through overhead speakers. I shoved my hands in my pockets and hunched against the noise as if it were freezing cold.

Was it snowing in Tilikum? Probably.

I stopped at the next intersection and waited while traffic went through. A woman stood next to me, holding the hand of a girl who looked a little older than Maddie. The kid wore a red velvet dress with a matching bow in her hair.

She looked up at me and her eyes widened. "Mommy."

The woman's attention was on her phone.

"Mommy." The kid tugged on her mom's hand, her wide eyes on me. "The Grinch."

"What?" She didn't look up.

"Mommy, it's the Grinch, except not green."

The woman finally tore her gaze away from her phone to look at her kid, then me. Her cheeks colored and she tugged her daughter closer. "Honey, no. That's just a man. I'm really sorry, I don't know what she's talking about."

I didn't answer, just let my eyes flick to the kid. Narrowed them.

"He's the Grinch in disguise," the little girl whispered. "He has mean eyes."

Clearly uncomfortable, the woman shifted her feet and let out a nervous laugh. "I'm sorry. She's six. Excuse us."

The light changed and she hurried her kid across the street, casting a wary glance back at me.

Ignoring them both, I stepped off the curb and crossed. The music faded as I walked up the next block only to surround me again as soon as I entered my building. Without acknowledging the garish lobby decor and hunching against the instrumental version of *Sleigh Ride*, I went straight to the elevator and up to my floor.

My neighbors' Christmas crap had started spilling out into the hallway. Wreaths hung on doors and someone had strung garland around theirs. Some other idiot had put up stockings, as if expecting Santa Claus to wander the hallways of a luxury downtown condominium on Christmas Eve.

I punched in my door code and went inside. Didn't bother turning on the lights. There was a chill in the air and despite the fact that I could almost hear Alice calling me cheap, I ignored that, too. I could put on a damn sweater if I got cold.

After putting my things away and changing into a clean t-shirt and sweats, I went to the kitchen and poured two fingers of whiskey. I swirled it in the glass and took a sip, relishing the bite as it slid down my throat.

My phone buzzed. The hope that it might be Isabelle threatened to melt the ice in my chest. But it was just Alice.

"Yeah?"

"Sorry to bug you but have you talked to Isabelle today?"

"No." My spine stiffened and I set my drink down. "Why? What's wrong?"

"I just got off the phone with Cole. Something happened to her dad. Cole was on the other side of the farm, so he didn't see what happened, and he hasn't heard from anyone yet. But there was an ambulance and they took Mr. Cook to the hospital. I was hoping you might know what was going on."

"I don't know. I haven't spoken to her."

Her voice was thick with worry. "I hope he's okay. Cole sounded so concerned. I'm tempted to drive over there, although that's ridiculous. Maddie goes to bed early and it's not like I know the Cooks very well. And I'm part of the entity trying to buy out their farm against their will, which you'd think would be more of a stumbling block for Cole, but he's so understanding."

"You're rambling."

"I know. What the heck is wrong with me? I share one thing with you and suddenly I'm talking to you like we're best friends."

We're not friends.

I almost said it. And maybe if my mind hadn't been spinning with concern over Isabelle and her father, I'd have had time to ponder why I didn't. Why I didn't want to lie to her.

Because somehow, Alice and I *were* friends.

When had that happened?

I didn't have time for that. I needed to find out what was going on with Isabelle's dad.

"I probably won't be in the office tomorrow."

"Oh, okay." She sounded surprised. "Let me know what you find out."

"I will." I almost ended the call but paused. "And Alice?"

"Yeah?"

"Thanks for calling."

"Of course. If Cole calls back, I'll let you know what he says."

"Thank you."

I hung up and swiped to Isabelle's number. Stared at the screen for a heartbeat or two.

Instead of calling her, I went to my room and threw some clothes in a bag. I'd call her from the road. Regardless of what she said, or what was happening to her father, I knew I needed to be there. Why? I had no idea. I wasn't supposed to care. Not about her, or her farm, or her parents.

But I still got in my car and headed for Tilikum.

18

ISABELLE

*M*y body ached with exhaustion but the beeping of Dad's monitor kept me awake. As did the hard plastic chair I'd been sitting in for hours. I shifted, trying to get comfortable, and only succeeded in making myself slightly less uncomfortable than before. Comfort wasn't happening tonight.

Dad dozed in the bed, a thin blue blanket pulled up to his chin. He looked so tired. So frail. I'd never thought of my dad as old before. I didn't like it.

I couldn't count the number of times I'd told Dad to stay off the roof. Had he listened? No, he hadn't. He'd gone up on the roof of the house—in the freaking snow—to put a cap on some vent that had blown off in the last windstorm. And he'd fallen.

Boom, hit the ground.

I hadn't seen it happen, which was probably for the best. Mom had heard it happen, which was both horrible for her and good for him, because at least someone had been around to call an ambulance. It had caused a bit of a scene at Christmas Village, especially as word swept through the visitors that it was Russell Cook being taken to the hospital.

Time seemed to move so slowly in an emergency room, as if the second hand on the clock could only tick at half-speed. The doctor had been in twice and assured me he was going to be okay. They'd admit him overnight just to be safe but he'd probably go home tomorrow.

Rumors were already flying around town, blanketing the Tilikum gossip line like a deep winter blizzard. He'd had a heart attack. A stroke. No, a stroke and a heart attack at the same time. He'd fallen and broken his back and was para-lyzed. Some people speculated foul play, although appar-ently no one could decide who would have targeted the sweet old farmer who ran Christmas Village. Thankfully for Annika, no one seemed to be attempting to connect it to the Haven-Bailey feud. That situation was already a bomb waiting to go off. They didn't need any more fuel on that fire.

Especially because it was just my dad thinking he could still climb around on rooftops in the snow, as if he were freaking Santa Claus.

My leg tingled, so I shifted again before the pins and needles could get worse. I'd sent Mom home for the night, assuring her I'd stay with Dad until they moved him upstairs. By some miracle, he hadn't broken any bones, but it had been a big fall. He was going to hurt—a lot—and maybe need physical therapy before he could get back to work.

That was going to stick in his craw. There were few things Russell Cook hated more than being laid up.

The nurse poked his head around the blue curtain. "Sorry for the wait. His room is almost ready. I'll be back to take him upstairs in a few minutes."

"Thanks."

"Can I get you anything?"

"No." I stifled a groan as I sat up. "I'm fine."

He left and I stretched my arms overhead. How long had I been there? Hours, although I didn't remember exactly when I'd arrived. Long enough that I was really done with this chair.

"You should go home," Dad said, his voice gravelly.

"Just rest, Dad. They'll move you upstairs soon."

"I already told them I don't need to stay. I'm fine."

"You fell off a roof. You're not fine."

He grumbled something incoherent—not quite admitting I was right, but at least he didn't try to get out of bed again.

The nurse came back with the news that a room was ready. I squeezed Dad's hand before they took him upstairs and I assured him Mom would be back first thing in the morning.

It occurred to me as I watched them wheel him toward the elevator that I didn't have my car. I'd driven over with Mom and she'd already gone home. I pulled out my phone and checked the time. It was late, but Marigold was probably still up. I'd make it up to her.

"What happened? Is he okay?"

My tired brain could not process that voice. It felt as if I were moving in slow motion, my eyes gradually rising to meet his. Elias stood in front of me, dressed in his wool coat over—were those sweats? Elias Stoneheart wore sweatpants?

This couldn't be real.

"Elias? What are you doing here?"

"I heard something happened to your dad."

"Heard how?"

"Alice talked to the Phillips guy."

I blinked. That made sense. Cole was clearly crazy about Alice, so it wasn't surprising that they were keeping in touch even though she'd gone home when Elias had. "But... why are you here?"

His cool façade cracked, the way it had when we'd been having dinner, and I saw a glimmer of warmth in his green eyes.

"I don't know." The simple honesty in his voice nearly took my breath away. "I just got in the car and drove. Is your dad okay?"

"Mostly. He fell off the roof. Miraculously, he didn't break anything. They're keeping him overnight just to be safe."

He shifted closer. "Are you okay?"

That almost made me crack. Tears threatened to gather in my eyes as the stress and exhaustion of the last several hours swept through me. With a quick breath, I sucked it all in. "Yeah. Although I just realized I don't have a way home."

"I'll drive you."

I held up my phone. "I was just about to call Marigold."

"Isabelle." The tone of command in his voice did not make my insides heat up. Not one bit. "I'm here. Let me drive you home."

He was right. There was no reason for me to bug Marigold when he could give me a ride. But something about the hint of warmth in his eyes, the closeness of his body, and the way mine was responding, set off alarm bells in my head. An entire choir of them, ringing out a warning.

Or was it an invitation?

Against my better judgment, I nodded. "Okay. Thanks."

He didn't touch me as we walked through the emergency department to the exit. No light hand on the small of my back or gentle grip on my arm. Not that I wanted any of that. My body absolutely did not crave contact with him.

I was getting worse at the whole denial thing.

He led me to his car in silence. Fat snowflakes drifted through the pools of light cast by the street lamps, coating the ground in white. I hugged my arms against the cold and gave myself a stern reminder that I was mad at this man. He was trying to buy our farm and close it down. He'd gone around me to get to my parents.

And he'd broken my heart when I was eighteen.

I got in his car, wanting to kick myself for thinking about that. The last thing I needed after leaving my dad in the hospital for the night was to let my emotions take me on a sleigh ride through the forest of old memories. Especially those ones.

We drove through town, past Christmas lights and the big town tree in Lumberjack Park. He turned onto the gravel driveway that led to my parents' house, then took the right fork that led to mine. It was weird, and also not, that he knew where I lived without asking.

My heartbeat quickened as he parked outside my little house. This was fine. He was just dropping me off. I still didn't understand why he'd come all the way to Tilikum— or more importantly, what it meant that he had—but I didn't have to deal with it tonight. I could be grateful that he'd been there when I'd needed a ride, go inside, and go to bed.

Alone.

Definitely alone.

Because anything else would be a Santa's toy bag-sized mistake.

"Thanks for the ride." I reached for the door handle.

"Isabelle."

Why did he have to sound so tortured when he said my name? It was killing me. I paused, almost afraid to look at him.

You're mad, Isabelle. So mad at this man.

"I'm sorry for talking to your parents without you. I shouldn't have done that."

The sincerity in his voice took the wind out of my sails— deflated the anger I was trying to hold. Now I was really afraid to look at him. If I met his eyes, I'd do something stupid. Like kiss him.

How could I think of kissing him? This was Elias. I had history with this man. Bad history. I couldn't be craving his lips on mine.

But I really was.

I didn't turn. "Thank you for apologizing. I forgive you."

He held still and silent, as if waiting for me to make the next move. Giving me the chance to decide.

His restraint nearly undid me, especially because I could feel the tension as he held himself back. From what, I didn't know. From saying something else? Asking to come in? Leaning over and taking my mouth with his?

What did I want from him?

I didn't know and maybe it was the not knowing that prompted me to speak. "Do you want to come inside for a few minutes?"

"Sure."

We got out and I fished my keys out of my purse. The porch light was off, as were the lights inside, but I managed to unlock the door. My heart felt jumpy as I led him inside.

I flipped on the switch. "So, this is it."

He took slow steps into the room and looked around. "No decorations."

"For Christmas? No. I have plenty but I never seem to find time to put them up."

"You live on a Christmas tree farm and you don't have a Christmas tree." One corner of his mouth lifted ever so slightly.

Don't do that to me tonight, Elias. Don't be cute and funny. "It's a travesty. But I'm also busy, so…"

He nodded as if he understood. "What was your dad doing on a roof?"

"Other than denying that he's too old to be up there? Trying to fix something."

"Phillips should have done it."

"That's what I said. That's what Cole said, too. But you know my dad. He's as stubborn as Horace."

"Horace is an ass."

I laughed and almost snorted. "Literally."

My smile faded and tension filled the air. The electricity sparking between us was impossible to deny. Did he feel it, too?

He cleared his throat and glanced around. "I don't remember what this looked like before. Was it finished?"

"Not really." I set my purse down and slipped off my coat. "It was rough. Not livable."

"You did it all yourself."

The way he said that—as a statement, not a question—sounded a lot like a compliment. A tingle of pleasure ran down my spine. "I did. It took a while, but I think it was worth it."

"It looks great."

"Thanks."

His eyes met mine again and for a second, I thought he was going to say he had to go. Conflict gripped me. I still didn't know what I wanted from him.

Or maybe I did and I was afraid to admit it.

But he seemed to make a decision. He took off his coat, draped it over the arm of the couch, and headed for the kitchen.

He really was wearing sweats.

Without a word, he started rooting through my cupboards. The sight of Elias in my kitchen, dressed so casually in a crisp white t-shirt and sweatpants, momentarily took away my ability to speak. I couldn't even ask what he was looking for. I just stared.

He took out two mugs and set them on the counter, then kept searching. Out came the tea kettle. He filled it with water and put it on the stove to boil. I was about to ask what he was doing when he turned and something about the way he moved reminded me why my friends and I had all agreed that a man in gray sweats was a thing.

Because, oh my sugar plum fairy, he filled out those sweats well.

"You should sit down," he said finally.

His low, velvety voice was impossible to resist. That, and my tired body wanted to sit on something that wasn't hard plastic. I toed off my shoes and sank into the couch, letting out a long breath as I relaxed.

It had been a long day.

And Elias was here. He'd heard my dad was hurt and he'd come.

Why?

The tea kettle whistled as I pondered that question. Why was he here?

I didn't have an answer. I had a feeling he didn't either.

A couple of minutes later, he came into the living room and handed me a mug, then sat down next to me with his. I leaned in and inhaled.

Hot chocolate.

I swallowed back the rush of emotion, hoping it didn't show. How many times had he made me hot chocolate at the end of a hard day? When we'd been studying for a test or working on our senior projects. When I'd started taking on more responsibility on the farm and worked myself to exhaustion.

When we lost—

Thinking about *that* was going to make me cry and that was absolutely not happening in front of Elias Stoneheart. Not a chance.

Thankfully, he broke the brief silence. "You don't have any marshmallows or whipped cream."

I glanced at the mug. "I'm surprised I had hot chocolate."

"I'm not."

Lifting the mug to my lips, I took a sip. It was rich and smooth, extra chocolatey just the way I liked it. "This is good. Thank you."

"I figured you needed it."

"Do you have a place to stay tonight?"

"I'll get a hotel."

Yes, a hotel. That was the right answer. Because I certainly wasn't inviting him to stay here. "Okay." I took another sip. It was so calming. "Thanks for coming all the way out here. You didn't have to do that."

"I know. I'm glad your dad is okay." He set his mug on the coffee table. "How was opening weekend?"

"Good but I wish it had been better."

"Maybe it'll pick up."

I had the strangest urge to tell him about my parents' plan to convert the farm to commercial agriculture but I stopped myself before I made the mistake of confiding in him. I probably shouldn't talk to him about the farm at all but his interest seemed personal this time. "It usually does. A lot of people wait to get their tree until Christmas is closer."

"Did you ever start the reindeer encounter program you were talking about?"

How did he remember that? Back in high school, I'd had the idea to extend our season by offering farm tours year-round, particularly to see the reindeer. Somehow we'd never made the time to develop the program. "We haven't but I still think we should."

"What's stopping you?"

"Time and money, I guess. Cole and I could give some of the tours, but we'd need to hire another person to help. I'm convinced it would earn more than enough to offset the costs, but it would take a while to get the word out."

"You're right to think long-term."

I nodded.

We lapsed into silence again. I drank my hot cocoa and wrestled with my feelings. His presence was so comforting, the stress of the day melting away the longer we sat together. He'd always had that effect on me, a way of making me feel better without saying a word.

He shifted on the couch next to me. Had he leaned closer? I kept my eyes on my mug, suddenly afraid to look. Heat raced through my veins and my skin tingled at the thought of his touch. He moved again and his leg rested against mine, causing a burst of sensation.

This was so bad. I couldn't let this happen.

Or could I?

I set my mug on the coffee table and with my heart in my throat, shifted so I was facing him.

His green eyes held me captive. I knew those eyes. The

icy mask was gone, revealing the man I remembered. Those glimpses hadn't been my imagination. He was still there.

He leaned closer, his gaze dipping to my mouth. My heart beat so hard, I could hear it in my ears, feel it pulsing in my wrists. Tingles swept through me and the butterflies in my stomach took wing without any anger to impede their flight.

Simultaneously, I braced for impact and loosened my grip on reason. Elias was going to kiss me and I was going to let it happen.

No, I was going to do more than that. I was going to kiss him back. Thoroughly.

The knock on my door startled me so much, I jerked away, tweaking my neck.

"Ow." Wincing, I grabbed the back of my neck. Was someone seriously at my door? *Now?*

They knocked again, harder this time.

"Sorry— I don't— Door—" I kept sputtering apologies as I got up. My heart still raced and I was probably as red as a cranberry. I went to the door and found Cole with his hand poised to knock again.

"I'm sorry to bug you, but I never got an update on your dad and you weren't answering your phone."

I glanced at my purse where I'd left my phone. "I'm so sorry. I thought Mom was going to call you but she probably thought I was. Dad's okay. He didn't break anything but they kept him overnight as a precaution."

Cole let out a breath. "Good. I'm glad to hear that. Are you okay? Do you need anything?"

Elias stood and cleared his throat. Cole's gaze shifted and his eyes widened.

"Oh. I didn't know you had company." He glanced over his shoulder. "Right, the car. I should have realized. Sorry."

"No, he's not..." I trailed off because what was I supposed to say? I didn't know what was happening, so how could I explain it to Cole? "He gave me a ride home."

"Could you update Alice?" Elias asked. "She was worried about Russell."

Cole blinked, like that surprised him. "Yeah. I'll give her a call right now."

"Thanks, Cole," I said.

"I'll check in with you tomorrow," he said.

He left and I shut the door behind him.

"I should go."

Disappointment flooded through me. Elias already had his coat on. Damn it, Cole. And damn it, me. If I would have called him earlier, he wouldn't have stopped by. "Sure, yeah. It's getting late. Are you heading home tomorrow?"

He opened his mouth to answer but he paused before speaking. "I don't know."

I nodded slowly and moved so he could step past me. "Okay. I guess I'll talk to you later."

"Goodnight, Isabelle."

"Goodnight, Elias."

He left and I shut the door behind him, wondering what in the world had just happened.

19

ELIAS

*H*ot chocolate had been a mistake.

Almost kissing Isabelle had also been a mistake, but somehow the hot chocolate was worse. I'd only taken one sip but that had been all it took. The rich, warm drink had slid over my tongue, warming my throat, and I'd realized I hadn't had a cup of hot cocoa in years.

Not since the last time I'd made it for Isabelle. The Christmas when everything had fallen apart.

I wasn't going to think about that. I refused.

A squirrel ran across the path between me and my car. It stopped, resting on its hind legs, and looked back at me.

That was weird.

It darted away and scurried up a tree.

Squirrels were everywhere in this town, so one random squirrel climbing up a trunk shouldn't have sent another burst of memory flooding through me. But all I could see was the Cooks' farmhouse, decked out in Christmas lights—the way it had looked on that awful night.

It hadn't been the moment our relationship had ended. We'd stayed together until graduation. But looking back, that Christmas Eve had been the beginning of the end. After that, nothing had been the same. Eventually I'd left Tilikum —and Isabelle—for good.

I got in my car and backed out. But the memories wouldn't fade. I couldn't freeze them out this time.

AGE eighteen

THE CHRISTMAS LIGHTS outside the farmhouse twinkled, bright enough to stand out even though it was still early in the afternoon. The front windows were dark and I'd caught sight of Isabelle's parents over in the village. They hadn't seen me, which was a relief. My relationship with them was shaky at best these days.

Not that I blamed them. I was the guy who'd gotten their daughter pregnant.

We'd known for a few weeks. It was still so early, she wasn't showing and she said she didn't feel much of anything. No morning sickness or food cravings. Not many people knew. Just her parents, my aunt and uncle, and Annika and Marigold. We'd have to start telling everyone soon, especially after today. People were going to ask questions and in this town, rumors would fly.

Not that I cared what anyone else thought.

While our classmates were getting ready for graduation, celebrating college acceptance letters and secured apprenticeships, we were trying to wrap our heads around being parents.

The weird thing was, I wasn't scared anymore.

A squirrel scurried through the brush and ran up a tree.

Ignoring it, I went around to the back porch and glanced in the kitchen window. Isabelle sat at the table, picking at a cookie on a plate.

I loved her so much.

That was why I wasn't afraid. I loved her and I loved the child we'd made. This hadn't been the plan—not even close. But it had happened. And now that it had, I'd realized something.

I wanted this. I wanted a family.

Obviously it would have been better if it hadn't happened now, while we were still in high school. We were young and this was throwing a wrench in our future plans. But since it had happened, we were going to make the best of it. I was going to take care of her, always.

With a deep breath to calm my racing heart, I slipped my hand in my coat pocket and touched the small package I carried. Her Christmas present, but so much more.

Here goes nothing.

I knocked and poked my head inside. "Hey."

She smiled but it didn't hide the sadness in her eyes. "Hey. Thanks for coming over."

"I was going to anyway, it's Christmas Eve." I went over to the table and sat next to her. "Are you okay? You look upset."

"I'm fine."

She wasn't. We'd met when we were eleven and started dating sophomore year. I knew her. Something was wrong. But because I knew her, I wouldn't push. She'd talk about it when she was ready.

Besides, I had a feeling I knew. Her parents were probably still mad about the baby. I wished they knew they didn't have to worry. Hopefully after tonight, they would.

I leaned over and kissed her cheek. "Wait here."

She stayed at the table, still picking at her cookie, while I got up and got the tea kettle going. It only took a few minutes to make us two mugs of hot cocoa, complete with big dollops of whipped cream. I added some red and green sprinkles to the top because it was Christmas.

"Merry Christmas." I set the mug in front of her. I had no idea why, but hot chocolate always made her feel better.

"Thanks." She slid the mug closer but didn't take a sip.

I sat down with mine and my hand strayed to the outside of my coat pocket. Again. I knew it was still there but I couldn't stop myself from checking. I almost took it out and set it on the table. After all, that little box wrapped in silver paper was why I'd come over. But she sniffed and I realized she had tears welling in her eyes.

Alarm flooded through me. I reached over and covered her hand with mine. "Belle, what's wrong?"

She sniffed again and her eyes stayed on the table. "I couldn't tell you on the phone when I called earlier."

"Tell me what?"

It took her a few seconds to answer, and when she did, her voice was barely above a whisper. "The baby."

Dread filled me, making it hard to speak. "What happened? Is the baby okay?"

She shook her head and tears spilled down her cheeks.

I scooted closer. "Belle, tell me. I'm here, it's okay. Tell me what happened."

"I woke up this morning and I just knew something was wrong. I don't know how I knew. Nothing was happening, just a bit of blood. Hardly any. I finally told Mom and she said we should go in, just to be on the safe side. They did an ultrasound. They had two doctors check to be sure." More tears trailed down her cheeks. "No heartbeat."

My heart stopped. Pain gripped my chest. I couldn't breathe. "What?"

Her eyes finally met mine and the hurt in them was unbearable. "We lost the baby."

"How? Do they know why?"

"No. They said this happens sometimes. It was early. It's not uncommon."

Those were someone else's words, phrases she was parroting, as if they would help her understand. Anger at whoever had told her that flowed through me like molten steel. Not uncommon? As if that made it okay?

I had no idea what to say. I wasn't good at offering comfort, not even to Isabelle. "There wasn't anything they could do?"

She shook her head. "No. They said it's not my fault."

"Of course it's not your fault."

"I guess it's probably for the best. We didn't mean to get pregnant."

For the best? This wasn't for the best. Something that hurt this much was *not* for the best. "Is that what your parents said?"

"No. They just said they're sorry. Mom cried."

Isabelle had been crying, too. I could see it now. The skin around her eyes was red and blotchy. She sniffed again and wiped the tears on the back of her hand.

I wanted to cry, too. It was the strangest sensation. I never cried. The last time I'd shed a tear, my father had sent me to my room. Told me I couldn't come out until I could be a man. I wanted to cry over this loss and I couldn't. The tears weren't there.

What was wrong with me?

"Belle, I'm so sorry."

"It's okay. I'll be fine." She wiped her cheeks again and finally took a sip of her hot cocoa.

She wasn't fine and neither was I. And I had no idea what to do about it.

We sat in silence for long moments, drinking our hot cocoa. Maybe that was what we needed. Just to sit here and be sad together. I was keenly aware of the box in my pocket but now everything had changed. Again. I didn't understand how that could keep happening. I'd been with her when she'd taken the pregnancy test and it had felt a lot like this. Like one moment had altered the course of the future forever. Here we were again, facing another sharp turn— one we hadn't foreseen.

The ground beneath my feet kept shifting. I'd spent so much time over the last few weeks making new plans, figuring things out. Was I supposed to undo all that now? Did we go back to being normal teenagers? Would we just graduate and go on with our lives, like this had never happened?

She pushed her half-empty mug away. "I should go help out at the village."

"Belle, no." I reached for her hand but she was already getting up. "You should rest."

"I already laid down for a while after we saw the doctor. I don't want to rest anymore. It'll drive me nuts."

I watched as she took our mugs to the sink and poured them out. "What did the doctor say?"

"That I can do whatever feels comfortable as long as I don't overdo it."

"Maybe we should just watch a movie or something."

"I need to do something, not sit around."

I'd never felt so helpless. The pain in my chest was crushing, like my ribs would snap and puncture my lungs. I didn't know what to do, how to cope. Isabelle put the canister of hot cocoa away and rinsed the spoon I'd used. Why had she bothered? Why did she care about the mess in the kitchen?

I stood and gently grabbed her arms—made her stop moving. "Belle."

She let me draw her against me. I wrapped my arms around her, wishing I could make this all go away. She hugged me back and I felt her deep exhale as she rested her head against my chest. Maybe I needed to give her the Christmas present anyway. Just because we weren't having a baby didn't mean we couldn't still—

But she pulled away and started fixing her ponytail. "I promise I'll be careful, but I need to go do a few things. Do you still want to come over for Christmas dinner tomorrow?"

I nodded. "Sure."

"Do you want me to come with you to tell Dale and Hattie?"

"No, I can tell them."

She met my eyes, but hers were dry. "Elias, I'm sorry."

"You don't have to be sorry. You didn't do anything wrong."

"I still am. I know this has been really hard." She shifted on her feet and fidgeted with her ponytail, the way she did when she was stressed. "I'll see you tomorrow for Christmas? We can talk more then. I just can't sit still right now."

I nodded again, wishing I could fix this.

But maybe she didn't want me to. Maybe she was relieved.

Now she wasn't stuck with me.

We said goodbye, and I turned and left out the kitchen

door, knowing already that I wasn't coming for Christmas dinner. She'd be mad, but I couldn't.

And maybe she didn't want me to.

Without really seeing where I was going, I walked to my car. Got in the driver's side and pulled the box out of my pocket. Opened it.

It wasn't much. Just a gold band. I didn't have a lot of money but I'd done my best. When I'd bought it the other day, I'd resolved to make something of myself so I could buy her something better. By our fifth anniversary—at the latest —she'd have a diamond on her finger. A big one.

But there wasn't going to be a fifth anniversary. Isabelle wasn't going to marry me. Because now she didn't have to.

A single tear slid down my cheek but like hell was I going to cry now. I swiped it away and closed the box, then tossed it on the passenger seat.

I turned on my car and backed out. My chest still hurt but I hardened myself against it. I let a sheen of ice form around my heart, encasing what was left of it.

Didn't matter. It wasn't beating anyway.

20

ISABELLE

I woke up feeling hungover. Instead of popping up and getting straight to work, like I usually did, I had to drag myself out of bed. I took a long shower, hoping the heat would ease the knots in my back and shoulders. But all I could think about as the water streamed over me was how close I'd come to kissing Elias last night.

Crazy. I was crazy.

Thankfully, Cole had interrupted us.

But was I thankful for his sudden appearance at my door?

I wasn't but I should have been. He'd saved me from making a huge mistake.

As the morning went on, I started to feel more like myself. Mom went to the hospital to be with Dad and I stayed behind to manage another busy day at Christmas Village. Losing myself in work helped. It always did. A few hours went by in a blink as I put out small fires and made sure everything ran smoothly. The WiFi glitched, leaving the vendors unable to process credit cards. Isabelle to the rescue. The kettle corn machine stopped working. I'd never worked on one before but somehow I fixed it. There were candy canes to deliver and hot chocolate to make for the tree customers.

And I didn't think about Elias at all.

That's a lie. I thought about him constantly.

I wondered where he was. If he'd stayed in Tilikum or left early this morning. Maybe even last night. I resisted the urge to text him and invite him to meet me for lunch. Or maybe dinner.

Busy. I needed to stay busy.

The scent of pine and sawdust surrounded me as I went to check on the guys manning the u-cut Christmas trees. This early on a weekday, there were only a few customers searching for the perfect centerpiece to their holiday cele-brations. A saw rang out as one of our guys cut a trunk for a more even fit in the tree stand. I checked in with the cashier and made sure there were enough fresh wreaths for the afternoon rush that would come later.

As I walked back toward the village, I kept an eye out for broken or misplaced decorations. Someone had left an empty coffee cup on a bench, so I took it to a nearby garbage can. Glancing around, I couldn't help but wonder what it would look like if we really did close Christmas Village. Instead of neatly trimmed paths lined with evergreen garland, lights, and red bows, there would be nothing but rows of crops. Dust in the air from the agricultural machin-ery. No cozy shops filled with handmade ornaments and cookies. No Santa's Workshop or wooden penguins smiling from drifts of snow. No reindeer to delight the kids of Tilikum.

But there was more to my determination to keep our farm and Christmas Village. This place represented some-thing to me. It was filled with the memory of a child who never was. Who didn't get the chance to be born and grow up here.

The child I'd almost had with Elias.

A pang of grief hit me. It was so strange how all these years later, I could still feel sad for something I'd never really had. I didn't think about the baby often, but once in a while, especially this time of year, I remembered.

I had two choices. Give up and be sad, or keep fighting for my family's farm and everything it represented.

The choice was obvious. And my conflicted feelings for Elias wouldn't get in the way.

Squaring my shoulders, I veered through the village and the growing crowd, mentally estimating today's potential attendance. Would it be enough to cover our costs? We did most of our business on the weekends, but today was already looking good. Maybe there was hope after all.

I glanced ahead and did a double take. Was that Elias? He sat on a bench, dressed in his dark wool coat and sweats. It looked like the same clothes he'd been wearing last night. His forearms rested on his thighs and his brow was deeply furrowed, like he was lost in thought.

Feeling suddenly wary, I approached him. He didn't seem to notice me coming. I slid my hands into my coat pockets—I'd actually remembered to put one on today— and stopped.

"Elias?"

His head jerked toward me and he straightened, but didn't say anything.

"Are you okay?"

He blinked. "I'm fine."

I tilted my head. "Are you sure?"

His eyes looked slightly wild and his hair was unkempt. Clearing his throat, he stood. "Yes. Fine."

"Did you find a hotel room last night?"

"Hotel?"

"Yeah." He was starting to worry me. "After you left my place you said you were going to a hotel. Did you?"

"Right, yes. I did. The Grand Peak."

He had the same haunted look in his eyes that I'd seen when we'd had dinner together. "Are you sure you're all right? You look like you saw a ghost."

"No. Just a squirrel."

"What?"

"Nothing. How's your dad?"

"Grouchy, according to my mom. They should be discharging him soon."

"Good."

"He's going to have to take it easy for a while." I started toward the reindeer barn and Elias fell in step with me. "My mom has her work cut out for her, convincing him to rest."

"And that's going to leave you shorthanded."

I sighed. "I'm still pretending that isn't going to be a problem."

He could have taken the opportunity to remind me that this would be another blow to the farm's finances. But he didn't. Just walked alongside me, as if he somehow belonged here.

Inside the barn, Cole was finishing up with a group of preschoolers, answering their reindeer questions. A little boy in the front raised his hand with urgency, practically jumping out of his shoes.

Cole pointed to him. "Go ahead, what's your question?"

"Does Rudolph live here?"

"Afraid not, my friend," Cole said. "None of our reindeer have red noses."

"Can they fly?" another child asked.

"Not that I've seen, although..." He glanced around, then leaned in as if about to share a secret. "Sometimes I wonder if they do it when we're not looking."

The children giggled and Cole grinned at them.

I didn't want to interrupt, so I waited near the barn entrance for Cole to finish up. He took a few more questions from the class, answering with his usual friendly smile. Elias stood next to me, not quite glaring at Cole, but his crossed arms gave him an air of opposition.

The teacher rounded up the kids and led them out the other side, where they could walk around the outskirts of the reindeer pen and see more of the herd. Cole cast a quick glance at Elias, his expression hard to read, before moving closer.

"Mom will bring Dad home as soon as they discharge him," I said. "He's supposed to rest, so we'll need to be a united front to make sure he actually follows doctor's orders."

"Don't worry." Cole stepped closer to me, his eyes warm with concern, and put a hand on my arm. "How are you holding up?"

"I'm okay. Trying not to panic at the reality of being down a person, especially going into the weekend."

"I know. We'll handle it. I've got your back."

"Yeah, thanks."

"I'll catch up with you later." He squeezed my arm and left.

"Why does he need to catch up with you?" Elias asked.

Was that jealousy in his voice? "We work together. That means we have to, you know, work together."

"He's hiding something."

"What?" I glanced the way Cole had gone. "No, he's not. What makes you say that?"

"No one's that nice unless they're hiding something."

I scoffed. "Actually, some people are that nice. Cole happens to be one of them."

"Then why—" Looking away, he closed his mouth.

"Then why, what?" I put my hands on my hips. "Why did we break up? That's none of your business."

"He's dating my assistant. That makes it my business."

My eyes lit up. "Are they really dating? I was hoping they'd get together."

"You were?"

"Why wouldn't I be? They make a great couple."

His brow furrowed and his green eyes flashed with anger. What was he so mad about? A tingle of jealousy wormed its way through me. I didn't have anything to be jealous of. There was no reason his apparent protectiveness of his assistant should bother me.

But it did.

"Look, I don't know what's going on with Alice and Cole, but he isn't hiding anything," I said. "Unlike you, he's very straightforward and uncomplicated. What you see is what you get."

"How am I complicated?"

"Really? How are you *not* complicated?"

He started to answer but paused, as if he didn't know what to say. Finally, he pointed an accusatory finger at me. "You invited me in."

"What?"

"You invited me in last night. That wasn't my idea."

"Are you trying to say that makes *me* complicated? I'm not the one who randomly drove out here and showed up at the emergency room."

"It's a good thing I did."

"Why, because I needed a ride home? I had other options."

He moved closer. "No, because you were doing that thing where you convince yourself you don't need anyone."

"I don't do that."

"Belle." He grabbed my chin and tilted my face up toward his. "You always do that."

"Don't pretend like you know me."

With his hand still gripping my chin, he inched his face closer to mine. "I do know you."

My pulse raced, and despite the chill in the air, a wave of heat swept through me. His touch was firm but gentle, his eyes insistent. He was right, he did know me. He always had, in a way no one else did.

But I couldn't let this happen.

I stepped back and he let me go. Reflexively, I tightened my ponytail. "I need to get back to work."

His jaw hitched and he growled, a low sound in his throat. Hooking his arm around my waist, he hauled me roughly against him. Before I could say a word, he grabbed my ponytail and took my mouth with his.

The heat of his kiss blazed, lighting me up from the inside. His tongue demanded entrance, delving into my mouth, making me gasp and whimper. My knees weakened but he held me tight, holding me against his hard body. He devoured me, holding nothing back.

I hadn't been kissed like that in a very, very long time. I was vaguely aware that visitors might be watching but I couldn't bring myself to care. All that existed was Elias's mouth on mine, his grip on my hair, and his strong arm pulling me close.

Slowly—almost reluctantly—his kiss went from deep to

shallow. Without releasing his grip on me, he pulled away, just enough for our lips to separate.

His nose brushed against mine and my breath came fast. I felt delirious, overcome by the intensity of kissing him.

Instead of doing the sane thing and forcing my brain back to reality, I did the crazy thing. I popped up on my tip toes, threw my arms around his neck, and kissed him again.

Someone behind me cleared their throat. Gasping, I stepped away and dropped my arms. Elias let go and his eyes widened.

Oh no. Who was he looking at?

"Sorry to interrupt," my mom said, her voice as casual as if she'd just walked in on us having tea, not making out in the barn. "I just thought you'd want to know your dad is home."

Swallowing hard, I turned around. "How is he?"

"Sore and tired. And angry with me for making him lie down but that's not unexpected."

"Can I help with anything?"

She shook her head. "No. I'll handle him."

My face felt flushed and my lips still burned with the heat of Elias's kiss. This was so embarrassing. "Mom, we—"

"Don't worry about it." She brushed off my attempt at an explanation with a wave of her hand. "Elias, would you like to join us for dinner tonight?"

I gaped at her. She was inviting him to dinner? "I don't know if he's staying."

She ignored me, her gaze on Elias, her expression friendly.

"Sure, I'd love to."

"Wonderful. We'll eat around six." She jerked her thumb behind her, pointing in the direction of the house. "I better go make sure Russell isn't trying to sneak outside. I'll see you two tonight."

I mumbled a thank you. It was the best I could do. My brain was still swimming in the heady stream of endorphins from being kissed so thoroughly. I hardly knew what was happening.

Elias took a deep breath and stepped back as my mom left the barn. His cool confidence seemed to have returned but there was no mistaking the heat in his eyes. "I'll let you get to work. I need to do the same."

"Yeah, work."

One corner of his mouth lifted. "I'll see you tonight."

I nodded.

His tongue slid out over his bottom lip, a quick gesture I almost missed. But I got the distinct impression he could still taste me. Without another word, he turned and walked away, leaving me bewildered.

21

ELIAS

I wasn't quite sure how I'd ended up invited to the Cooks' place for dinner. At first, Faye's interruption in the barn had seemed like a disaster. For a second I'd been a teenager again, horrified at having been caught making out by my girlfriend's mom. But I'd quickly come back to myself.

And something about kissing Isabelle had shaken me out of my earlier stupor. I'd come to the farm without any sense of purpose. I hadn't even gotten dressed beyond putting on my coat against the cold. Isabelle had found me sitting on a bench in Christmas Village and I'd hardly remembered how I'd gotten there.

But kissing her had brought back my sense of control.

It had also awakened something in me. A deep desire I'd been denying.

I wanted her. And I wasn't sure how much longer I'd be able to fight it.

Dinner with her, and her parents, was probably not the best idea. What I should have done was leave Tilikum. Gone home to get my head together, not booked my hotel room for another night and left a message with Alice that I'd be working remotely again the next day.

But that was exactly what I'd done.

I walked through freshly fallen snow and knocked on the Cooks' front door. A garland of evergreen boughs interspersed with red berries decorated the door frame and the wreath had a large red bow. Their Christmas tree sparkled in the window, the white lights reflecting off shiny ornaments.

Faye answered, dressed in a blue sweater with white snowflakes. She smiled. "I'm glad you made it. Come in."

Her friendliness was both disarming and unsettling. A part of me wanted to relax into the familiarity of the Cooks' farmhouse. The comforting scent of food filled the air and a fire crackled in the wood stove. I had to admit, their holiday decor was charming rather than garish, with lights, garland, and candles creating a cozy ambiance. Even the instrumental Christmas music playing softly in the background beckoned to me.

But I also didn't know what to make of her hospitality. Was she attempting to lull me into a false sense of security?

Either way, I was there. And at least there wouldn't be any squirrels scampering by, inexplicably leading me down unwanted paths into the past.

She took my coat and I followed her into the kitchen. Isabelle stood at the stove whisking what looked like a pot of gravy. She'd changed out of her work clothes into a dark green sweater and jeans with a pair of candy cane striped socks.

I wanted to march across the kitchen, scoop her into my arms, and kiss her like I had earlier. But Russell sat at the table and leveled me with a hard glare.

This was going to be interesting.

"No business tonight," Faye said, pointing at me, then Russell. "We're having a nice, holiday dinner."

"It's not a holiday," Russell grumbled.

"It's the holiday season, so it still counts. But if you'd prefer, I can heat you up some canned soup instead of the turkey and mashed potatoes."

"Now, honey."

Faye just smiled.

"Mom, when did you find time to roast a turkey?" Isabelle asked.

"Oh, a turkey couldn't be easier. You just prep it, pop it in the oven, and wait. It wasn't any trouble." She gestured toward the stove. "Keep whisking."

Isabelle went back to stirring. Her eyes flicked to mine but she glanced away. She was cute when she was flustered.

I liked that I'd done that to her. It made me want her more.

Russell kept glaring at me, as if he could read my mind and knew all the things I wanted to do to his daughter.

Awkward. But I didn't let it bother me.

Old habit made me offer to help and under Faye's direction, Isabelle and I got dinner on the table. Russell tried to get up several times only to be scolded by his wife or daughter. Considering he'd fallen off a roof, he looked healthy, although I could tell by the winces he tried to hide that he was banged up and sore.

"How long will you be in town?" Faye asked when we were all seated and dishing up.

"I need to head back tomorrow."

"That's too bad. But I'm sure you'll be back for the parade."

I bit back a groan. The annual Christmas parade. They

still did that? Of course they did. Tilikum had always loved its traditions.

"I doubt it," I said.

Faye looked oddly disappointed while Russell seemed to be trying to ignore my presence at his table. Isabelle kept her eyes on her dinner.

She was thinking about me kissing her. I was sure of it.

Faye changed the subject, engaging her husband in conversation about the farm. I took a bite of my gravy-slathered turkey and had to stop myself from moaning with pleasure. The meat was tender and juicy, the gravy full of flavor. I'd forgotten how intensely satisfying comfort food could be.

The rest of the meal was just as good. Creamy mashed potatoes with what had to be an absurd amount of butter. Sautéed green beans, probably harvested earlier in the season from Faye's garden—a simple dish but packed with flavor. And crusty bread that practically melted in my mouth.

I hadn't realized how much I'd missed this. I ate well at home, but it was often takeout or simple meals I'd thrown together. I hadn't even bothered with a Thanksgiving dinner, brushing off the invitation from my aunt and uncle to spend it with them. I'd eaten Thai food, alone in my condo. At the time, I hadn't thought much of it. But something about the pleasure of this meal brought back more memories—good ones, of holiday dinners followed by pie and hot cocoa.

Instead of leaving me bewildered and frustrated, the quick flashes of remembrance gave me a strange sense of peace.

I met Isabelle's eyes across the table. She wiped away a crumb from the corner of her mouth and licked her lips.

Desire for her smoldered inside me. I hadn't wanted a woman like this in a very long time. I was a man; I had needs. But I tended to avoid indulging in them. Attachment was such a hassle, it was never worth it in the long run.

Isabelle would be.

True to her warning, Faye didn't allow any mention of business as we finished our meal. She asked benign questions about my job and where I lived as if she were simply catching up with an old friend. Russell even joined the conversation to ask about my Tesla and how it handled in the snow.

"I'm so sorry I don't have a proper dessert." Faye stood and started gathering our empty plates.

I'd practically licked mine clean. "I'm too full anyway."

"Me, too." Isabelle stood to help clear the table. "Thanks for such a great meal, Mom. That was amazing."

"My pleasure."

Russell stood with a wince but held up his hand as if to ward off any assistance. "I'm not an invalid. I can rinse off dishes."

"I guess that won't hurt you," Faye said. "I'll help."

I thanked Faye for dinner and Russell gave me a nod. It wasn't quite friendly but it was better than a glare.

"I'll walk you home," I said to Isabelle.

She opened her mouth as if to argue, but I raised my eyebrows. If she told me no, I'd leave—go back to my hotel and nurse my sexual frustration. But I knew she wasn't going to.

"Okay, thanks."

I helped her with her coat, then put on mine, and led her out into the cold.

We walked in silence as snowflakes drifted around us. The blanket of white dulled the sound and reflected the light of the moon, making the night unnaturally bright and quiet.

The windows of Isabelle's house were dark. I followed her inside and as she flipped on the light I was struck with how *her* it was. The decor was cozy without being trite, tidy without being stark.

I could also tell she didn't spend much time here. It was almost too clean and organized.

She took off her coat and tossed it on a chair. Although she hadn't actually invited me to stay, I did the same.

We could keep dancing around it, but I knew how this night would end. She wanted it as much as I did. I could see it in her eyes, in the way she licked her lips. A slight flush crept across her cheeks as I stared her down, a predator sizing up his prey.

"Elias, maybe—"

Decisively, I crossed the distance between us and cut her off with a kiss.

If there had been any reluctance in her, it vanished the moment our mouths crashed together. She threw her arms around my neck and pressed herself against me. Heat seared through my veins at the feel of her.

I backed her up toward what I hoped was the bedroom. Clothes came off, discarded and forgotten as we stumbled through a doorway. We were hot and frantic, our kisses wet and messy. Something hit the floor with a bang but neither of us cared. The tension between us was at the breaking point.

My hands roamed, tearing off the last of her clothes. In between kisses I muttered something about a condom and stopped long enough to grab my pants off the floor, fish one out of my wallet, and put it on.

I pushed her onto the bed and climbed on top of her.

The familiarity of her scent washed through me, making me want her all the more. Her skin was warm and soft against mine, her mouth eager.

We joined with groans, with hands clutching flesh, temptation turning to sensation. Her hips moved, her body writhing beneath me. She felt so good, I was overcome.

I'd missed her so much.

I didn't want to think about that. Not now, while I was inside her. I wanted to sate my lust, feed this intense desire. Nothing more.

We flipped over, knocking throw pillows to the floor. She was glorious, so beautiful I wanted to devour her. Our bodies moved in sync like we'd been made for this.

Made for each other.

Intensity built. My heart pounded in my chest and the heat and pressure were overwhelming. She reached her climax and threw her head back, taking me with her. I grunted hard, my hands digging into her hips as I unleashed.

So fucking good.

She slumped against me, breathing hard. Instinctively, I slid my fingers through her hair—her ponytail had come out somewhere along the way—and kissed her neck and shoulder.

That was probably a mistake. Kissing like that was too intimate. This was just sex. But her skin tasted good and I wasn't ready to untangle myself from her yet.

After a long moment, she rolled off me and I got up to deal with the condom. When I came back, she was half-dressed.

Good. No confusion. No intrusion of feelings. We'd both wanted this—needed it—and it didn't have to mean anything other than that.

She tossed my underwear at me. "I guess that was dessert but if you want, I have more hot cocoa. I even bought whipped cream."

I needed to leave. Staying was only going to make this complicated.

But for some reason, I couldn't. I tugged on my underwear and slid my shirt over my head. "Can't say no to that."

She finished getting dressed and went to the kitchen. I could still taste her on my lips, smell her intoxicating scent all over my skin.

I took a deep breath. This wasn't a problem. We were both adults, we could enjoy sex while I was in town. And it didn't have to change anything.

Heading into the kitchen, I pushed aside the nagging feeling that it already had.

22

ELIAS

$\mathcal{I}$sabelle moved around her small kitchen with practiced ease. A voice in the back of my head warned me, again, that I shouldn't stay. There was a familiarity to all this, from the sense of well-being after sleeping with her to the sound of cupboards and boiling water, that threatened to melt the ice around my heart.

She had the power to make me vulnerable and that was the last thing I needed.

Still, I stayed.

I told myself that it was enough to push aside the instinct to touch her again—to walk up behind her, put my arms around her, and kiss her neck. I wouldn't go that far. It would be too intimate.

Unlock too many memories.

She handed me a mug of cocoa topped with a pile of whipped cream covered with red and green sprinkles.

"How am I supposed to drink this?"

"Do your best." She took a sip of hers and the whipped cream smeared over her nose and top lip. "Okay, maybe that was a little overboard. But it's so good."

I chuckled softly as she got a paper towel and wiped off her face. I took a drink, doing my best to keep the whipped cream off my nose, and was pleasantly surprised when it didn't produce a rush of memories.

Maybe this was what I needed. It was like exposure therapy.

Isabelle gestured to the living room, so we moved to the couch, each sitting in one corner. She tucked her legs beneath her and cradled her mug in her hand.

"So can you just kind of take off and not show up for work? How do you not get fired?"

"My position offers a lot of freedom. Unless I have meetings in the office, I can work remotely."

"That's a nice perk." She took a drink, this time without getting whipped cream on her face. "I guess this means you didn't have any meetings today."

"No. For some reason, everything slows down this time of year."

"Well, yeah, it's the holiday season."

I rolled my eyes. "That's just an excuse."

"What do you expect people to do? Just ignore that it's Christmas?"

"When it gets in the way of business, yes."

She shook her head. "When did you become Ebeneezer Scrooge?"

"I'm not."

"You kind of are. Everything is about the numbers. I can imagine you sitting in a cold house, refusing to turn the heat on, while you count gold coins and lock them up in a box."

Her refusing to turn the heat on comment hit a little too close to home. "I wouldn't do that."

"But it does seem like you aren't into the holidays."

"That's true."

I thought she was going to ask why, but she just took another drink of her cocoa. I did the same.

She stared into her mug. "My parents are planning to close Christmas Village after this year."

My brow furrowed. "I thought they were trying to keep the farm."

"They are. That's why they think they have to close the village. It takes up a lot of space and they think they can make the farm more productive if they use it for crops. You know, convert to commercial agriculture."

There was some sense in that. I didn't know the industry well enough to have the numbers in my head, but it stood to reason that commercial crops would earn the farm more income than what they were bringing in now. It still seemed like a long shot, with their debt level, but it might have been a viable alternative to selling.

For some reason, I hated the idea.

If they found a way to keep the farm, it would certainly cost me the deal and probably my promotion. Obviously that wasn't ideal, but it didn't account for the surge of discontent I felt at the idea of Christmas Village closing.

It made no sense. I didn't even like Christmas Village.

I glared at my hot cocoa and put it on the coffee table. Maybe it was getting to me again.

Isabelle didn't seem to notice my lack of response. "I probably shouldn't be talking to you about the farm but I don't know if it really matters at this point. It is what it is. I'm working as hard as I can to prove to them we don't have to close the village but I feel like it's a losing battle. I'm not even sure what's worse, an ugly data center if we sell to you or tearing everything down and planting some cash crop."

"Who said the data center would be ugly?"

"Wouldn't it be?"

I had to concede. "Probably. Those types of facilities are usually built for function and security over aesthetics."

"See? It's ugly either way."

I wanted to make her feel better but there wasn't much I could say. I didn't have the solution she wanted. I couldn't save her family's farm.

But could I help in the short term?

"If you need an extra set of hands tomorrow, I can come by."

Her eyebrows lifted and her lips twitched in the hint of a smile. "That would help a lot, actually."

"Then I'll be there."

An inexplicable urge to stay swept through me. I wanted to take Isabelle back to bed and sleep with her warm body next to me.

But that would be taking things too far.

So once again, I forced myself to get up and leave. After saying goodbye, I headed back to my hotel.

And went to bed alone, with her scent still on my skin.

I woke up early and headed straight for the farm. More snow had fallen overnight but the main roads had already been plowed, so I didn't have any trouble getting there. When I arrived, Phillips was busy plowing the parking lot outside the u-cut tree area. He seemed to be the only person there, although I knew Isabelle had to be around somewhere.

After parking closer to the village, I found her fixing a portion of the fence around the reindeer pen. She was bundled up against the cold in a heavy winter coat, knit hat, and gloves. Her leather tool belt hung at her waist and her jeans already had a smear of mud on one leg.

She pounded a nail into a cross board then pulled on it to test its strength.

"Has Horace been kicking the fence again?" I asked.

With a laugh, she slipped her hammer into the loop on her tool belt. "I wouldn't be surprised. I don't know how the board got loose but you know him, once he finds a weakness he won't leave it alone."

"Well, I'm here. What do you need me to do?"

She looked me up and down. "Is that what you're wearing?"

I glanced at my clothes. Obviously this wasn't a slacks and a button-down shirt kind of job, so I'd worn my wool coat over a t-shirt and sweats. "It's all I have."

"You might want to run into town and get some work clothes."

"Is there anything open this early?"

"Friendly Farm and Feed opens at seven."

"Isn't that a farm supply store?"

"Yeah."

"They sell clothes there?"

"They have pretty much everything there."

I eyed her skeptically.

"You can wear that if you want, but I'm betting that coat was expensive and you're going to get dirty. Not to mention wet. It's supposed to snow all day and trust me, you don't want to be in those shoes in a foot of snow."

She had a point. I had no idea when I'd ever wear farm clothes again, but it was probably worth it to avoid the misery of freezing wet feet.

"All right. I'll be back."

She pulled her hammer out of her tool belt. "You can change at my place when you get back. Good luck."

I left and went to Friendly Farm and Feed. It was right off the highway, just south of town. The faded sign on the warehouse style building was shaped like a cow and despite the early hour, there were several pickup trucks in the parking lot. A rusty tractor that probably hadn't run in decades was draped with multicolored Christmas lights.

The large doors were wide open and hot air blew down from overhead heaters just inside the entrance. Bags of chicken and livestock feed were stacked along the walls and the air smelled of pine and hay.

I glanced around the sprawling store. They did seem to have a bit of everything—tools, pet supplies, animal feed, snow blowers, and even Christmas decorations. A section near the back looked promising, so I headed that direction.

Their clothing selection was appropriately utilitarian. I sorted through an ocean of plaid flannel and thick cotton canvas. With a sense of resignation, I chose a blue flannel shirt, brown canvas pants, a thick work coat, and a pair of boots. On the way to the register, I grabbed a set of gloves and a black knit hat.

It wasn't going to look good, but at least I wouldn't be miserably cold all day.

With my farm wardrobe sorted, I headed back to the farm. Christmas Village seemed to be waking up, with vendors and workers arriving. A woman in a red and green elf costume strolled by, as if that were a perfectly normal outfit to be wearing in public.

At least I didn't have to wear that.

I went to Isabelle's house to change. The shirt fit better than expected and although the pants were thick and stiff, they weren't terrible. I laced up the boots, put on the coat and hat, and headed out into the snow.

Isabelle had finished the fence repair. I found her at the cabin where customers paid for their trees, knocking icicles off the eaves of the roof with a big stick.

Lowering her stick, she smiled at me. "Look at you."

I held out my arms. "Go ahead. Do your worst."

"No, this rugged thing works. They say some men clean up well, but maybe we should dirty you up more often."

Desire smoldered inside me and I moved closer. "Maybe I should dirty you up."

She bit her bottom lip but put a hand on my chest and stepped back, putting more distance between us. "I don't know if we should do that again."

I knew we shouldn't, but if anything, that made me want her more. Still, I wasn't a total animal. I could maintain control of myself. For now.

"What do you need me to do? Anything but deal with Horace."

"What's wrong with Horace? He's a sweetheart."

"Horace hates me."

"When was the last time you saw him?"

"You don't think he'll remember me?"

"Actually, he probably would. Donkeys have really long memories. But that's fine, I need help hauling in more pre-cut trees. You can take the UTV, it has a trailer already hooked up. They're all in the outer fields and Cole should have flagged the rows where he cut a tree down."

"I can handle that. Bring them here?"

"Yeah, over there to the pole barn with the equipment." She pointed. "The guys will put them on the shaker to get the excess needles out and prep them for sale."

"Got it. Keys are in the UTV?"

"They should be. You remember how to drive it?"

"Of course."

She paused for a second and smiled. "Thanks again."

Her gratitude felt good—warmed a corner of my heart. And for once I didn't immediately freeze out the feeling. "No problem."

She left, taking the path that led to the village. I turned and headed for the UTV. The keys were in it and although it started on the first try, the engine sounded rough, like it needed to be serviced. I drove out past the closest u-cut lot and into the next field.

The UTV didn't have a heater and the cold air bit at my skin. But it was refreshing. I found the flags marking the rows where trees had been recently cut and started loading them into the trailer.

It was hard work but it felt good to be outside, trudging through the snow, sweating under my warm clothes. Gym workouts had nothing on hauling trees and I had a feeling I'd be sore the next day. But I liked it—the way my muscles strained and the satisfaction of driving in load after load of Christmas trees to the pole barn.

I took the UTV out one last time to see if I'd missed any. Unless there were more in another area of the farm, I'd gotten them all. I drove back and parked the UTV where I'd found it and went in search of Isabelle to see what was next.

Christmas Village was teeming with visitors. Families with young kids, couples, and even a group of teenagers wandered down the decorated paths between the shops. The scent of sugar filled the air, either from the bakery selling Christmas cookies or the kettle corn stand—or both.

I stepped off the path just outside Santa's Workshop so I could text Isabelle and find out where she was. A family with two young kids—a boy who was probably ten or eleven and a little girl who looked to be around Maddie's age—stopped outside the small building.

"Is Santa home?" the girl asked.

The dad pointed to a sign on the door. "That sign says he'll be back in ten minutes. Should we wait?"

The girl jumped up and down. "Yes! Santa!"

Her brother jumped with her, exclaiming in excitement. She let go of her parents' hands and ran up to the building, trying to look in the window. Her Dad followed and lifted her up so she could see inside.

The boy glanced over and gave me a sheepish grin. "I already know."

"You know what?" I asked.

He lowered his voice to a whisper. "That Santa's not real. I'm supposed to pretend for my sister. Dad says I'm part of the magic now."

"Avery, look inside," the little girl said. "There's a tree and presents."

"Coming." He shrugged, but he was smiling, like he enjoyed indulging in his little sister's belief in Santa.

The whole scene was oddly endearing. And at least the kid hadn't called me the Grinch in disguise.

Isabelle hadn't replied, so I headed for the reindeer barn to see if I could find her. She wasn't there, but the Phillips guy was.

He did a double take. "Elias?"

"Have you seen Isabelle? I'm supposed to be helping her."

"No, but if you're here to help, can you go bring Horace into the other barn? I just heard that Russell was spotted out at the u-cut lot. I need to go help Faye convince him to go home and rest."

I bit back a groan. No, I didn't want to wrangle Horace

into the barn. But like hell was I going to back down. If this guy could handle it, so could I.

"Sure, I've got it."

"Great. He's in the outer pen. You know where he goes?"

"I think so, yeah."

"Thanks, man."

Shit.

I watched him walk away with a sense of dread in the pit of my stomach. The last time I'd been near Horace, he'd tried to bite my junk. I wasn't looking forward to this.

23

ISABELLE

*T*he day had been busy enough that I'd almost been able to outrun the snowstorm of feelings that kept trying to overtake me.

Almost.

When Elias had first appeared earlier that morning, I'd been fine. Okay, so my lady parts had tingled, as if they knew they were in the presence of greatness, but I'd managed to keep my hormones in check. Sure, we'd slept together. But it wasn't a big deal. It wasn't even the first time.

But jingle my bells, it had been amazing. Even better than I remembered, and what I remembered had been great.

Still, it was just sex. The tension between us had been building and we'd given in. Now we could go back to normal.

If there was such a thing as normal when my ex was in town trying to buy my family farm and my mom was being weirdly hospitable and I was quickly realizing I still had a lot of feelings for him. And now we'd slept together.

Maybe I was kidding myself about outrunning the snow-storm. I was knee deep in a blizzard of emotion.

When he'd come back from the farm store, decked out like a rugged farm hand, I'd almost lost it. How had I forgotten how delicious he looked in Carhartt? Elias Stone-heart no doubt wore a suit extremely well but there was something about him in work clothes with a few days' stubble on his jaw. He could melt an iceberg looking like that.

Fortunately, I'd been able to send him off to the tree lot all morning. Which had given me time to get my head together and tell my lady parts that Elias and I would not be walking in an orgasm wonderland again.

Unless?

No.

I checked my phone and realized I had a bunch of unread messages. One was from Elias, letting me know he was done with the trees. The rest were from my mom and Cole. There'd been a jailbreak. Dad was on the move.

With a sigh, I veered toward the tree lot. He'd been spotted there, which was to say one of our seasonal employees had ratted him out. I'd have to find out who had tipped off my mom and make sure he or she went home with a box of cookies.

Snow was still falling and I made a mental note to have someone shovel the walk leading to the village and check to be sure the parking lot had been salted. That was probably a job Elias wouldn't mind doing.

I was so touched that he'd offered to help. He didn't have anything to gain from spending his Saturday here. It was in his best interest that we fail; if things went badly enough this season, it would be a lot easier to talk my parents into selling.

So why had he come?

I couldn't imagine it was because we'd slept together. As much as I'd have loved to believe I had that kind of magic between my legs, that was just silly.

It didn't take long to find my dad. He was in the pole barn, standing next to the baler with his arms crossed. Cole was there, as was my mom, both apparently trying to convince him that he couldn't help bale trees.

"Dad, what are you doing out here?" I went into the barn and the scent of pine and sawdust surrounded me.

His stance was solid and defiant. "I can help run the baler."

"Or you could rest and heal faster."

"I won't heal by sitting around."

"Yes, you will. That's how healing works. You get hurt, you rest and give your body a chance to recover."

He scowled at me.

"Russell, I love you, but you're impossible." Mom shook her head and walked out.

"Dad." I moved closer and tucked my arm through his. "You're stressing out Mom. Your fall really scared her. I know you feel up to working but why don't you indulge her and rest today. It'll make her feel a lot better."

He took a deep breath and it was like hearing the wind go out of his sails. "I don't want to make things worse for your mom."

"Of course you don't." I squeezed his arm. "If you feel up to it, cook her dinner tonight. She'd appreciate that. And we're doing fine out here. Business is good today."

"It's true, we've had a great turnout already," Cole said. "We've got things covered."

"You're right." He sounded reluctant, but I was pretty

sure he'd listen. For today at least. Tomorrow would be another story.

"Thanks, Dad."

I gave him a hug and he headed back toward the house.

"Do you mind following him?" I asked Cole. "At a distance so he doesn't notice. He might still try to detour and go do something he shouldn't."

"Yeah, I got it. By the way, what is Elias doing here?"

"Mom invited him to dinner last night." *And then I invited him into bed. No, don't say that.* "He offered to help out since Dad is supposed to be resting."

"Huh." He scratched his beard. "I asked him to move Horace into the barn, so he's probably still there."

Oh no. "Elias is trying to move Horace?"

"Yeah, he said he'd handle it."

"I better go check on him."

Cole left to make sure Dad didn't get himself into trouble and I headed straight for Horace.

The sound of braying carried through the air. Horace was generally friendly with people but crowds could stress him out, so during the day, we kept him in a pen away from Christmas Village. He'd usually go into the barn quite happily, knowing it meant food was coming. But once he decided he didn't trust someone, it was very hard to convince him otherwise.

And donkeys did have notoriously long memories.

I found Elias in the pen. Horace stood about ten feet away, facing him. His ears twitched. Speaking softly, Elias took a step closer and Horace immediately moved back. I watched with growing amusement as they continued the dance, Horace matching Elias's steps, keeping the same amount of space between them.

Elias stopped. "Horace, it's time to go into the barn."

Horace brayed, as if to say *you can't make me.*

I covered my mouth, trying not to laugh.

"Damn it," he muttered and tried to get close to Horace again.

This time, Horace didn't move.

Elias crept closer. "Good donkey. That's it. Come with me."

As soon as Elias reached for his bridle, Horace dipped his head and side-stepped. He brayed again, and I realized Horace wasn't being difficult because he was stressed or upset. He was playing with him.

I stifled another giggle as Horace pranced around him in a circle. Elias finally got a grip on his bridle and the donkey stopped in his tracks. It was as if Horace's feet had been suddenly planted in concrete. Elias tugged on the bridle but Horace absolutely refused to move.

"Fucking donkey." Elias pulled but Horace didn't budge.

"He's messing with you." I went through the gate and shut it behind me.

"I'm aware of that," Elias said through gritted teeth.

Horace brayed.

I approached and ran my hand down Horace's neck. "Hi, good boy. Are you having fun with Elias?"

Elias let go and Horace turned to nuzzle me.

I stroked him gently. "There's my good boy."

"He's a good boy for you. With me, he's still a stubborn ass."

"He wasn't being stubborn. He was trying to play."

"Great game." Elias's voice dripped sarcasm.

I laughed and took the bridle. "At least he wasn't trying to nip at you."

"That's something."

"Come on, Horace. Time to go in."

I led him into the barn where Cole had already prepped his lunch in the feeding trough. He started happily munching on his straw as I closed the gate to keep him in.

"You make that look so effortless," Elias said.

"He knows me. That helps. Donkeys have a reputation for being stubborn, but really they're just intelligent and concerned for their own safety. Trust is key. They're also really playful and I think he likes messing with you."

Elias let out a long breath. "No kidding. So, what's next? Hitching up the reindeer to Santa's sleigh?"

My stomach growled. I pulled out my phone and checked the time. It was well after one o'clock. No wonder I was hungry. Had I eaten yet today? Maybe not.

"I'm going to grab some lunch. If you have to go, it's fine."

"I can stay."

"Are you sure?"

"As long as my next job doesn't have anything to do with Horace."

"Deal. Let's go raid the leftovers at my parents' house. We can make turkey sandwiches or something."

His mouth hooked in a grin. "I'm in."

That smile of his did terrible things to my insides—made them tingle and swirl. If we ate quickly, there'd be time to go to my place and—

No. That wasn't happening.

He fell in step beside me and we headed for my parents' house. I knew I was playing a dangerous game, but there was something about him I couldn't resist.

24

ELIAS

*A*fter helping at the farm again on Sunday, I drove home that night. Reluctantly. But being out of the office too much would give Damien more opportunities to undermine me. I couldn't let that happen.

Especially because I had no idea what I was going to do about the Cooks' farm. If he figured that out, I'd be screwed.

Spending the weekend working with Isabelle had been oddly satisfying. I was stiff and sore but it wasn't like having a headache after a long day at the office. I didn't want to swallow a few ibuprofen with a glass of whiskey to take the edge off. I felt good—accomplished in a way I hadn't in a long time.

The work week brought its usual crises and challenges. I stayed at the office late every night, catching up from my time spent in Tilikum. Damien seemed to avoid me, which suited me fine. I wasn't interested in an open confrontation.

And I still didn't know how I was going to beat him.

Friday came and I found myself anxious for the day to be over. Technically, I didn't have a reason to go to Tilikum for the weekend. But I'd stopped trying to convince myself I wasn't. I also didn't book a hotel room, hoping Isabelle would just let me stay with her.

Because damn it, I wanted her. One taste had not been enough.

I was surrounded by Christmas—on the streets, in my building, in my office—and every ornament, every bow, every candy cane reminded me of her. She was everywhere. I even let the overly cheerful barista in the lobby coffee shop talk me into an eggnog latte.

It was a Christmas drink. I hated those.

But it was delicious. And of course it reminded me of Isabelle.

There was a knock on my office door and Nigel poked his head in. "Have a minute?"

I hid the sinking feeling in the pit of my stomach behind an icy mask. "Sure."

He came in and shut the door behind him. He'd been out of town all week and I'd been hoping I wouldn't have to talk to him in person yet—not until I had a chance to figure out what to tell him. Because I knew exactly what he was going to ask.

He didn't sit down, but stood casually next to the chair on the other side of my desk. "Just looking for an update on the land deal."

"I realize it's taking longer than it should. The family is determined."

He nodded slowly but I couldn't read his expression. "Interesting."

What was interesting? That the Cooks were holding out on selling or that I hadn't closed the deal yet? "It's a busy time of year for them. I suspect the relative influx of cash from their tree farm is making them overly confident in their ability to remain a going concern."

"Probably. But I don't want to have to wait until their cash dries up to get this done."

"Agreed." I hesitated, uncertain whether I should bring up alternative solutions. Would that make me look incompetent? Had Damien already suggested other site locations and Nigel had rejected them? I should have found out but I'd been so confident I'd be able to put this deal together. And now my promotion was at stake.

Still, it couldn't hurt to feel him out. "Are there any other sites we should consider? Ones with owners who are more amenable to selling?"

There was a flash of something in his eyes. Frustration, maybe? He was a man who was used to getting what he wanted.

"I have yet to come across anything better. And with real estate prices on the rise, we need to get this nailed down."

"Understood."

He met my eyes and nodded before leaving. He didn't have to say another word. I knew what the look meant. Close the deal or no promotion.

I let out a long breath. Damn it. This was beginning to feel more and more like a no win situation.

My phone buzzed with a text.

Isabelle: *I have a question but I probably shouldn't ask*

Me: *Go ahead*

Isabelle: *Are you coming out here this weekend?*

Me: *I was planning on it*

Isabelle: *Okay*

Me: *I'm staying at your place*

Isabelle: *Wow, way to invite yourself over*

Me: *Admit it, you want me to stay*

Isabelle: *Um...*

Me: *Don't deny it, Belle*

Isabelle: *Fine, you can stay at my place*
Me: *I'm leaving soon but with traffic, it'll be a while*
Isabelle: *I'll leave the light on*

The corners of my mouth lifted at the prospect of a night in Isabelle's bed. I didn't know how to solve my problem, but at least I had that to look forward to.

THE NIGHT with Isabelle proved to be even better than anticipated. She had indeed left the light on for me and answered the door in a sheer red nightie. I overlooked the fact that it made her look like a Christmas present and tore it off her as quickly as I could.

Sleeping over, which had seemed too intimate last weekend, felt strangely normal. We settled into bed together, sated and satisfied, and woke up with the dawn. It was the best night of sleep I'd had in a long time.

Pulling her back into bed for morning sex wasn't bad either.

Afterward, we got dressed and went to work. There was no shortage of tasks to be done. The parking lot had to be plowed and the aisles between the rows of trees had to be cleared of snow so people could walk safely. The reindeer needed tending, as did Horace, although no one asked me to help with him again. Damn donkey.

People started arriving to wander through Christmas Village or to buy Christmas trees. The scent of sugar from the kettle corn machine permeated the farm, mixing with the fresh wood of the trees. I replaced fuses on Christmas lights, hauled bales of straw that were supposed to have been delivered during the week, and took a turn on the baler, wrapping Christmas trees with twine to make them easier for customers to transport.

"Merry Christmas," a customer said after I'd helped load her tree into the bed of her pickup truck.

"Merry Christmas," I muttered in reply.

"Aw, look at you giving out holiday greetings," Alice said behind me. "Did it hurt?"

I whirled around. Alice stood with her daughter, both bundled up in winter coats and hats. Maddie leaned on her crutches and grinned up at me.

"What are you doing here?" I asked.

"I brought Maddie for the Christmas parade. But I think the bigger question is, what are you doing here? And what are you wearing?"

I tried to think of a smart-ass reply but nothing came to me. "Isabelle's dad got hurt so I offered to help."

Alice shook her head slowly. "Just when I think you couldn't possibly surprise me more."

"Don't tell anyone in the office."

"Obviously. What would Damien do if he found out you're helping the family you're supposed to destroy?"

"We're not out to destroy them. Don't be dramatic."

"But seriously, this outfit?" She gestured up and down. "Amazing."

I glanced at my clothes. "What's so amazing about it? I'm wearing an itchy flannel and stiff work pants."

"Exactly."

Maddie hadn't stopped grinning at me.

"Why is she smiling like that?" I asked.

"I'm going to see Santa," Maddie said.

I eyed her. "Let me guess. You're going to wish for world peace."

She giggled. "No. I want a `merica doll."

My brow furrowed. I had no idea what that meant.

"She means an American Girl doll. They have one with crutches but they're not exactly affordable. I guess whether or not Santa can bring her one depends on whether Mommy gets a holiday bonus this year." Alice gave me a smug grin.

My gaze moved from her to Maddie. She still smiled at me with those big, hopeful eyes. "Well played. You'll get a bonus."

"Thanks, boss." She looked down at her daughter. "Well, Miss Maddie, we should go see if we can find Cole. What do you think?"

If the girl could have jumped up and down, she probably would have. Instead, she wiggled and nodded her head. "Yay! Cole!"

"Merry Christmas, Elias," Alice said and I didn't miss the hint of smart-assery in her voice.

"I'm not wishing you a Merry Christmas back."

"That's okay, I just wanted the bonus."

Maddie waved. "Merry Christmas."

I ground my teeth together and growled, but I couldn't bring myself to blow off that sweet little voice. "Merry Christmas."

"Kid, you're magic," Alice said as they turned and walked off.

A loud bang came from the pole barn. Instinctively, I ran to see what had happened. Russell better not have gotten hurt again.

Inside the barn, two of the employees were busy looking over the baler. A tree was halfway through, with the bottom branches neatly wrapped with twine but the top still sticking out the other side.

Isabelle came running. It was like she had a radar for these things. "What happened?"

"Baler got stuck," one of the guys said. "It won't start up again."

"Great," she muttered. "Can we get this one out and hand-wrap it so the customer doesn't have to wait?"

Without a word, I jumped in to help one of the other guys pull the tree out of the baler. He cut the twine and while Isabelle started looking the machine over, I worked on wrapping the tree. We took it out and loaded it into the customer's truck.

When I came back, Isabelle was lying on the ground beneath the machine, as if she were working on a car.

"It needs to be replaced," one of the employees said quietly. "Needed a new one for a while."

"Add it to the list," the other guy said.

Isabelle scooted out from under the baler and got to her feet. "That might have done the trick. Let's test it."

The two employees loaded a small tree into the baler and one of them turned it on.

Nothing.

"We can just hand wrap for today," one of them said.

Isabelle sighed. "Yeah, just do your best for now. Thanks, guys."

She turned to leave and I followed her out.

"I knew we needed a new baler," she said as we walked. "I was just hoping this one would last the season. It saves so much time."

"How much do they cost?"

"I don't think a lot but I'll have to do some research. Of course, it might not matter if my parents convert the farm."

"Or if my company buys it."

She stopped and put her hands on her hips. "Really? Are we going to have this conversation again?"

"Belle."

"Don't do that. Don't try to make this about us."

"Should we just pretend the farm isn't in trouble?"

"I know it's in trouble."

"We're not at odds, here. If we work together, we can figure out a solution that's good for everyone."

"Any solution that involves closing Christmas Village isn't good for anyone, especially this town." A few visitors glanced at her and she lifted her hand. "We're not closing. We're open every day until Christmas." She glared at me.

"I don't want to argue with—"

"Good. Then don't." She whirled around and stalked off.

I knew better than to follow her.

A squirrel ran by, crossing the shoveled path and bounding up a tree. Why the hell were there so many squirrels in this town?

"They don't hibernate," a gravelly voice said behind me.

A deep groove formed between my eyebrows and I turned around slowly.

Harvey Johnston grinned at me. He was bundled up in a down jacket and instead of his usual wide brimmed hat, his shaggy graying hair was covered by a knit cap that looked homemade. Badly homemade. The thing was a mess.

I wasn't sure that I wanted to have a conversation about squirrels—or anything else—with Harvey. He'd probably start talking about the past catching up with me again and I'd wind up falling down another rabbit hole of memories.

"They stay in their nests," he said, as if I really needed to know this information. "In trees. But they come out sometimes when they know they can find food. And there's lots of it around here."

"Good to know."

He reached up as if to tip his hat, but didn't find the brim. "Merry Christmas."

"Merry Christmas."

Harvey wandered away down the path toward the parking lot and I glanced around, worried that another formative scene from my past was about to overtake me.

But nothing happened. It was just Christmas Village—the Christmas Village of now, not of my childhood or my teenage years. Probably its last year in existence, which seemed sad as I looked around. Where would Maddie go to see Santa Claus next year?

I dismissed that thought. It didn't matter. There were guys dressed like Santa everywhere. It wasn't like she wouldn't get her Christmas wishes if she couldn't come here. I was the one giving her mom a Christmas bonus. Santa didn't have anything to do with it.

Another squirrel ran by and a familiar sense of mystical dread poured through me. I glanced around warily, but I wasn't plunged into more unwanted memories of Christmas past. The squirrel just scampered up the path.

And for some reason, I went the same direction.

25

ELIAS

I wasn't following a squirrel. I was just walking off my frustration.

The fact that a squirrel happened to be bounding up the path in the same direction I was going was nothing but a coincidence.

The path was mostly clear of snow but rolling drifts covered the landscape between the shops and coated the trees with white. Very winter wonderland.

That song popping into my head did nothing for my mood.

Why did Isabelle have to be so reactionary? We both knew the situation with her farm was still an issue. Sleeping together hadn't changed that.

I shoved my hands in my pockets and kept walking, passing happy families and kids pointing out the signposts leading the way to Santa's Workshop and the reindeer barn. I was heading in the wrong direction, deeper into the farm and away from the parking lot, but I still didn't turn around.

The squirrel disappeared, veering off the path and up a tree. I ignored it and kept walking. The path turned right and the sound of music and voices emanated from a refurbished barn. A sign outside read Tilikum Historical Society Christmas Party.

A Christmas party. My back tightened and my lip curled in a sneer. I hated Christmas parties.

But for reasons I couldn't explain, I approached the wide-open doors and looked inside.

The old barn had been cleaned out and transformed into an event space. It was rustic, but with Christmas decorations everywhere, it was at least festive. Propane heaters kept it warm, a tall tree with white lights stood in the far corner, and more lights were strung across the ceiling. Tables were set with red and green tablecloths and holly centerpieces. Christmas music played in the background and guests mingled around the buffet or sat at tables chatting.

I vaguely recognized some of the people. I'd probably met them when I'd lived here before—friends of my aunt and uncle or people who lived in town. A laugh caught my attention and I noticed my aunt and uncle were there. They stood with another couple—Neil and Barb Halverson if I remembered correctly—all holding glasses of champagne. Hattie was dressed in a red and green sweater and she and Dale wore matching Christmas light necklaces.

Nobody seemed to notice me and I was strangely transfixed by the scene. Were Dale and Hattie members of the historical society? Had they been when I lived with them? Was this a typical holiday tradition for them?

I had no idea what they usually did around Christmas. They didn't have any kids of their own to come visit, but they'd always liked celebrating the holidays.

"You should have come to our place for Thanksgiving," Barb said.

"That would have been nice," Hattie said. "Although we did have a lovely dinner, even though it was just the two of us."

"I thought Elias was back in town," Neil said.

"He stopped by earlier in the month," Hattie said. "But he wasn't here for Thanksgiving."

"What about Christmas?" Barb asked. "Will he spend it with you?"

"He usually stays home," Hattie said.

"He's a busy man," Dale said. "And I don't think he has the same love of Christmas that we do."

"That's too bad," Barb said. "Whatever happened to his parents?"

"Hattie talks to his mother now and then," Dale said. "We haven't heard from his father in a long time."

"They must be divorced?"

Dale nodded. "They split a number of years ago. Joan remarried but I don't think Vincent ever did."

"That's so hard on a child," Barb said. "I always felt bad for him."

My back stiffened. I didn't want her pity.

"Thankfully, we talked his parents into letting him come live with us before the worst of their split happened," Hattie said. "Joan is my sister and I love her but she didn't do right by her son. Neither of them did."

Wait, they'd talked my parents into letting me live with them? It had been my aunt and uncle's idea?

I'd never known that.

"No, they really didn't," Dale said. "I hate to think of where he would have ended up if we hadn't taken him in."

"He was lucky to have you," Barb said.

"Doesn't seem like he knows it," Neil said.

Barb nudged her husband. "We don't know that."

"I'm just calling it like it is," Neil said. "They didn't have to open up their home to him the way they did. You'd think he'd show a little more appreciation, especially around the holidays."

"We understand. His work does keep him very busy," Hattie said. "And he's doing incredibly well for himself."

"We're proud of him," Dale said. "He was on the wrong path but he turned it around. Now he's on his way to out-earning his father, and that's something."

I felt like I'd just been stabbed right through the chest. Proud of me?

Until that moment, I hadn't realized how much I wanted that kind of approval from my uncle. But hearing those words almost made my knees buckle.

I staggered back, away from the barn entrance. My aunt and uncle didn't seem to have noticed me—probably because I was dressed like a farm hand—and I didn't want them to. I didn't know what to say to them.

They'd wanted me. They were proud of me.

And I'd never been anything but a dick to them.

I turned around and headed back through Christmas Village. Past snowbanks and red bows and twinkle lights. I needed to get out of there. This place was messing with my head again. I got to my car and left but quickly realized my mistake. The main road through town was closed for the parade. Even in the cold, people were congregating on the sidewalks along the route, waiting for it to start.

Damn parade.

I veered down a side street, passing stores and restaurants decked out for the holidays. Every door had a wreath and windows were lined with lights. It was all so cozy and cheerful, it made me sick.

Turning down another street, a sign caught my eye. Timberbeast Tavern.

A tavern. Not a lounge or a bar. Not the sort of place that served craft cocktails with clever names. I'd never been in the Timberbeast Tavern, but from the outside it looked like exactly the sort of place I needed. A tavern with sticky floors and cheap whiskey. And the best part? Not a single Christmas decoration in sight.

The parking lot was almost empty. Also perfect. I wanted to hunch over a drink at a bar by myself and nurse my shitty mood.

I walked in and groaned. A string of lights ran along the length of the bar and there was a tree in the corner. Cheery Christmas music played in the background and the bartender wore a fucking Santa Claus hat.

What was with this town? Even the lumberjack tavern was celebrating?

But I still wanted a drink, so I took a seat at the bar.

"What can I get you?" the bartender asked. He was a big guy dressed in red buffalo plaid. Thick, hairy arms stuck out of his rolled-up sleeves.

"Whiskey."

"You got a preference?"

"No. Just get me a drink."

He put a glass on the bar and filled it with amber liquid, then slid it over to me. "Are you in town for the parade?"

I downed it in one swallow. "No."

He grunted and refilled my glass, then left me to my whiskey.

Hunching over my drink, I tried to ignore the music. *I'll Be Home for Christmas.* Really? I had to sit here and be guilt tripped by Bing Crosby?

Of course, the guilt was probably warranted. Since I'd

moved out, I hadn't spent a single Christmas with my aunt and uncle. Not one.

Did it matter? It was just another day.

Then again, maybe it wasn't. At least, it wasn't to them.

Just like the farm wasn't just a piece of land to Isabelle.

Damn it.

How had this gotten so complicated? I'd gone into this situation convinced that I could get what I wanted out of Isabelle—namely, the Cooks' signatures on a purchase and sale agreement. And here I was, dressed like the Phillips guy with dirt on my boots and a growing set of callouses on my hands, drinking cheap whiskey in a small-town tavern.

What would my mentor have done? That was an easy answer. Jake Marlon would have slept with Isabelle, using sex to manipulate her, and bowled over any resistance from her parents. He would have used every trick up his sleeve, and he would have won—secured the land deal and the promotion.

He certainly wouldn't have found himself where I was—confused, frustrated, and fighting a growing mess of inconvenient feelings.

I'd admired him for his drive and ambition. He'd taught me to stop at nothing to get what I wanted.

Then again, he'd dropped dead on a golf course. He hadn't even finished his game.

And Isabelle wouldn't have given him the time of day. She'd have seen through his bullshit.

That thought made me crack a smile. Damn Isabelle and her sass. I wondered if she had any idea how tough she was. I'd always loved that about her.

The song changed. *Blue Christmas*. It was still a holiday song but at least it better matched my mood.

I blew out a long breath and swallowed the whiskey. It

was terrible. The bartender met my eyes, silently asking if I wanted another. I shook my head. I'd sit at the bar a little longer before subjecting myself to the nonsense of the Christmas parade. But that was where Isabelle would be and I needed to go find her.

26

ISABELLE

*U*sually work was my go-to method for dealing with stress or frustration. But today it wasn't helping. It didn't matter how many tasks I checked off my to-do list, how many fires I put out, or how many things I fixed. I was a bundle of stressed-out energy.

Damn it, Elias.

I shouldn't have slept with him last night. Or this morning. Lines were blurring and I was feeling increasingly confused. His mention of buying the farm had simply taken my already wound-up emotional state and made it snap.

I felt a little bit bad about that.

Christmas Village had started to clear out as people made their way to downtown Tilikum for the annual Christmas parade. Annika and Marigold had both texted, nudging me to come watch with them. They knew I could get away but probably wouldn't if they didn't make me.

They were such good friends.

I didn't bother changing clothes. It was cold, so I needed to stay bundled up anyway. I left the farm and drove downtown, finding a parking spot a few streets away from the parade route.

Tiny snowflakes drifted from low-lying clouds—just enough to add to the holiday ambiance without threatening everyone's ability to drive home. It was so nice when the weather cooperated. You never knew what to expect this time of year in the mountains.

Both sides of the street were jammed with people anxiously awaiting the start of the parade. Dads lifted kids onto their shoulders for a better view and moms held tight to little hands so they wouldn't get separated. One family had matching reindeer headbands and I saw Elias's aunt and uncle across the street, decked out in blinking Christmas light necklaces.

It was all so wholesome. So sweet. Families, friends, and neighbors gathered to watch a silly small-town parade that probably hadn't changed much in decades.

"There you are," Marigold said, popping up out of nowhere in front of me. She looked adorable, as always, in a chic wool coat with her hair down around her shoulders. "I was hoping we'd find you."

Annika came through the gap in the crowd, holding hands with her son, Thomas. She wore a cream colored winter coat and matching hat. Thomas was dressed in blue and bits of hair stuck out from the bottom of his stocking cap. He was such a cute little guy, his expression perpetually serious.

"Hey! Merry Christmas!" I hugged my two friends. "It's so good to see you."

Annika picked a piece of straw off my hat. "You, too."

I brushed my hand over my head in case there was more. "Thanks. Hi, Thomas. Can I pick you up?"

He nodded and reached for me. I picked him up and settled him on my hip. "Are you excited to see Santa?"

His brow furrowed and he shook his head.

"He's not so into the whole sitting on a stranger's lap thing," Annika said.

"That's fair. Are you excited for Christmas?"

He nodded.

"Awesome. Look, buddy." I pointed. "The parade is starting."

The first float rolled by. It had a multi-colored train with cars full of presents.

"Aw, how cute," Marigold said.

"I love the Christmas parade," Annika said. "Thomas, what do you think?"

"Big cock!" he exclaimed.

"Um, what?" I asked.

Annika laughed. "That means big truck. He sees the fire truck coming."

Sure enough, up next was the Tilikum Fire Department. Their engine came by, decorated with lights—and fire fighters. Including Levi Bailey.

"We-vi's big cock," Thomas said, his voice serious.

"Oh, he's saying Levi," I said. "I get it."

"We-vi!" Thomas waved. "We-vi have a big cock!"

"Does he now?" Marigold asked, nudging Annika.

Levi seemed to catch sight of Annika and gave her a wink. Then he waved at Thomas.

"Bye-bye, We-vi," Thomas called. "Bye-bye We-vi's big cock!"

"Wow, okay," Annika said, reaching for Thomas. "Everyone saw the big truck, buddy. Look, here come polar bears."

The next float looked like a big iceberg with several polar bears wearing red and green scarves.

"Oh," Marigold said, looking at something—or someone —behind me. "Annika, we should see if Thomas can get a better view over there."

"Why? Oh." She nodded. "Good plan. We'll see you later, Isabelle."

"Wait, where are you guys going?"

They didn't wait to answer me—just disappeared into the crowd.

That was weird.

And then I felt him behind me.

I didn't know how I knew it was Elias and not just another random parade-watcher. But I did.

A little thrill made my stomach tingle. I tried to squash it down but it refused to stop, especially when I turned around.

Why couldn't I just stay mad?

Sigh.

I couldn't get enough of him in that coat with a knit hat and work boots. Why did he have to make that look so sexy? Cole wore stuff like that every day and I barely noticed.

One look at Elias's green eyes and I knew he had a lot on his mind. Whether or not he'd share any of it with me was another story. But I could see through that icy mask he kept trying to wear—past the façade of indifference he wore like armor. Something was troubling him.

"This is..." He gestured to the parade. "Something."

The next float was just Harry Montgomery in his pickup truck. He'd decorated it with multicolored lights and a big red bow in the front. Half a dozen of his goats milled around the bed, each adorned with a red ribbon around their neck.

"It's not fancy but it sure is cute."

One of the goats bleated at the crowd.

"Why isn't Horace in the parade?"

"We tried once but he refused to walk. It's a shame, too, he looked so handsome in his ugly Christmas sweater."

"A donkey ugly Christmas sweater? Those are the worst. I'm on Horace's side."

"What's wrong with ugly Christmas sweaters? They're funny."

"They're hideous."

"That's the point. You need one with a Grinch on it."

The Tilikum High School marching band came next, playing a jaunty rendition of *Jingle Bells*. Some kids nearby started yelling the lyrics at the top of their lungs. Elias opened his mouth like he was going to say something else, but closed it again, wincing slightly at the noise.

Finally, the band moved on and the kids quieted down.

He leaned close. "I'm sorry about earlier."

"It's okay. Sorry I snapped at you."

"Don't worry about it. I'm the asshole."

A little boy stared up at Elias, a look of abject horror on his face. He slowly brought a finger to his lips and shushed him. "Careful."

Elias's brow furrowed. "Excuse me?"

"Santa's coming. You'll get on the naughty list."

"Oh, he's already on the naughty list," I said.

The little boy's eyes widened. "You better fix that. There's still time."

One corner of Elias's mouth lifted. "How do I fix it?'

He wrinkled his nose, as if he were thinking hard. His face brightened. "Say sorry and do something nice. That's what I have to do when I'm mean to my sister."

"That's probably good advice. I'll be right back." Elias disappeared into the crowd, going back the way he'd come. I started to ask where he was going, but he was gone before I could get the words out.

The next float ambled by—a giant snow globe—and the boy turned to watch.

I waited with my hands tucked in my coat pockets, wondering where Elias had gone. A gingerbread house float went by, followed by a pretty nativity scene.

Cole drove past, towing our float. It looked cute, with a big decorated tree and a vintage-style sign for Christmas Village. I hoped it would entice more people to come to the village after the parade was over.

It might be their last chance.

I pushed aside the rush of sadness and waved at Cole. He waved back and I realized he wasn't alone. He had Alice's little girl, Maddie, on his lap. She had her hands on the steering wheel, as if she were driving, and the smile on her face was so precious it almost brought tears to my eyes.

"Here." Elias reappeared, seemingly from nowhere, and held a to-go cup in front of my face.

I took the cup. It was warm. "What's this?"

"Hot cocoa. With whipped cream on top."

I tried not to smile but it was hard. He was melting my heart and it was absolutely killing me. "Thanks. Is this your attempt to get on the nice list?"

"It's a start."

"Good timing." I nodded toward the next float—a big sleigh with Mr. and Mrs. Claus waving at the crowd.

"Lucky me."

We stood on the sidewalk sipping hot cocoa as the rest of the parade went by. I saw my parents on the other side of the street and waved to them in between the floats. Mom smiled and waved back. Dad furrowed his brow at Elias but finally offered me a wave.

To be fair, I didn't blame him for his reluctance when it came to Elias. I didn't know what was happening between us, so I certainly couldn't fault my dad for his skepticism.

The last of the parade went by and the crowd started to thin as people made their way back to their cars or went to the shops and restaurants around downtown Tilikum. Elias and I wandered toward Lumberjack Park. The snow had stopped and although it was cold, the air was still.

Lights twinkled all around us. Tilikum itself was almost as festive as Christmas Village. A wreath hung on every door and bows, garlands, and other decorations reminded everyone that it was the merriest season of the year.

Cole stood with Alice and Maddie at the entrance to the park. Our float was parked along the curb and it looked like Maddie was describing her parade adventure. She pointed enthusiastically to the float, then to Cole.

She noticed Elias and her eyes brightened even further. "Mr. Rock—I mean Mr. Stone. Mommy, what's his name?"

"Mr. Stoneheart, honey."

"How about you just call me Elias." He crouched down in front of her. "Did you see Santa yet?"

She nodded. "Yes. He said I was a good girl."

"I bet he did."

"I was in the parade. Did you see me? I drove the truck."

"You did a great job. Looks like you're ready for your driver's license."

Maddie giggled. "No, I'm too little."

"Are you sure? How old are you? Twenty?"

She laughed harder. "No. I'm five."

"Really?"

"Yes, five." She held up her hand with her fingers and thumb splayed wide, as if to prove her point.

Alice and Cole watched the exchange with expressions

of bewilderment. I didn't blame them. It was like seeing a totally different side of Elias.

"Okay, I believe you." Elias stood.

"I need to get the float out of here," Cole said. "Maddie, do you want to help drive it back to the farm?"

"Yes! Please, Mommy?"

Alice glanced at Cole. "Are you sure you won't get pulled over or something?"

Cole grinned. "It's not far and I have to go parade speed anyway."

"Small town living," I added with a shrug.

"There's room for all three of us," Cole said.

If anyone had ever looked completely lovestruck, it was Alice. She gazed at Cole with wonder in her eyes and nodded. "Okay."

"Yay! I get to drive!" Maddie exclaimed.

In one smooth motion, Cole scooped her up and grabbed her crutches. I didn't miss the wink he gave Alice. She watched him take her daughter to the truck, her lips parted, as if she were too stunned to move.

"He's always been great with kids," I said.

"He's amazing," Alice said, her voice awed.

"Are you staying the weekend or do you have to go back tonight?" Elias asked.

"We're staying. Maddie is going to need an early bedtime after all the excitement today. And I was kind of hoping—"

"I already said you'll get your bonus," Elias said.

She laughed softly. "No, I was hoping Cole and I could go on an actual date tomorrow. He said he could get away for a couple of hours but I'm not sure what to do with Maddie. I thought about Dale and Hattie but I hate to ask them for yet another favor."

"I'll do it," Elias said.

Alice and I shared a glance.

"You'll watch Maddie?" she asked.

"Sure. Why not?"

Alice's eyebrows drew together and she regarded Elias for a long moment. "She does like you for some reason."

"You can bring her over to my place," I said. "Elias can watch her there."

"Okay. Thanks. I'll confirm the time with Cole and text you."

Elias nodded.

"Thanks again." Alice went to the truck and got in with Cole and Maddie.

"Damn," Elias said under his breath.

"What?"

"I'm definitely going to lose her to the farm guy."

"They do make the cutest little family."

"I keep telling myself that assistants are replaceable but I don't think she is."

"But you still offered to watch her daughter so she can go on a date."

"I don't know what's wrong with me lately."

I laughed. "Neither do I. Do you have dinner plans? Not that I can eat now. I have to get back to the village. But later?"

He turned and met my eyes. His were deep green and full of feeling—no ice to be seen. "I'm in town for you."

My breath caught in my throat and my stomach flipped. It was either the beginning of a Christmas miracle or I was in big trouble.

27

ELIAS

*M*addie sat on Isabelle's couch, her hands folded in her lap and her legs sticking straight out. She watched me with an inexplicable grin on her face, as if she were expecting me to do something funny or interesting.

I stood with my arms crossed wondering what the hell I was doing.

Kids were not my thing. Not because I had a particular disdain for children. I'd just never been around any. The kids I encountered tended to be like the little girl in the red dress who'd called me the Grinch in disguise. They didn't like me.

But Maddie just sat there, smiling up at me, like she had all the confidence in the world that I'd be a good babysitter.

My brow furrowed. "So what do we do now?"

Her skinny shoulders lifted. "I don't know. Where's the tree?"

"What tree?"

"The Christmas tree. Christmas is coming and there's no tree."

"You don't talk like you're five. You know that, right?"

She giggled.

I shook my head. "I don't know why Isabelle doesn't have a tree. She's been too busy, I guess."

"Where are all the presents going to go?"

"I don't know."

"Can Santa come down that chimney?" She pointed to the wood stove.

I glanced at the round pipe that went from the top of the stove out through the ceiling. My first thought was to say, *you don't still believe in that crap, do you?* But I paused. It would probably be a jerk move to ruin the kid's belief in Santa. I'd leave that to her mother.

"Of course he can."

"How?"

"Magic or something? Can we talk about something else?"

She giggled again. "What do you want for Christmas?"

Isabelle.

I pressed my lips together so I didn't say that out loud. What the hell was wrong with me?

"A promotion."

"What's a po-motion?"

"Promotion," I said, enunciating the word. "It means a better position at work."

"Why?"

My brow furrowed again. That was a dumb question. Although she was only five.

And why did I want that promotion so badly?

"It's a grown-up thing. Ask your mom."

"I want a `merica doll. The one with crutches."

"I remember."

She glanced around the room and started humming

Jingle Bells while she tapped her legs in time with the tune. I figured I should probably find something for her to do. She couldn't sit on the couch for the next couple of hours. But I had no idea what to do with a five-year-old girl.

"Can we bake Christmas cookies?" she asked.

"I don't know how to bake cookies."

"Use a recipe."

Maybe that wasn't a bad idea. I slipped my phone out of my pocket. There had to be a million cookie recipes on the internet. "Do they have to be Christmas cookies?"

"Yes."

I grunted. Of course they had to be Christmas cookies.

A quick search for *simple Christmas cookie recipes* yielded a ton of results. I went to the kitchen to see if Isabelle had any ingredients. That might have stopped our cookie baking plan in its tracks, but she had the basics. I didn't know how old the stuff was, but it would have to do. She even had red and green sprinkles, leftover from our hot cocoa.

Maddie waited patiently on the couch, watching me with that inexplicably happy smile on her face.

I didn't know how to make this work. She was too small to reach the counters but I didn't know if she'd be safe standing on a stool. Or if Isabelle had a stool. I figured I'd just have to pick her up, so I got out the ingredients, some measuring cups and spoons, and a few mixing bowls.

"You're going to have to do most of it." I went back to the living room to get Maddie. "I'm not exactly a baker."

"I know how. I bake cookies with Mommy."

I picked her up and she draped an arm lightly over my shoulder. We went into the kitchen and I pulled up a recipe for sugar cookies on my phone.

"Cole works at a farm," she said as I turned on the oven.

That was a random thing to say. Again, she was little.

Random was probably normal. And her mention of Cole made me curious. What did she think of the man her mom was dating?

"It looked like you had fun at the parade with him." I measured the flour and let Maddie pour it into the large mixing bowl.

"I got to drive."

"You sure did. Was Cole nice?"

"He's always nice. He smiles a lot. Not like you."

That almost made me laugh. "I guess not."

She took the cup of sugar I handed her and dumped it in the bowl. "He kissed my mommy."

"Did he?"

She wrinkled her nose. "On the mouth. Don't tell Mommy. It's a secret."

"I won't." I scooped out some baking powder and handed her the spoon. "Is it okay with you that Cole kissed your mommy?"

She dumped it in the bowl. "Yes. Do you kiss Isabelle on the mouth?"

I cleared my throat. "Um, yes?"

She erupted in a fit of giggles and covered her mouth. "Ew."

I shifted her to my other arm and checked the recipe again. "You won't think it's ew when you're a grown-up."

"Yes I will."

"Okay, kid. What's next?"

"I don't know. I can't read big words. Only small ones."

"It's easy to forget you're only five."

She just laughed.

Following the recipe, we finished making the cookie dough. It said to let it chill in the fridge for an hour, but that was bullshit, so I stuck it in the freezer. I'd give it ten minutes.

I set Maddie on the counter while we waited. She told me, in intricate detail, all the reasons she wanted her `merica doll`, including the outfits she wanted and how she planned to name the doll Rosie. Five minutes later, she'd changed her mind and wanted to name her Isabelle. I told her I liked Isabelle a lot better than Rosie.

The recipe said to roll out the dough and use cookie cutters. I searched through Isabelle's cupboards, but didn't find any, let alone any in Christmas shapes.

"We're going to have to freehand these," I said. "Can you use a butter knife?"

"If I have super-zizzun."

"Do you mean supervision?"

"That's what I said." She grinned at me.

"Okay, I'll supervise. You cut out the shapes."

I rolled out the dough on the counter next to her and let her go to town with a butter knife. She stuck out her tongue while she worked, carefully tracing shapes into the cookie dough. I did my best to scrape them off the counter with a spatula—luckily for me, I remembered from my aunt to put flour down so the dough wouldn't stick—and set them on the baking sheet.

When I'd placed the last cookie, I tilted my head and eyed our work. One looked like it might have been a stubby candy cane. Another blob vaguely resembled a tree. As for the rest, I'd have to assume Maddie knew what she'd meant to cut out and hope a bunch of red and green sprinkles would be good enough to make them pass for Christmas cookies.

I held out the two bottles of sprinkles. "Go for it, kid."

With a big smile, she took both and shook them over the

cookies. When all the blobs of dough, and most of the baking sheet, were covered, I had her stop. She waited on the counter while I put them in the oven and set the timer.

"Can I give Mommy and Cole some cookies?"

"Yeah. You made them, you can give them to whoever you want."

"You should give some to Isabelle."

I wanted to give Isabelle a lot of things tonight, and cookies were just the beginning.

Although it was Sunday. I needed to get back home. Go to the office tomorrow.

But another night with Isabelle was too tempting. I could work remotely for another day.

"Sure, I'll give some cookies to Isabelle."

In minutes, the scent of sugar filled the house. I checked them a few times to make sure I didn't let them burn. She'd done a good job, I didn't want to be the one to ruin them at the last minute. Finally, the timer went off and they looked done to me. At least, I hoped they were done under all the sprinkles.

But I hadn't burned them. That was something.

I moved Maddie to the table and found her some paper and a pen. She drew while we waited for the cookies to cool, humming Christmas songs the entire time.

There was something about the kid. Life had dealt her a shitty hand, between her cerebral palsy and an asshole father. But she was so damned happy, like even at five, she could see the bright side to everything.

Or maybe she was just really excited for Christmas.

I checked the cookies and figured they were cool enough to try. I put one on a plate for Maddie and slid it across the table to her.

"Do you have milk?" she asked.

"Good question." I checked the fridge, but Isabelle didn't have anything to drink other than a bottle of white wine and some cans of sparkling water.

But she did have cocoa.

"No milk but can I make you hot cocoa?"

She clapped. "Yes, please!"

I heated up the water and remembered that it was probably too hot for a little kid. So I added some cold water from the tap and mixed in the hot cocoa powder. I added a generous dollop of whipped cream and some sprinkles on top.

"Thank you."

"You're welcome. How's the cookie?"

She took a bite and seemed to consider as she chewed. Then her face broke out in a wide smile. "Yummy. We're good bakers."

I got her more paper out of a drawer and let her have three more cookies. That was probably too much sugar, but that was what Alice got for leaving her kid with me.

There was a knock on the door and Alice came in. "Hey, Maddie-doodle!"

"Mommy! We made cookies!"

She shut the door and came over to the table. "I can tell. It smells amazing in here."

"Elias let me help."

"You did all the work," I said. "I just helped you reach."

She looked at me with that big, bright smile and laughed.

"Thanks again for watching her," Alice said.

"It was no problem. She's a great kid."

It was Alice's turn to smile, just as big and bright as her daughter. "She really is."

"I have to go potty, Mommy."

"Sure, honey. Where are your crutches?"

"Living room," I said, darting to the couch to get them for her.

Alice helped her off the chair and I handed her the crutches. She headed down the hallway to the bathroom.

"Do you need help?" Alice called after her.

There was a pause. "No. I got it."

"She can do that by herself?" I asked.

"Usually," Alice said. "She's good at hoisting herself up, although she won't be able to reach the sink to wash her hands. So, how was she?"

"Great. She asked to bake cookies, so I figured why not. I probably let her eat too many."

She smiled. "That's okay. I assume she'll eat too much sugar when she's with a babysitter."

Her phone rang and she dug it out of her purse. As soon as she looked at the screen, her face fell. "Hang on, I have to take this."

I waited in the kitchen while she went to the living room.

"Yeah?" she answered. There was a long pause. "I realize it's expensive. I pay half, remember?"

Was that her ex? I didn't mean to eavesdrop, but the house wasn't very big. I listened for Maddie in case she needed help washing her hands.

"I really don't need this right now," Alice said, keeping her voice quiet. "It's almost Christmas and I can't—"

Another pause. She paced back and forth in front of the door.

"I get it, but she needs this. It's not optional."

Damn it, I wished I could hear the other side of that conversation. What the hell was he saying to her?

"No, we don't need to shop around. That's not how this works."

"Mommy, I need help!" Maddie called from the bathroom.

Alice glanced at me, her eyebrows raised, and mouthed, *can you help her*? "I can't afford it on my own," she said as I got up and went to the bathroom.

I knocked on the door. "Maddie? Your mom's on the phone. Can I help?"

"Okay. I can't reach the sink."

I paused before going in. "Are you dressed?"

"Yes."

I found her standing with her crutches in front of the sink. I went in and picked her up so she could wash her hands. She scrubbed them carefully with soap, rinsed, and dried them on a fluffy hand towel. I set her down and she situated herself with her crutches again.

"Thank you."

"Do all little kids have such good manners?"

She shrugged. "I don't know. Can I have another cookie?"

"You'll have to ask your mom."

I followed her back to the kitchen. Alice was slipping her phone back into her purse.

She took a deep breath and turned around. "Ready to go?"

"Can I have more cookies?"

"I'm pretty sure you've had plenty. And we have a long drive."

"But I need to give one to Cole."

Alice smiled but there was a tiredness in her expression that hadn't been there before. "That's fine. We can find him before we go."

I'd seen plastic bags in one of Isabelle's drawers, so I got one out and let Maddie put cookies in it for Cole. While she stuffed the red and green blobs into the bag, I moved closer to Alice and lowered my voice. "Is everything okay?"

She sighed. "Yeah. Or no. I don't know. My ex is pushing back on paying his share of her physical therapy. He thinks we should find someone else, like you can find a discount physical therapist or something. He's already late in paying for last month and if we get too far behind, I'm afraid they'll cancel her appointments."

I didn't know what to say. What kind of asshole refused to pay for his kid's medical care? Especially a kid like Maddie?

The same kind who didn't even see his kid.

I ground my teeth together.

"Come on, Maddie, that's enough cookies." Alice took the bag and ushered her toward the door. "Thanks again, Elias. Will you be in the office tomorrow?"

"No, I think I'll work from home."

She glanced over her shoulder and raised her eyebrows. "From home? Or from here?"

I glared at her.

She just laughed and led Maddie out the door.

I grabbed a cookie and took a bite. It was actually pretty good, even with the thick coating of sprinkles. A few fell on my shirt and I dusted them off as I chewed. I wanted to find out where Alice's ex lived so I could go over there and rearrange his face. I wasn't usually a man prone to violence, but the way he treated his daughter made me want to rip him to pieces.

The pictures she'd been drawing caught my eye and I picked one up. Stick figures. Not exactly a Picasso, was she?

One had a big Christmas tree surrounded by a heap of rectangles that were probably supposed to be presents. Another had a big stick figure with a frown and angled eyebrows next to a small stick figure with a smile. Both had round blobs in their hands.

It was me and Maddie holding cookies.

I gazed at it in wonder and the ice around my heart cracked a little bit more.

28

ELIAS

I stayed with Isabelle that night.
And the next.
And for the rest of the week.

I spent the majority of each day helping on the farm. Her dad was back to work but there was more than enough to do. I fed the reindeer—but stayed away from Horace— hauled more Christmas trees, shoveled snow, and even handed out hot cocoa to smiling customers.

Not that I smiled back. Much.

Every night, Isabelle and I went back to her place together. Despite being tired from a long day, we always found the energy to rip each other's clothes off. And after untangling myself from her warm, sleeping body, I'd go out to her kitchen, turn on my laptop, and try to keep up with my actual job.

It was almost Christmas, and although the crowds at the village didn't seem any bigger, the energy in the air had changed. I'd always thought people got more frazzled as the big holiday approached—plagued by stress and dread over all the shopping, cooking, parties, and get togethers. But everyone at the village seemed to be enjoying themselves.

In fact, they weren't just enjoying themselves. They were downright happy. Not an in-your-face excited sort of happy —except for some of the kids in line to see Santa. It was more peaceful than that. A sense of joy that seemed to permeate not just Christmas Village, but the entire town.

It was weird.

What Isabelle had told me weeks ago about Christmas cheer kept echoing in my mind. It was real and it mattered. I couldn't have explained why, but I was beginning to wonder if she was right. If it wasn't all sentimental bullshit designed to part people from their hard-earned money.

I also couldn't stop thinking about my aunt and uncle. What they'd said about me, and how I'd treated them over the years. I'd stopped by their house the other day, not quite sure what I was going to say or do, but they hadn't been home. I'd noticed a pile of wood on the side of the house that had needed to be chopped and stacked, so I'd stayed and done it. It certainly didn't make up for years of indifference but it was better than nothing.

And Maddie. That sweet, spunky little girl who didn't seem to let any of the challenges facing her—and they were considerable—dim her light. What would happen to her if her father stopped paying his share? Would Alice be able to afford everything Maddie needed?

I'd already put in a request for a raise for Alice but I didn't know if it would be enough. Or if HR would approve it.

This was why I wanted to be the boss.

Okay, it was mostly for the sake of my bank account and the prestige of being in charge. But if I were CFO—or better yet, CEO—I wouldn't have to worry about convincing another department to pay my assistant more.

Saturday morning came and I woke up late. Isabelle was gone, no doubt already working. With a groan, I hauled myself out of bed. I'd only been sleeping a few hours a night and it was starting to catch up with me.

I got dressed, donning a green flannel and clean pair of work pants. Somehow, I'd found myself with an entire wardrobe of farm clothes—flannels, cotton canvas pants, thick socks, and several pairs of gloves. It wasn't because I was going to do this for much longer, of course. It just made sense. My clothes got dirty while I worked and it wasn't practical or efficient to do laundry every day.

The air outside was cold and a fresh layer of snow covered the ground. That meant there'd be plowing and shoveling to do. I figured Cole had already cleared the parking lot—he usually did—so I stopped by the Cooks' shop to grab a snow shovel and started on the walkways in the village itself.

Vendors were arriving to open their shops for the day. They passed by with smiles and holiday greetings. I nodded to them and mumbled the occasional Merry Christmas.

I kept shoveling, making my way toward the reindeer barn. A snow blower would have been nice—certainly more efficient. I'd seen one in the shop but it didn't work.

Yet another thing on the list to be repaired or replaced.

I caught sight of Isabelle as she disappeared into the barn. As if I couldn't help myself, I followed. A memory flashed through my mind—me as a lovesick teenager, chasing her into that same barn, hoping no one else would be in there so I'd have the chance to kiss her.

The same need drove me now.

She stood alone in front of one of the reindeer pens,

talking softly to the animal. Another reindeer snorted at me as I walked in. I cast a glare at it but it just snorted again.

Isabelle glanced in my direction and the way her eyes lit up filled me with warmth. She was melting more of the ice around my heart, and in spite of the fear of what she'd find in the hole in my chest, I couldn't stop it.

Maybe I didn't want to.

Without giving her a chance to say a word, I slipped my arms around her waist, drew her close, and kissed her.

We'd been avoiding this kind of public display of affection. Although we were sleeping together, we hadn't talked about what it meant—if anything. We certainly weren't dating in any real sense. It was more like taking advantage of our physical proximity in the off hours in a way that was mutually pleasing. It wasn't like this was a relationship.

That's what I was telling myself, at least.

But kissing her like this made me wonder what was really happening between us. Her lips were silky against mine, her mouth deliciously warm. She felt so good pressed against me.

Too good.

But knowing this could be a mistake wasn't enough to make me stop.

I let myself indulge a moment longer before slowly pulling away.

"Wow. All I want for Christmas is another one of those." The corners of her mouth turned up. "What was that for?"

"Just making your Christmas wish come true."

She laughed softly. The reindeer she'd been petting grunted and another answered with a similar guttural sound.

"I'll let you get back to work." I brushed another light kiss across her lips before letting her go.

"Okay," she said, her voice breathy.

I left her there and went back to the shoveling. When the walkway was cleared, I put the shovel away and went in search of the next task. Some of the lights strung between Santa's Workshop and the Peppermint Parlor had fallen overnight, so I got out a ladder and went to hang them back up.

Isabelle was outside the Peppermint Parlor, talking to the vendor who used the shop. I paused and watched her, momentarily distracted by the way her mouth moved. The memory of myself as a lovesick teenager returned. I probably looked like an idiot, gazing at her like that, but I couldn't help it. She was mesmerizing.

A man approached as the vendor said goodbye to her and went back into the shop. I did a double take and narrowed my eyes. What the hell was Damien doing here?

He glanced my direction, but his eyes passed over me without recognition—dismissive of the unimportant farm hand. He clearly didn't realize it was me.

"Isabelle Cook?" he asked.

"Yes."

He held out a hand toward her. "I'm Damien Barrett."

She crossed her arms, leaving his hand in midair. "What are you doing here, Mr. Barrett?"

He flexed his fingers and withdrew his hand. "First and foremost, I'm here to apologize."

"For what?"

"For not coming to meet with you in person sooner. And for my colleague."

"Which colleague would that be?"

"Elias Stoneheart. He's under the impression that this project was handed to him, but it's really just a misunderstanding." He waved his hand as if to push the topic away.

"Internal politics, nothing you need to be concerned about."

"I see."

He gave her what was probably an attempt at a compassionate smile. "Is there somewhere we could go to chat?"

"Not really."

I swallowed back a laugh. She was such a badass.

"You wouldn't prefer to get out of the cold?" he asked.

"No. I have a lot of work to do."

"I'm sure you do but we need to discuss the future of your family's farm."

She sighed. "I don't have anything to discuss with you."

"I know that selling isn't your first choice. But ignoring the facts won't change them."

"You could take your own advice and stop ignoring the fact that we keep turning you down."

"Ms. Cook, I realize you and your family have a sentimental attachment to..." He glanced around. "All this. But nostalgia doesn't pay the bills and you're up to your eyeballs in debt. The numbers are clear."

My jaw hitched. It was like having my own words flung back in my face. How many times had I said the same things to her? And it was all true, so why did I hate hearing it so much?

"I'm well aware of my family's financial situation. But there's more to all of this than money and that's something none of you seem to understand."

"I have no doubt you've worked incredibly hard to keep this place running. It's all very charming." His voice dripped with smug disdain and he gestured vaguely at the decorations around them. "But there's a lot more to running a business than sugar plums and magic reindeer."

"Oh, is there? I had no idea. I'm glad you were here to

enlighten me. Now if you'll excuse me, I have to get back to work."

She tried to walk away but he grabbed her arm. And I almost came unglued.

I jumped down from the ladder and darted toward them. Damien's eyes widened as I planted a hand on his chest and shoved. "Get your fucking hands off her."

He stumbled back a few steps and put up his hands. "Who the—Elias? What the hell are you doing here? And what are you wearing?"

I moved so I stood between him and Isabelle. "Why are you here?"

"To see Ms. Cook. Not that it's any of your business."

"I think she made it clear that she doesn't have anything to discuss with you."

The vein in his forehead popped out. "You need to stay out of my way."

"This isn't your deal anymore."

"We'll see."

I lowered my voice. "I suggest you be careful, Barrett. Trying to go around me is a very bad idea."

"So was backstabbing me. I'm not going to let you or a couple of hick farmers pretending to own the goddamn north pole ruin my career."

Instinctively, I held out an arm to keep Isabelle back. She collided with it.

"You jerk," she hissed.

"This place is circling the drain. Look at it." He gestured around him. "It's laughable."

"You need to leave," I said, still blocking Isabelle from clawing out Damien's eyes.

He looked me up and down. "I don't know what your game is, Stoneheart, but you better hope it works. I don't know why Nigel wants this piece of shit farm so badly, but he does. And he doesn't care who hands it to him. We both know what's at stake here." His eyes moved to Isabelle. "You're going to lose the land. It's just a matter of when and whether or not you and your family walk away with anything. I don't know what this guy is promising you, but I can make sure you do have something to show for it. Or you can let it go to foreclosure and wind up with nothing. Up to you."

I seethed with anger as I watched him turn and walk away.

Isabelle stopped pressing against my arm. She stepped back and straightened her coat. "You should have let me at him."

"I can't believe he had the balls to show up like that."

"He didn't know you'd be here, did he?"

"No."

She gazed at me for a moment and I wondered what she was thinking. "Well, I have enough to do without worrying about him. I have to figure out how to conjure up a Christmas miracle so we don't lose our farm."

I wanted to say it. I'm not going to let you lose the farm.

But how could I say that to her? I wasn't here to save the farm, I was here to talk her into selling it.

The problem was, the Cooks were going to lose their farm, whether my company bought it or not. Isabelle really did need a Christmas miracle.

And miracles didn't exist.

29

ISABELLE

*A*fter a weekend that had been busy, but probably not busy enough, I spent most of Monday cashiering with my mom at the u-cut farm. We did decent business for a weekday, although this close to Christmas, I'd been hoping for better. There were still too many precut trees that hadn't sold and dozens more that were ready for harvest but hadn't been cut yet.

I had to face the fact that things weren't looking great.

As usual, my response to stress was to work harder. When things slowed at the u-cut farm, I took care of the reindeer, shoveled snow, sorted through cut evergreens to make more wreaths, and chatted with customers, trying my best to keep up my Christmas cheer.

At the end of the day, tired and hungry, I trudged back to my place in the dark. I wondered where Elias had been all afternoon. I hadn't seen him since around noon.

That kiss in the barn the other day—and others like it—burned hot in my memory. As did the nights we'd been spending together. I didn't know what it all meant—if anything—but the more time we spent together, the more I craved him.

The more I wanted him to stay.

But thinking like that was only going to get me, and my heart, in trouble. Serious trouble.

The porch light was off but the front window glowed. In fact, it didn't just glow, it sparkled. There was a wreath with a big red bow on the front door that I hadn't put there. I'd been so focused on work, I hadn't put up any decorations. Maybe my mom had been by. It seemed like something she would do.

I went inside and my breath caught in my throat. A beautifully decorated Christmas tree stood in the living room. White lights gleamed, reflecting off shiny ornaments. There was even a tree skirt around the base and a gold star adorned the top.

As much as I loved Christmas, I almost never put up my own tree. I never seemed to find the time, and although every year I told myself it didn't matter, I always wound up feeling a little sad when I woke up Christmas morning without a pretty tree to enjoy.

I stood in the doorway, gaping at the beautiful tree, oblivious to the cold air I was letting in through the open door.

Elias came out from the kitchen holding two mugs. "Do you like it?"

"It's beautiful." I glanced between him and the tree. "Wait, did you do this?"

"Yeah. It's Maddie's fault. She was complaining about there being no tree."

I laughed. "I always mean to put one up and I never seem to get around to it."

"I figured." He gestured with one of the mugs. "You might want to close the door."

"Oh." I turned around and shut it, then took off my coat and boots. Elias handed me one of the mugs—hot cocoa with whipped cream and sprinkles. "Thank you. This is really nice."

He shrugged, like it was no big deal. "I just thought you'd like to have a tree. Your mom showed me where to find the decorations. You didn't have a star, so I bought one over at the Rustic Noel. I got some more ornaments there, too. Pretty handy to live right outside Christmas Village. If you're into this kind of thing."

I laughed at his nonchalant tone. He kept trying to act grumpy about Christmas, but I could see through it.

We sat on the couch with our cocoa. He'd made a fire in the wood stove and the rest of the lights were off, leaving just the glow of the Christmas tree. It was all so cozy and Christmassy, it made my heart swell. I scooted closer to him so I could lean against his shoulder and tucked my legs beneath me.

"Thank you for this."

"You're welcome." He paused. "Merry Christmas, Belle."

I took a deep breath, savoring the warmth of the mug in my hand, his body beside me, and the way my old nickname sounded on his lips. "Merry Christmas, Elias."

We sat in silence for a long while, sipping our cocoa and listening to the fire crackle in the wood stove. The tension in my body eased, the stress of the day melting away, and another sensation began to awaken.

Desire.

As if he could read my mind, he took our mugs and set them on the coffee table. Then he maneuvered me onto my back and settled between my legs.

He kissed me deeply and something was different. Most evenings, we went at each other with undisguised urgency, as if our sole aim was to satisfy our lust.

This wasn't urgent. His kiss was slow and indulgent. I savored the feel of his mouth tangling with mine. My hands explored the hard planes of muscle in his shoulders and back, and I breathed in his scent.

He was so male. So profoundly masculine. From the deep timbre of his voice to the strength of his hands to the way his body pressed into me, he spoke to me on a primal level. My hormones reacted in a dizzying surge. I wanted him—all of him—and I wanted him now.

Once again, he moved as if he already knew what I needed. He pulled off my shirt and covered my skin with hot kisses. I tore at his clothes, needing more—more skin, more contact, more heat.

My nerve endings fired, sensation overtaking me as our bodies came together. My hips rose to meet his and moans escaped my lips, mingling with the soft crackle of the fire. He groaned as he thrust into me, as he took me for his own.

He gave me everything I needed and so much more.

I clutched at him and our movements grew frenzied. Passion swept through us, as if we were not only joined in body, but in spirit. We moved together, moaned together, breathed together. The intensity sent me spiraling and I let it sweep me away, heedless of the consequences.

Tonight, Elias owned me.

His piercing green eyes met mine and our movements slowed. We were hot, breathing hard, ready to burst, but in that moment, I felt something. This wasn't just sex anymore. We weren't here to sate our lust and move on.

I almost said it. Almost gave voice to the words my heart whispered.

I love you.

But I didn't. Fear held me back and instead of leaning into the uncertainty and throwing caution to the wind, I reached for the desire that had brought us here. I raked my fingers through his hair and brought his lips back to mine. Rolled my hips against him and moaned into his mouth.

He responded, driving into me with renewed fervor.

My eyes rolled back as climax overtook me and I lost myself in the waves of pleasure. I felt him reach his peak and he spurred me to new heights, his grunts and growls and the strength of his body overwhelming me.

We finished, still breathing hard. His eyes reflected the gentle glow of the Christmas tree. He brushed my hair back from my face and pressed soft kisses on my lips.

Emotion swept through me. I felt so vulnerable. So close to him, yet so afraid. His nose brushed mine and he kissed me again, as if he were in no rush to separate himself from me.

I didn't want him to. I didn't want this moment to end.

After a few more kisses, he finally got up. I felt warm and languid, like I was floating on a cloud of bliss. I couldn't remember ever feeling so deeply satisfied.

We cleaned up and threw together a quick dinner. But the *something different* permeated the evening. He drew close to me while we cooked, brushing my hair aside to kiss my neck. His arms wound around me with familiarity and closeness. It was as if we'd taken a step, brought our relationship—if it was, indeed, a relationship—to a new level, without saying a word.

I didn't quite know what was happening but I didn't want to break the spell.

Tired from a long day, we went to bed early. I settled into bed in his arms, my body curled up with his, and tried to ignore the way my heart felt slightly unsettled. I'd enjoy this for what it was while it lasted. Tonight, I couldn't ask for more.

I woke up cold.

My toes were peeking out of the covers, so I bent my knees and pulled my feet beneath the comforter. No light shone through the small gap in the curtains and I told myself it was the middle of the night and I needed to go back to sleep.

Turning over to find a more comfortable position, I realized I was cold because I was alone.

Where was Elias?

And had I already grown so accustomed to having him in my bed that I'd wake up at his absence?

My brain was too sleepy to contemplate what that meant. I looked toward the bathroom door, but it was ajar and the light off. He wasn't in there.

Pushing the covers aside, I got up, slipped on a robe, and crept out of the bedroom. The house was dark except for the Christmas tree—he must have turned it back on—and the glow of his laptop screen. He sat at the table with his computer, his open briefcase, and a few files.

He was working. All week I'd assumed he'd taken time off. But he'd been helping me on the farm all day and staying up late to do his actual job.

He'd been doing all this for me, without saying a word. Without complaint or asking for anything in return. Sure, we'd been sleeping together, but there was no way a man like Elias would sacrifice like this just to get a woman into bed. He'd have no problem getting in some girl's pants, if that was all he wanted.

Did he actually want me?

It had certainly felt that way earlier. The way he'd felt when he was inside me and the way he'd looked at me with so much intensity in his eyes. And now this? Staying here in Tilikum to do a job that wasn't his, while his career was on the line.

I was dumbfounded.

Something deep inside me, something beyond emotion and reason, wanted Elias.

But I didn't want him for a night, or a weekend or a handful of weeks strung together while he poked around my farm.

I wanted him. All of him.

Which meant I really did need a Christmas miracle. Not just to save the farm, but to save my heart. Because it would be all too easy for Elias to break it again.

30

ELIAS

*I*sabelle shifted, rousing me from sleep. I groaned, not ready to wake up. The room was dark but it was probably early morning, which meant she'd slip out of bed soon.

I slid my arm around her waist and drew her close, tucking her against me. With a slow exhale, she relaxed. A hint of the winter cold outside was in the air, but nestled in her bed together, we were comfortable and warm.

After long moments, she stirred again. "Morning."

"Morning," I said, my voice husky with sleep.

"I should probably get up, although I don't really want to."

I placed lazy kisses on her shoulder. "Me neither."

We lingered a while longer, but eventually we had to get up. We both had a busy day ahead of us.

But waking up with Isabelle in my arms satisfied a deep need I'd been ignoring for a long time. A need for connection. I'd tried to lean into that need once. Taking that risk had cost me. I didn't know if I was ready—or willing—to take that kind of risk again. And yet, there I was.

While Isabelle got ready for the day, I drank some coffee and checked my work email. I was half-expecting a message from Nigel, telling me he was pulling me from the project and giving it back to Damien. Could that have been why Damien had come to Tilikum? Had Nigel promised him the promotion if he put the deal together?

If Nigel had been willing to hand the project to me to get what he wanted, he'd certainly be willing to take it out of my hands just as quickly.

Which meant I needed to figure out what the hell I was going to do.

I couldn't live in denial much longer, especially now that Damien had seen me at the farm. I hadn't been in the office in over a week. I was sleeping with the woman I was supposed to be convincing to sell. And the longer I spent working alongside her, the less convinced I was that I could do what I'd come here to do—talk her into selling her family's land.

I'd been doing research on other properties that would be suitable for our datacenter. It seemed to me that there were several solid options. One wasn't far from Tilikum, just north of town. The terrain wasn't as optimal for construction purposes, but from what I'd gathered, it looked like it would work.

And I wondered why Nigel hadn't already abandoned his plan to buy the Cooks' farm and gone for this property instead.

Probably cost. Although this piece of land was actually for sale, it was priced higher than what we'd likely pay for the Cooks' farm. Still, if I could make a compelling case to Nigel and talk the seller down from their asking price, it would solve a lot of problems.

Isabelle emerged from her bedroom, dressed in a long

sleeve shirt and those damn denim overalls that shouldn't have been so sexy. But they were.

She wound her arms around my neck from behind and leaned in close. "I'm heading out."

"I have some things I need to get done here first."

"Of course." She kissed my cheek. "I'll see you later."

I got to work on a proposal for the potential new location. The data was compelling but I'd need to drive out and view the site for myself, make sure there weren't any issues I was missing.

My phone buzzed with a text from Alice, letting me know she couldn't come in to work today. Normally, I would have grumbled about the inconvenience she was causing me, but for some reason, a new thought popped into my brain. Was something wrong?

Was it Maddie?

Instead of texting back, I called her.

"Please don't give me crap about missing work," she said by way of answering.

"I'm not giving you crap. What's going on? Is Maddie okay?"

"I think she has an ear infection. We're on our way to urgent care."

"Is that normal? Will she be all right?"

"Yeah, sometimes kids get ear infections. It hurts but she'll be okay." She paused. "Look, I don't have any more PTO, so—"

"Don't worry about it. I'll take care of it."

"Thanks," she said, her voice thick with relief. "I'll check in with you later."

I said goodbye and ended the call. Despite Alice's assurance that Maddie would be okay, I still felt a twinge of worry for the kid.

And what was going on with her physical therapy? Had her shitty father paid his part of the bill?

There wasn't anything I could do about that at the moment, so I decided to drive out to the other property and take some photos. I called the real estate agent on the listing and got more details. He said I could go walk the property if I wanted. The boundaries were clearly marked with stakes, and part of the perimeter was lined with a wire fence. I'd take some photos to include with my proposal and try to anticipate any objections Nigel might have. This needed to be airtight if it was going to work.

I drove out to the site and although it was covered with snow, I could already tell it would work. Most of the property was an empty field, fairly flat, although the back side went up the side of a hill. Still, there were no existing structures to demolish and not too much grading. It was close enough that on-site staff could easily live in Tilikum or one of the other nearby towns.

This seemed like a slam dunk, but Nigel had prioritized the Cooks' farm over this. What was I missing? Access to infrastructure? Construction costs?

I'd have to keep digging and figure it out.

I got back in my car and out of habit, checked my email. I had a message from HR about Alice's raise.

Denied.

What the fuck? Why the hell had they rejected her raise?

Anger flooded through me. This was bullshit. I needed to call Nigel and—

Except I couldn't come in hot over this if I wanted to stay on Nigel's good side. And I had to stay on his good side or my proposal would be dead in the water before I got the chance to convince him.

Once again, to get what I wanted, I had to play the game. I'd figure out Alice's salary later. I didn't have a choice.

But I was still pissed about it.

I drove back to Tilikum in a bad mood. The Christmas decorations blanketing the town grated on my nerves. Did they really have to adorn every light post with a giant candy cane? What was the point?

Every wreath and string of lights deepened my annoyance. The town Christmas tree in Lumberjack Park made me grind my teeth together and a group of carolers singing as they walked down the sidewalk made me want to stop in the middle of the street and tell them to shut the hell up and stop bothering everyone.

And then I saw him. Motherfucking Damien Barrett.

I drove past as he went into the Copper Kettle, but there was no doubt it had been him. Why was he still in Tilikum? He should have left yesterday after I chased him out of Christmas Village.

So it wasn't much of a surprise when my phone lit up with Nigel's call. Of course he'd call me now.

With a deep breath to collect myself—*play the game, Elias*—I answered. "Stoneheart."

"Are you in the office?"

"No, I'm out, but I can ex—"

"That's fine, we can do this over the phone."

Shit. Do what over the phone? "Sure. What do you need?"

"I talked to Damien this morning. Apparently he's in Tilikum to meet with the Cooks. But I suppose you know that."

I decided to wait to see where this was going before offering an explanation. "Yes."

"He tells me he saw you helping at the Cooks' farm. Is that true?"

"Yes, but—"

"Interesting angle. Unconventional, but interesting. I'm impressed. But..." His pause felt ominous. "If you aren't any closer to getting this deal nailed down, I'm giving the project back to Damien. He seems to think he can get signatures before the holiday."

"He's full of shit."

Nigel laughed. "He said the same thing about you."

"I'm sure he did. I was there yesterday when he approached Isabelle Cook. She wouldn't even shake his hand, let alone meet with him."

"Her parents are the owners."

"I realize that, but they're a close family. It's Isabelle who's really calling the shots."

Although they all had so much to lose.

"This project has been a thorn in my side long enough. I'd like to spend Christmas with my family without worrying about where I'm going to build the goddamn data-center. This should have been done months ago."

"Maybe it's time we consider other options."

"No." His voice cracked like a whip. "I want that farm."

For a second, I thought about pushing back. But I was in my car, not in any position to make a compelling argument for the alternative site. Besides, I wanted to do it in person. Nigel was easier to reason with face to face.

"Then I need Damien out of my way. If he shows up at the farm again, he's just going to piss them off. They don't like him and I can guarantee you they won't deal with him. If you want this to come together, you need to let me handle it."

"Fine. But I want the signed contract on my desk before Christmas."

I swallowed hard but kept my voice even. "Understood."

He ended the call and I blew out a long breath.

What the hell was I going to do now?

31

ISABELLE

*H*appy holiday music played in the background of the Copper Kettle, and the servers bustled around the restaurant, bringing trays of mouth-watering food to their customers. Lights twinkled and a cute little Christmas tree decorated with acorns, red buffalo plaid, and tiny wooden squirrels stood near the front door.

Marigold sat across from me, cheerfully perusing the pages in a binder.

A wedding binder. For Annika and Levi.

The whole town was abuzz with the news that Levi Bailey had proposed to Annika Haven. Not only were a Haven and a Bailey getting married—something no one thought would ever happen—they were getting married soon. New Year's Day, in fact.

The date was symbolic of new beginnings and I loved the significance. They were so in love and so ready to start their life together. And Marigold was in wedding-planning heaven, even with the crazy time line.

"This is coming together so well," she said, shutting the binder with a satisfied smile.

"Did anyone have a doubt?"

"Well, me at first. Although I do love a challenge."

I smiled. "Obviously. I'm glad things are coming together, though."

"It helps that Annika is so easy-going and Levi just wants to marry her. They're not too concerned about the details, so that gives us some flexibility."

"It's so romantic, don't you think? Two feuding families brought together by love?"

She sighed. "It's beyond romantic. I love it so much. Honestly, someone should write a book about it."

"I'd read it."

"Same. Off topic, but thanks again for having lunch with me. I know you're so busy right now, but it's really good to see you."

"I'm glad you called. I think I needed a little break and we both know I wouldn't have taken it on my own."

"Isn't that the truth. Has anyone told you recently that you work too hard?"

I lifted my eyes, as if I'd find the answer on the ceiling. "Not today."

"Consider this your reminder."

"Thanks, Mari. Although, to be fair, I haven't been killing myself as much as usual. I've had extra help."

"Have you?"

"Elias offered to lend a hand after my dad's fall and he's kind of been helping ever since."

"Elias? Helping on the farm? You're kidding."

"No. And can I just admit out loud how hot he is when he's hauling Christmas trees and moving straw bales?"

"I'm having a hard time picturing it."

I laughed. "I know, but he used to help on the farm a lot back in the day. It came back to him."

"Wait." She leaned forward and lowered her voice. "You're sleeping with him, aren't you?"

I scoffed, as if she'd just suggested I'd told all the kids in town that Santa Claus wasn't real. "Of course not."

She raised her eyebrows.

"Fine. Yes. He's been staying at my place."

"I know I don't need to tell you to be careful. But oh my friend, I hope you're being careful. And I don't just mean using protection, although that, too."

"I'm being as careful as I can be, on both counts." I let out a breath. "I realize I'm taking a big risk, here. It might turn out to be just sex while he's in town and when he goes back to his life, nothing will come of it."

"And you're okay with that?"

"I hear the skepticism in your voice."

"Well, can you blame me? You were in love with him and now he's back in your life under pretty sketchy circumstances."

"You're completely right and I know I need to be cautious. How stupid would I be if I let him break my heart twice?"

"I would never say you're stupid, even if he did break your heart again. Although if he does, I need your permission to ruin him."

I tilted my head. "Mari, you're the sweetest person in existence. You don't have it in you to ruin anyone."

She shrugged. "I'd find a way. Is he still trying to buy the farm or did he decide to back off?"

"We haven't talked about it much." I sighed. "His jerk of a co-worker showed up at the farm yesterday and he wasn't happy about it."

"What happened?"

"The guy grabbed my wrist when I tried to walk away, and Elias came up and shoved him."

"I know I shouldn't say this, but that's kind of hot."

"I'm glad you said it because I was thinking it."

She laughed. "How's the village been doing this season? Do you think it'll be enough to carry you guys through next year?"

"I don't know. I'm afraid to look at the numbers."

"I'm sorry you have to deal with this." She reached over and squeezed my hand. "But I believe in you."

"Thanks."

Her phone buzzed and she glanced at the screen. "I'm so sorry, but this is wedding related, so I need to take it."

"Of course, go ahead."

Marigold got up and went outside to take her call, putting on her coat as she went.

A man came in just as she was going out and the sight of him made my jaw drop. It was Damien Barrett, the jerk from Elias's company.

What was he still doing in Tilikum? I figured he'd left yesterday when I'd refused to talk to him—especially after Elias had put him in his place.

The hostess showed him to the booth right behind mine but he didn't seem to notice me. As soon as she walked away, he answered his phone.

Maybe it was just me, but how rude. He couldn't have gone outside like Marigold? As if the entire restaurant wanted to hear his conversation.

"Hey, Nigel. Yeah, I am."

Nigel. That name sounded familiar. Was that their boss?

"You know you can't trust him; he's full of shit." He sounded annoyed. "That's absolutely not true. It's a delicate situation but I know what I'm doing."

I wondered if he was talking about our farm. Whatever it was, I certainly wasn't meant to hear. But it wasn't my fault. I wasn't even trying to listen.

"He said what?" There was a pause. "He might have embedded himself with them but a lot of good it's going to do. I don't think they're going to be fooled. Except maybe the daughter. I think there's something going on between them."

A sick feeling spread through my stomach. The daughter was obviously me. Embedded with them? Was he insinuating that Elias was helping on our farm to manipulate us into selling?

Was that why he'd been doing it? Was it all just a means to an end?

"There's a clear conflict of interest going on here, Nigel. You have to see that."

I had no reason to trust anything this Damien guy said. He didn't know why Elias was really here.

Although I wasn't sure if I did either.

Maybe I was kidding myself that something real was blossoming between us. Maybe he had embedded himself on our farm so we'd trust him. So we'd think he was on our side.

I didn't want to believe he was capable of that.

But I'd trusted him once, and he'd left. Could I trust him now?

I didn't know what to think.

32

ELIAS

*S*hoveling straw wasn't helping.

I'd decided to take a page from Isabelle's book and work off some stress in the barn. Horace was in his enclosure, eying me with what was either amusement or hostility. I couldn't tell which. As long as he stayed on one side of the gate and I stayed on the other, we'd be fine.

A trickle of sweat dripped down my back and dust from the straw hung in the air. I hardly noticed the animal smell anymore. Weird how it had hit me like a freight train the first time I'd come back to the farm and now it barely registered.

The faint hum of activity in Christmas Village carried into the barn. People still strolled up and down the paths, buying last minute gifts and treating themselves to baked goods and candy. It hit me out of nowhere that I didn't have a gift for Isabelle for Christmas.

Did I need to get her one? Would we exchange presents? The impending holiday was an in-my-face reminder that although I was sleeping with Isabelle, we hadn't exactly defined our relationship. Was it a relationship? Or were we just indulging ourselves temporarily?

What did I want from her? More importantly, what did she want from me?

I shoveled more straw and Horace brayed at me.

"Shut up, you ass."

He brayed again.

"You know, I don't actually have to let you have any of this straw. I could leave you in there and you'd just have to stand there and stare at your lunch."

That shut him up.

There was also the rather large elephant in the room—a looming truth even bigger than the farm.

Isabelle was my ex.

We had history and we'd never addressed it.

As much as I wanted to believe the past was in the past, I had the sinking feeling that crazy old Harvey Johnston had been right. The past was going to catch up with me.

But there wasn't anything I could do about that now. I had to figure out how to save my career.

Horace brayed at me again.

"Yeah, yeah. I'm almost done."

"Horace, be a good boy," Isabelle said behind me.

I set the pitchfork down and turned. She wasn't wearing a coat, just her long sleeved shirt and overalls. "Aren't you cold?"

"Yeah, but it's fine. I left my coat in the car. I'll get it later."

Something was wrong. I could see it in her eyes and in the way she kept her distance. "Is everything okay?"

"I don't know. Probably. I should go get my coat and get to work."

"Belle."

"Really, it's fine. I had lunch with Marigold, so I'm behind on a million things. I'll catch up with you later."

"Don't do that."

"Don't do what?"

"That thing you do where you walk away and pretend being busy will fix everything."

She put her hands on her hips. "And what are you doing? I'm sure you're not shoveling straw for Horace because it's fun."

As if in answer, Horace brayed again.

"I'm just trying to get my head together."

"Which is exactly what I'm going to do."

My jaw hitched. I was being pulled in too many directions. Isabelle, the farm, Damien, Nigel. I didn't know how to make it all work, how to get what I wanted without letting go of things I wasn't willing to give up.

"Fine, go get your head together," I said. My phone started ringing, but I ignored it.

"Why are you here?"

The gravity of her words made me stop short. It was *the* question, wasn't it? What was I doing here?

Was I here to help Isabelle? Or was I just trying to find a way to get them to sell so I could secure the promotion?

"I don't know."

The disappointment in her eyes gutted me. "Damien's still in town. I overheard him talking to Nigel. That's your boss, right?"

"Yeah."

"They seem to think this is some kind of inside job. Like you've been spending all this time here just so you can find a way get our land."

"Belle."

"Is it true or not?"

"Not entirely."

"What is that supposed to mean? It's either true or it isn't."

"It's more complicated than that. I'm not trying to manipulate you."

"You could have fooled me. Are you still trying to buy our land or not?"

I hesitated.

And that was the wrong choice.

"Damn it," she said, spitting out the words. "I should have known better. Why did I let myself get tangled up with you again?"

"Belle, no—"

"Stop calling me that. I should have known this was a mistake."

My phone started ringing again. Damn it. I pulled it out of my pocket, ready to throw it against the wall. But it was Alice.

My brow furrowed with concern. I already knew she was out of the office because of Maddie's ear infection. Had something happened? Was it worse than they thought?

Despite the fact that things were about to blow up with Isabelle, I answered. "Is everything okay? How's Maddie?"

"She's fine, that's not why I'm calling. I just got a call from your father's lawyer."

"What did he want?"

She took a deep breath. "Elias, your father passed away."

I hesitated, waiting for a reaction—shock, sadness, anything—but I just felt numb. "How? When?"

"A heart attack. It was a few days ago but no one found him right away. I'm so sorry. The lawyer asked me to have you call him. You're the only family he had, so they need someone to authorize all the arrangements. Then there's the will and everything. I'll send you his number."

"Thanks."

"Are you okay? Do you need to talk?"

"No. I'm fine. I'll take care of it."

"Okay. Maddie says hi."

Despite everything, that almost made me crack a smile. Almost. "How's her ear?"

"Better. A heating pad helps and the antibiotics should kick in soon. Let me know if you need help with travel arrangements or anything. I can do it from home."

"Just take care of Maddie."

I ended the call and pocketed my phone. Isabelle watched with concern written all over her face.

"What happened?" she asked.

"My father died."

"Oh my god. I'm so sorry."

"It's okay. We weren't close."

"I know but that's still hard."

No, it wasn't. It should have been, but I felt nothing. "I need to go call his lawyer. Arrangements and all that."

"Yeah, of course. Can I help with anything?"

"No. I'll handle it."

Without another word, I turned and walked away.

TWELVE HOURS LATER, I was in New York.

It was the middle of the night, so I went to my hotel and tried to sleep. Pointless. I just stared at the ceiling, frustrated and unsettled. After an hour or so, I gave up. Pacing around the room wasn't any better but I couldn't sit still.

I didn't feel any grief for my father. There was clearly

something wrong with me if I couldn't muster even a hint of sadness at his passing. We hadn't had much of a relationship but he was still my dad. Shouldn't I have felt something?

Maddie had said my heart was beating but I wasn't so sure she was right.

Eventually the sun came up. I showered and dressed for my meeting with my father's lawyer. I had to go to his apartment, which for reasons I couldn't explain, filled me with a sense of dread.

My phone rang as I was buttoning up my shirt. It was my mother. I took a deep breath before answering. This was going to be interesting.

"Hi, Mom."

"Elias, your father is dead."

Way to break it to me gently. "Yes, I heard. I'm in New York now."

"Good. I'm glad they finally called you. I kept telling them it wasn't my problem. That's what a divorce is for."

"What do you mean? When did you find out?"

"I suppose it was a few days ago."

"And you didn't call me?"

"Well, I'm sure that wasn't my job. The lawyer was supposed to get in touch with you. You're his next of kin."

I let out a breath. There was no point arguing with her. "His lawyer called me yesterday. I'll take care of everything."

"See that you do. I don't want any more calls about this."

"You won't."

I didn't bother with any niceties, just ended the call. She'd known for days and she hadn't bothered to call me? Who the hell did that?

My mother, apparently.

Pushing her out of my mind, I left the hotel and took a

cab to my father's building. I'd never been here; he'd been living in an apartment he'd purchased after the divorce. The lawyer—a guy named Diego Ridgeway—had sent me the code to get in, so I didn't wait for him to show up. I took the elevator up to his floor and went inside.

It was cold. I shut the door behind me and checked the thermostat. It was on but set to sixty degrees. I had a flash of memory, hazy from when I was very young. My dad telling me to put on a sweater if I was cold, rather than turn up the heat.

Despite his wealth, he'd always been cheap.

His furniture was old and worn and the walls were bare. Not what most people would have expected from a man whose net worth had to be in the millions.

I wandered around but there wasn't much to see. Nothing on the kitchen counters except a few dirty dishes and an empty bottle of wine. His office was tidy and just as stark as the rest of the house. No photos or artwork on display. Just a laptop and some mail.

The bed wasn't made in the master bedroom. He'd died in there, alone. I didn't go in.

The spare bedroom was empty except for a stack of moving boxes he'd never unpacked. How long had those been sitting there? They were unmarked and I didn't bother looking to see what might be inside.

I heard the front door open, so I went out to meet Diego.

We shook hands and offered the customary introductions. I brushed off his condolences and to his credit, he got straight to business.

"Thanks for coming on such short notice," he said. "I apologize for the delay in contacting you. Apparently there was some miscommunication with your mother."

"You assumed she'd call me and she didn't."

"Something like that."

"With anyone else it would probably have been a safe assumption."

He gestured to the dining table and invited me to join him.

"I'm not sure if your father kept you updated on the details of his estate plan."

"He did not."

"I see." Diego hesitated, tapping the paperwork a few times before continuing. "That's why I wanted to meet with you in person. As the executor of his will, it's my job to make sure his property and assets are distributed according to his wishes."

"Of course."

"And I understand if, given the fact that you're his only child, you assumed his assets would pass to you."

"I take it this means that's not the case."

"No, it's not. His estate is to be split between several women—Cynthia Lopez, Tiffany Park, and Lorelei Oron. Do you know any of them?"

"No."

"It's my understanding your father had a relationship with each of them."

"At the same time?"

"Yes."

"Do they know about each other?"

"They do now. I'm not sure if they did before. But none of them seemed particularly concerned about anything other than the money he left them."

"Unbelievable." I glanced around. "Obviously none of them lived here."

"No. He provided apartments and a stipend for their expenses and they—" He paused as if choosing his words carefully. "They made themselves available to him when he required."

I shook my head slowly. Leave it to Vincent Stoneheart to keep three mistresses rather than having a real relationship with someone.

The news that my father hadn't left me a cent should not have surprised me. But it pierced deep—much deeper than I wanted to admit. It wasn't that I cared about his wealth. That, in and of itself, was a surprising revelation as I let the lawyer's words sink in. I really didn't care about the money. A few months ago, I would have.

What hurt was knowing that he'd left me out on purpose. He'd willed everything he had to his three mistresses, rather than to his only son.

There wasn't much else to say, so I took care of the paperwork from the funeral home. He'd written into his will that he didn't want any funeral services and there didn't seem to be a reason not to respect his wishes. If any of the women wanted to do something in remembrance of him, they could do as they pleased.

Diego left and I wandered through his apartment one last time. In a few days or weeks, it would be emptied, his belongings sold or donated. It wouldn't be long before someone else lived in his apartment, all traces of him gone.

And what traces had he even left? What had he done with his life that was worth remembering? He'd lived a cold and empty existence and now he was gone.

My chest tightened as a stark realization hit me. This was where I was headed.

How much did my condo look like his? Frugal furnishings, minimal decorations, almost no personal touches. Because my life back home was as cold and empty as my father's.

I'd spent the last decade obsessed with success. With hoarding money like a miser. With power and influence and social status. I'd wanted to be seen as someone of importance—someone with power.

But this was where that road led. To loneliness and irrelevance. To a death with no one to mourn. No one to care. And nothing to show for my life except a cold, empty apartment and a number in a bank account.

With an almost frantic sense of urgency, I pulled out my phone. I needed to book a flight. I had to get back to Tilikum. Back to Isabelle.

I had to make things right before it was too late.

33

ISABELLE

*W*ith only a few days before Christmas, I was starting to lose hope.

I'd spent the morning helping my mom catch up on the bookkeeping and the numbers weren't looking good. Between the poor tree harvest, the rising costs of doing business, and our debt level, we were way behind. My belief that if I just worked harder, I could fix the farm's problems was on very shaky ground.

But the season wasn't over yet. We needed someone to cashier at the u-cut farm, so I headed there to take a shift. The little cashier's booth had a space heater, which was good because I'd forgotten my coat at home—again. After making sure there was enough hot cocoa for the afternoon customers, I settled in to sell Christmas trees.

And immediately lost myself in thoughts of Elias.

He'd left two nights ago and I'd only heard from him once—a terse text to let me know he'd arrived in New York. I felt awful about his father. The fact that their relationship had been somewhere between strained and non-existent probably didn't make this any easier. In fact, I wondered if their difficult relationship made the loss harder in a way. There was no more hope of reconciliation or closure. His father was just— gone.

To say I was plagued with mixed feelings would have been an understatement bigger than Santa's toy bag. I was deeply sympathetic to his loss and a part of me hated that he'd gone to New York to handle all the arrangements alone. But I wasn't his girlfriend. That was crystal clear. Whether I was a means to an end or just a convenient distraction, I didn't know. But I'd never wanted to be either of those things.

And I hated that I'd let it happen.

Someone rapping on the window startled me out of my thoughts.

A woman in a hunter green hat and black winter coat held up a tag from one of the trees. "Are you open?"

"Sorry. I was dreaming of a white Christmas, I guess."

She handed me the tag and I rang her up. "Merry Christmas."

"Merry Christmas."

I let out a long breath. That had been slightly embarrassing. I wondered how long she'd been standing there before she knocked on the window.

What I needed was a job that didn't let me spend so much time thinking. I needed to go shovel snow or fix something.

Except I couldn't fix it. I couldn't fix the farm.

I couldn't fix Elias either.

Was that why I'd let him get close again, despite knowing it was probably a mistake? Was I trying to fix him?

Another customer came and thankfully I noticed him right away. I tried not let myself dwell on our slow sales or the disappointing numbers this season. But it was hard. It seemed as if my brain wanted to fixate on either my confused feelings about Elias, or the imminent doom of our farm and Christmas Village.

Neither were particularly happy topics.

As if my mom could read my mind, she came out to take a shift. I hugged her and told her how much I appreciated it. I'd started to feel like I might go crazy if I had to stay shut up in the booth for much longer.

I walked down the path through Christmas Village, past the cute shops and decorations. The walkways had been cleared and the snow piled up on the sides added to the festive ambiance. I wandered by the ice skating penguins, the decorated trees, the wreaths and bows and candy canes.

Was Elias right about this place? Was it a waste of resources?

It did take up a lot of space. My parents had expanded the village over time, adding more shops and inviting new vendors to sell their holiday items. Santa's Workshop always had a steady stream of customers, people bringing their kids or pets—or both—for photos. But was it enough to offset the cost of the building? The electricity? The maintenance?

I walked through the village, looking at everything with calculating eyes. Was this place really worth it? What was I fighting for?

Maybe my parents were right and tearing it all down was the only way. What was the alternative? If we lost the farm, we lost everything.

I found myself in the reindeer barn. Several of the animals were in their pens. Lolly, one of our females, stuck her nose out over the gate, hoping for attention. I leaned against the slats and stroked her soft fur.

"Where would you go, if we had to find you a new home? You're all part of our family. I can't imagine losing you."

She bobbed her head as if to say she agreed, although she really just wanted me to keep petting her.

"What would you do, huh, Lolly? Would you keep fighting or surrender to the inevitable?" I left my next question unspoken. *Would you risk your heart for a man who probably couldn't love you back?*

A gust of wind blew through the open barn doors and I shivered. I needed to go find my coat. It was too cold to be outside in just my long-sleeved shirt and jeans.

"Did you leave your coat at home again?" a man's voice behind me asked.

Not just a man. Elias.

My heart jumped and I turned. "I thought you were in New York."

He was dressed in his wool coat with slacks and black shoes. It was almost strange seeing him in his usual attire again.

"I was. I had to come back."

"Did you get the arrangements made for your father?"

"Yeah, there wasn't much to do."

I nodded, not sure what to say. The instinct to slip into his arms—to hold him and let him hold me—was almost overwhelming. But I held back, hugging myself against the cold.

He unbuttoned his coat and came closer as he shrugged it off. "Here."

I started to protest but he put it around my shoulders. I slid my arms in and let the warmth—and the scent of him—surround me.

"Better?" he asked.

"Thanks."

"Belle, I need to talk to you."

My flight response kicked in. I didn't know if I was ready

to hear what he had to say and it made me want to take off his coat, throw it at him, and leave. Go lose myself in work like I always did.

I started shrugging off his coat. "Not right now. I need to—"

Cole burst into the barn, breathing hard. "We have a missing kid."

I sprang into action, fumbling to find my phone in my back pocket beneath the too-large coat. Kids didn't go missing in the village often, but it had happened, and we had a protocol. I needed to alert the staff, have them monitor the entrance and parking lot, and get a search organized. "Do we have a description?"

"It's Thomas Haven."

I stared at him. "Annika's son? My Annika?"

Cole nodded.

My heart started to race. "Where was he last seen? What's he wearing? I need details."

He filled me in and I called my mom, then a few of our seasonal workers. Cole left to make sure someone was watching the entrance and to search the parking lot.

"I need to go find Annika," I said, pocketing my phone. "She must be losing her mind."

"Let me help," Elias said.

No matter what was happening—or not happening—between us, I wasn't about to turn him down.

"Let's go."

I took off at a jog into the village with Elias beside me.

We stopped to alert the vendors along the way and see if anyone had seen Thomas. No one remembered seeing him, except Doris Tilburn. She'd sold his grandparents a cookie for him but she hadn't seen him since.

I found Annika with Levi Bailey, outside the Peppermint Parlor.

"Annika," I called to her as I approached. "I have the staff checking the parking lot and watching the entrances. Any sign of him?"

"Not yet."

The poor thing looked terrified, although when her gaze moved to Elias, her eyes widened with surprise.

"Is that?"

I sighed. "Don't ask."

"Elias Stoneheart," he said, nodding to Annika.

"I remember."

"We've alerted the employees. They're watching the entrances and keeping an eye out for him throughout the village itself," I said, realizing I was more or less repeating myself. But I was frazzled. "But so far, no one remembers seeing him except Doris Tilburn who sold your mom the cookie."

Josiah, Luke, and Zachary Haven—three of Annika's brothers—arrived followed closely by two of Levi's brothers, Logan and Gavin Bailey.

Tension surged through the small group. These two families did not like each other and I wondered how both sets of brothers were dealing with the imminent marriage of Annika and Levi.

Not very well, by the looks on their faces.

"We looked over by the reindeer barn, but we didn't see him," Logan said.

"We checked everywhere they sell cookies or candy," Zachary said. "He wasn't there."

"Or at least he wasn't when we looked," Luke said.

"Good point," Levi said. "If he's on the move, it's going to make this harder."

"Find him yet?" Another Bailey brother, Asher, joined the group. He had his young son in a baby carrier on his back and another of the Baileys, Evan, was with him.

"Not yet," Levi said.

Two more Haven brothers arrived—Garrett and Theo—asking questions before they'd come to a stop. Voices rose as everyone tried to ask more questions or offer explanations. I tried to cut in with suggestions of places to look for Thomas, but no one seemed to be listening to anyone else, least of all me.

Levi stepped into the middle and raised his voice. "We need a plan."

"Who the fuck put you in charge?" Zachary asked.

"Who cares, dickhead," Gavin said. "He's not wrong."

Elias groaned, as if the situation were pissing him off, but before he could say anything, Levi spoke up again.

"Knock it off."

Everyone froze and I had a feeling we were all wondering the same thing. Were the Havens and Baileys going to go at each other, right here in Christmas Village?

Elias slipped his arm around my waist and gently drew me back, as if to keep me out of harm's way.

"This isn't about the goddamn feud," Levi said, his voice full of authority. "We need to find Thomas."

Josiah Haven met his eyes and gave him a solemn nod. "What's the plan?"

"Let's divide the village into sections and split up. Call me or Annika if you find him or find anyone who thinks they've seen him. Isabelle, you know this place better than anyone. Divide us up."

A sense of resolve poured through me. "Okay, Garrett and Theo, take the parking lot. Luke and Zachary, double check the shops. Josiah, you should go with them. There are a lot of places a little guy could hide. And don't forget to check Santa's workshop. Logan and Gavin, go back to the reindeer barn, but don't try to ride one."

Everyone's eyes moved to Gavin. He'd climbed onto one of the reindeer when he was a kid and ridden it straight through the village.

"What?" he asked. "I wouldn't do that, I'm totally mature now."

Asher snorted.

"Asher and Evan, take the north section of the tree farm," I continued. "Levi and Annika can take the south section. The quickest way is down that path." I pointed. "Elias and I will head for the main house, in case he wandered out of the village itself."

"I don't know where Mom and Dad are, but if anyone sees them, tell them what we're doing," Annika said.

"Okay, people," Levi said. "Let's find Thomas."

Everyone broke off, heading for their section of the village or surrounding area. Elias and I went straight for my parents' house, slowing to search more carefully as we got closer.

"Thomas!" I called, making sure to check around the larger trees where a little boy could hide. Although there was so much snow, I didn't think he would have waded through it.

"Thomas, are you out here?" Elias's voice boomed.

"He's only two. How far could he get?"

"Maybe not far on his own, but someone might have taken him."

My stomach went queasy at the thought. "I hope that didn't happen. That's horrifying."

"There are awful people in the world."

I knew he was right, but it was hard to believe something

that terrible could happen in our sleepy little town. Especially at Christmas Village.

We got to my parents' house, but there was no sign of him. No little boy footprints in the snow, nothing. I called my mom and then Cole to see if they'd made any progress, but they hadn't found him. No one seemed to have seen anything and there was no evidence of a two-year-old boy anywhere. It was like he'd disappeared into thin air.

My stomach felt even sicker.

Elias and I kept looking and my sense of dread grew. We didn't say anything and I was grateful he didn't try to minimize what was happening. My best friend's child was missing and it was very possible something unthinkable had happened. The last thing I needed was him telling me everything was going to be okay.

Finally, the call came in. Levi and Annika had found him.

I breathed out a heavy sigh of relief, although I still felt like I might puke from the stress. I passed on the message, making sure Cole, my parents, and the rest of the staff knew Thomas had been located.

Elias looked at me as I put my phone away and the look in his green eyes nearly undid me. He opened his arms and I collapsed into them. I probably needed to pull away, keep a boundary between us. But come what may, in that moment, I needed him. I needed his comfort, and his arms had never felt so good.

34

ELIAS

*A*fter the crisis ended and the little boy had been found, we gathered at the Cooks' house. I sat, crowded around the table, with Isabelle, her friend Annika, plus several of Annika's brothers, and Levi Bailey. Faye had brought out hot cocoa and apple cider for everyone, although no one seemed to be drinking it.

Thomas sat in his mom's lap, eating a snack, calm and happy now that he was back with his family.

It was clear someone had taken him but the rest of the story didn't make much sense. He'd been found in a barn outside the tree farm—alone and unharmed. I had no idea why someone would grab a two-year-old kid, bring him out to a barn, and leave him there. Hopefully the police would find out.

I was glad the kid was okay. Although I didn't know him, I remembered his mom from high school, and she'd always been nice. Plus, he was an innocent child. I would have had to have been a monster not to care, regardless of who he was.

"Can we stop pretending like we don't know who did this?" Zachary Haven asked.

"We don't know who did it," Annika said.

"I hate to tell you this," Zachary said. "But your boyfriend just pulled the worst prank in the history of Tilikum."

"I'm her fiancé, and it wasn't me," Levi said. "I didn't have anything to do with it."

"No? How about your brother?" Zachary shot back. "Having another guy with your face is sure convenient. And we already know he was here."

"None of us would ever mess with someone's kid like that."

Zachary and Levi kept arguing. Isabelle nodded to the living room. I understood. We needed to get the kid out of here.

Isabelle reached for Thomas. "How about we go in the other room and watch a movie?"

Thomas lifted his arms. She stood and picked him up.

"Thanks," Levi said.

"No problem," Isabelle said. "We'll be in the next room not listening to the grown-ups act like children."

That almost made me laugh. I ignored the rest of the group—Isabelle was who I cared about now that the kid was safe—grabbed Thomas's snack, and followed her into the other room.

My chest ached a bit at seeing Isabelle with a child in her arms. It was a good look.

He was a cute kid with dark blond hair and big blue eyes —looked a lot like his mom. I didn't know who his biological father was, but the way Levi had protected him today, it was clear who his dad was.

Lucky kid.

Isabelle set him down on the couch and asked him if he wanted more crackers. He shook his head and by the way his eyes drooped, I had a feeling he'd fall asleep in no time.

"Okay, Thomas, do you want to watch a Christmas movie?"

He nodded with a big yawn.

Yep, tired.

I didn't blame him. He'd had a big day.

She turned on the Charlie Brown Christmas show and Thomas curled up on the couch with his head on a red and green plaid throw pillow. In less than a minute, his eyes closed.

I took a seat on the other end of the couch and beckoned for Isabelle to join me. Her eyebrows drew in and she hesitated. I understood why. She didn't trust me. I hadn't given her a reason.

Yet.

"Belle." I dared to use her nickname and reached for her. "Come here."

She let out a breath and although she didn't take my hand, she did sit beside me. It was a start.

I angled myself toward her but she spoke first.

"Thank you for helping look for him. That was scary."

"I'm glad I was here."

"Me, too. Do you think they'll find the kidnapper?"

"I hope so." I took her hand and considered it a win that she didn't pull away. "I really need to talk to you. That's why I came back."

"About what?"

"Everything." I hoped she understood the gravity of that word. I meant it. From what we'd been through in our past, to the years we'd spent apart, to what was happening between us now, to what I desperately hoped we could have in the future—we needed to talk about it all.

The lights from her parents' Christmas tree glimmered in her eyes. The hope in them made my chest tighten. But she didn't need to worry. I wasn't going to let her down. Not anymore.

"Ever since I left Tilikum after high school, I've been chasing the wrong things. I thought I needed to prove myself and that money was the only way to do that. Do you remember what you said to me the first time I came back to the farm?"

"To leave and never come back?"

"Probably. But you also said I wasn't happy. And you were right. I didn't even realize how unhappy I was. But I was miserable. It wasn't just because I'd let greed drive me for so long, although that was part of it. I was miserable because I didn't have you."

"Don't," she said, her voice almost a whisper. "Don't do this unless you mean it. My heart can't take it."

I leaned closer and pressed my palm against her cheek. "I mean it. I love you, Belle."

She gasped. I didn't wait for her to reply. Just surged in and kissed her.

The feel of her mouth on mine was like a soothing balm—such sweet relief. I kissed her softly, savoring her lips.

Without warning, she jerked away and jumped to her feet. Levi and Annika stood in the doorway. I'd been too absorbed in her to notice.

I licked my lips. Annika gaped at us but Isabelle gave her friend a quick shake of her head. Levi's mouth twitched as if he were holding back a smile. He tipped his chin to me and gathered Thomas into his arms. The poor kid didn't even stir, just rested his head on Levi's shoulder as he carried him out with Annika beside him.

They did make a cute family.

"Sorry," Isabelle said. "I'm just kind of overwhelmed right now."

I got up from the couch. "How about we go for a walk? You'll feel better if you're moving."

"Yeah, that would be good."

I insisted she wear my coat while we walked to her house to get hers. The temperature was dropping as the sun set and by the time we were both bundled against the cold, it was dark.

We wandered down the path toward Christmas Village and I took her hand in mine. We passed people admiring the lights, doing last-minute shopping, and soaking up Christmas spirit. Maybe I was imagining it, or maybe it was just being with Isabelle, but there was a peace in the air that was almost palpable.

Despite that sense of peace, I still felt an urgency to talk to her. It seemed like so much had happened in such a short time. I had clarity in a way I'd never experienced before.

"I've realized a lot of things since I've been back in Tilikum," I said, breaking our brief silence. "And one is that I can't escape my past. I can't ignore it either. Harvey Johnston was right, the past always catches up."

"Harvey?"

"Never mind. What I mean is, I need to face what happened to me when I was a kid. And more importantly, what happened between us."

I felt her stiffen. It was a painful subject for both of us but we'd never truly addressed it. And that had been our downfall.

"I wanted our baby," I said. "We were too young and it

felt like having a baby was going to mess up all our plans for the future. But I still wanted it."

"You did?"

"I never told you, but on Christmas Eve, when you told me we'd lost the baby, I'd been planning to propose."

"Oh, Elias. I never wanted you to settle for me just because I got pregnant."

"No." I stopped and gently took her by the arms so she was facing me. "No, Belle. I wasn't settling. I wanted you."

"Then why didn't you tell me?"

"I thought you were relieved that you weren't going to be stuck with me. I didn't think I was good enough for you."

"Why would you have thought that?"

I glanced down at the ground. "It felt like you just wanted to move on. We lost the baby and you just— went to work. And I was too young and stupid to see the truth. That you were hurting and that was how you coped."

"I was so sad that day." Her eyes glistened with tears. "Not just that day, but for months afterward. You're right, every time I felt sad, I found something to keep me busy. And you thought that meant I didn't want you anymore?"

"Yes. That's exactly what I thought."

She shook her head slowly. "I thought you didn't want me anymore. I thought *you* were relieved to not be stuck with *me*. I started avoiding you because I didn't think you wanted to be with me anymore. And then you left town as soon as you could after graduation and I thought I'd been right all along. You'd never really wanted me."

My chest felt like it was caving inward with the weight of what I'd done to her. "I'm so sorry. I had all these feelings and I had no idea what to do with them. I didn't know how to cope. I should have just told you."

"I should have done the same. I should have told you how hurt I was instead of trying to bury it all in work."

"Tell me now. Tell me everything."

She took a deep breath. "When I found out we'd lost the baby, I was devastated. But then I felt like I shouldn't be. We were too young and having a baby was going to change everything. Suddenly we weren't, but I was so sad. And afterward, it seemed like our relationship unraveled so fast. We stopped spending time together and when we did, we barely talked. Instead of trying to work through it, I started avoiding you. I didn't realize how that must have made you feel."

I steeled myself for what I needed to say. This was going to be hard to admit. "I thought you wanted to be rid of me. Like my parents. But that's no excuse for what I did. You buried your feelings in work, but so did I. Not just in work, but in ambition."

She reached up and placed her hand on my cheek. "You just wanted someone to love you."

"I didn't give you a reason to love me. I'm so sorry."

"I'm sorry, too. You were really going to propose that day?"

I nodded. "I had a ring in my pocket."

Tears broke free from the corners of her eyes. "I had no idea."

"I know. It's another thing I should have told you. Maybe I should have proposed anyway. It would have saved me from wasting a lot of time."

She smiled. "Everyone would have thought we were crazy."

"Probably. People will say we're crazy now, but I'm tired of worrying about what other people think. For years that's all I've cared about. I wanted everyone to think I was successful and important, but it doesn't mean anything. People feared and respected my father but he died alone. His life was so empty." I let out a breath. This was going to be a difficult truth to say aloud, but I knew I needed to say it. "I always thought he didn't care about me because I wasn't good enough. But the truth is, he was hollow. He couldn't give me what he didn't have."

"That's so sad."

"It is. I thought I hated him, but after seeing the emptiness of his life, I feel sorry for him. And Belle, I don't want to end up like him. I don't want to waste the rest of my life on pointless ambition. What good is the corner office if I'm alone? If I don't have you?"

She put her arms around my neck as I leaned down to kiss her. Relief poured through me. I could have missed this. I could have left her behind and died alone, hollow just like my father.

But that wasn't going to happen now.

She pulled away and smiled. "I'm glad you came back."

"Nothing could have kept me away."

"What a day." She took a deep breath. "I guess all's well that ends well. Now if I could just find a way to save the farm."

The corner of my mouth turned up. "Let me see if I can help with that."

35

ISABELLE

Two days before Christmas and the weather was perfect. Light snow fell on Tilikum, just enough to create the perfect holiday ambiance in the village. Tiny flakes drifted through the air, Christmas lights sparkled, most of our pre-cut trees had sold, and Doris Tilburn had brought in a batch of cookies that made the entire village smell like gingerbread.

Maybe things were starting to look up.

Elias and I had jumped into the farm's finances the day before, looking for solutions that didn't involve either losing the land or closing Christmas Village. He was still working, creating spreadsheets and charts with projections and forecasts. I focused on closing out the season on a high note and keeping morale up. Rumors had spread through town that we might close, so I did my best to counter those with assurances that we'd be back next year, with our usual abundance of Christmas cheer.

And I meant it.

For the first time in weeks, I had real hope that we'd figure this out.

It probably helped that I was floating on a sparkly holiday cloud of happiness, my heart full because I was in love.

So in love.

And he was in love with me.

Best Christmas present ever.

Everything had changed since Elias had come back from New York. The ice in his eyes had melted and we'd finally faced the heartbreak of our past. Facing it together, with honesty, had gone a long way toward healing those old wounds. There was still work to be done—trust to be built —but we had love.

That meant we had everything.

In the meantime, we had to find a way to save the farm.

I came back to my parents' office, where Elias was hard at work, to see if he wanted to break for lunch. He sat at my mom's messy desk, his eyes intent on the computer screen. I wound my arms around his shoulders and kissed his neck.

"Do you know what these payments are?" he asked, pointing to a list on the screen.

I looked over his shoulder. "That's probably the private loan my dad took out."

He winced.

"What? Is it bad?"

"The interest rate is sky high and they've already missed a lot of payments. According to the loan document they drew up, there's a balloon payment due soon."

My shoulders slumped. "Dad failed to mention that part."

"Not until next year, but it's a lot of money."

"Just when I thought the news was getting better."

He turned and took my hands. "Don't worry. I have some ideas."

I pulled up a chair and we went over our options—debt consolidation, potential farm subsidies, even the possibility of bringing in an investor. He'd looked at where we had inefficiencies and could improve and come up with ideas for how to bring more income to the farm without the need for big up-front investments.

He'd thought of things we hadn't, his outside perspective and knowledge giving him insights we'd missed. Overall, it looked great. We'd need to review it all with my parents, and do a little more research into the specifics, but it was the beginning of a solid plan.

"My parents need to see all this," I said.

"It's not foolproof, and I can't guarantee it'll be enough, but I think there's hope."

I smiled. "Hope is what we need. Thank you. And speaking of hope, let's hope your boss doesn't find out about this."

He waved off my concern. "Don't worry about him. I'll deal with it. Let's go talk to your parents."

We found them downstairs in the kitchen. They'd probably come in for lunch—they'd both taken off their coat and boots—but they sat at the table without any food in front of them.

Something was wrong. I could feel it in the air.

"What's going on? Is everything okay?"

Dad cast a worried glance at Mom. "I just spoke with the lender, the one who gave us the private loan."

"Dad, I know about the balloon payment. It's okay, Elias and I figured it out. If we can just—"

"Izz," he said, his voice serious, and I closed my mouth. "I appreciate that you tried, but it's over."

"What do you mean, it's over?"

"Even if we could make that balloon payment, which we

can't, it doesn't matter anymore. Someone else is buying out the loan."

My brow furrowed. "I don't understand. Who would buy out your loan?"

"DataStream. Or they will unless we can pay it in full by the first of the year."

"What? That's crazy. It's not due yet. They can't do that."

"Unfortunately, they can. It's in the terms that they can sell the loan to another party. There's nothing we can do about it."

"He's right," Elias said. "I read the loan agreement."

My heart sank. "So this is it? There's nothing we can do?"

Elias shook his head. "I don't get it. Buying out that loan will effectively get DataStream your land, but it's going to cost more and take longer. I sent my boss a proposal for a different piece of property that's arguably better than this one and he flat out refused. I don't know why he's so fixated on your farm."

"I do," Mom said softly.

"You do?" I asked. "What are you talking about?"

She sighed and Dad reached over to take her hand. "Your boss, Nigel Ferguson?"

"What about him?" Elias asked.

"I knew him a long time ago—in college. In fact, he and I were something of an item."

I gaped at her. "Wait, what? Are you saying you used to date Elias's boss?"

She nodded. "He was very charming and ambitious. But he wanted a different life than I did. I was young, but I was smart enough to realize we didn't have a future. I broke up with him and soon after, I started dating your father. Our romance was something of a whirlwind and before long, we were married. Nigel didn't take it well."

Dad snorted. "That's an understatement. I put a fist in his face once, I'll do it again."

I couldn't believe what I was hearing. "You hit him?"

"He started it. I just finished it."

Mom's lips twitched in a grin, although she tried to hide it. "Nigel confronted your father in some sort of caveman attempt to win me back. It didn't go well for him."

"And now all these years later he's trying to steal your farm?"

"To be fair, he's trying to buy it," Mom said.

"Let's not argue semantics," I said. "You're telling me this whole time Elias's boss has been trying to get back at you for breaking up with him and marrying Dad? And you never said anything?"

"It's not something I wanted to brag about," Mom said. "It was a tumultuous time in my life that I wanted to leave behind. I hoped we could settle this without losing the farm and without you ever having to know."

"No wonder he's been so fixated on this piece of land," Elias said. "And it means this is personal. He won't walk away."

The back door opened and Cole came in. "We have a problem."

"Another one?" I asked. "Just add it to the list."

"This one needs to go straight to the top. Burl Sanderson just called and said he can't be here for more Santa photos and he won't be at the Christmas Eve bash."

"Is he okay?"

"He's fine. He said it's on account of the Lyme disease outbreak among the reindeer."

"I'm sorry, what? The reindeer don't have Lyme disease. What's he talking about?"

"He heard they do and apparently enough people are saying it, half the town already believes it."

"Who would start telling people the reindeer have Lyme? That's not even how Lyme disease works."

"I have no idea. But people around town are talking about skipping the Christmas Eve bash and not just because of the reindeer. In the last day or two I've heard people say it was canceled, that half the shops burned down in a fire, and that the Baileys and Havens are planning a feud battle and everyone needs to stay home. I swear, it's like there's someone spreading rumors on purpose so the bash won't happen."

"Who would—" I stopped and met Elias's eyes. "Damien. And in this town, it wouldn't take much to get rumors spiraling out of control. Do you think Nigel put him up to it?"

"He could have, hoping to make the farm fail publicly."

"Either way, this is bad. We need to figure out damage control." I started ticking things off on my fingers. "We can post to the community page online. Put up posters and hand out fliers. Maybe get some quick postcards printed and ask businesses to put them out on their front counters."

"I can whip up some posters," Mom said, although I could tell her heart wasn't in it.

"Good," I said. "That's a start."

Dad said he'd help and Cole offered to do what he could to counter the rumors. But it felt like it was all going to be too little, too late.

Elias and I left and headed for my house. I felt so defeated. Just when I'd thought we were getting somewhere

—like maybe my Christmas miracle was about to happen—
it had all come crashing down.

I was still hungry, so I wandered into the kitchen. Elias
went back to the bedroom and came out a few minutes later
with his suitcase.

"What's going on?"

"I have to go back to Bellevue."

"Now? Tomorrow is Christmas Eve."

"I know but I have to take care of some things that can't
wait. Work stuff. Trust me I wouldn't leave now if I didn't
have to."

I couldn't blame him for trying to salvage his job nor
could I expect him to commit career suicide over the farm.
The fight was over. It made sense for him to try to secure his
job before it was too late.

Still, I was disappointed. I didn't want him to go.

"When do you think you'll be back?"

He laid his palm against my cheek. "As soon as I can. I
promise."

I nodded. He kissed me and we said goodbye. And my
last hope that I could save our farm melted away, like a
snowman in the sun.

36

ISABELLE

I woke up Christmas Eve not feeling very Christmassy. I wasn't usually one to succumb to pessimism, but I was feeling pretty defeated.

It didn't matter how hard I worked, I couldn't save the farm.

DataStream, and Nigel, would get what they wanted. Next year, instead of a festive village filled with Christmas cheer, there would be a cold, impersonal data center filled with racks of blinking servers. My parents would lose the farm they'd spent a lifetime building and I'd lose the only home I'd ever known.

The home I'd always loved so much.

It was hard to motivate myself to get moving. Christmas Eve was the last big day of the village and the Christmas Eve bash was the culmination of Tilikum's holiday celebrations. It was usually the best part of the year. After working so hard all season, we'd finally get to enjoy the festivities ourselves, celebrating the holiday with our community.

But I had a feeling this year's bash was going to be disappointing and sad, thanks to the hijacking of the Tilikum gossip line. The small crowd would be another in-the-face reminder that I'd failed.

I wasn't looking forward to it.

Still, I got up. Staying in bed all day wasn't going to help. I'd put on my big girl panties and get to work. Whether or not anyone came to the Christmas Eve bash, Horace and the reindeer needed to be fed and pastured, walkways needed to be cleared, and a myriad of other chores needed to be done.

It was late afternoon before I stopped moving. Elias wasn't back yet—and I hadn't heard from him—so I decided to find my parents to see how they were doing.

They were at home, in the kitchen. I paused at the back door and watched them for a moment. The way they moved around the kitchen together was so familiar. So sweet. It gave me a little bit of hope that they would be okay. No matter what this next season of life threw at them, they had each other.

I opened the door and the scent of sugar cookies wafted out to meet me.

Mom turned with a smile. "Merry Christmas."

"Merry Christmas," I said. "It smells great in here."

"Cookies make everything better," Mom said. "Especially when it's Christmas."

"You don't see me arguing," Dad said. He took a drink of water from a tall glass. He'd recovered well from his fall and thankfully, hadn't been on any more roofs.

"How are you two holding up?" I asked.

"We've been through worse," Mom said.

Dad raised his eyebrows. "Have we?"

She waved off his question. "Sure we have. We'll get through this."

"I wish there was more I could do." I lowered myself into

a chair at the kitchen table. "It would have been nice to at least go out with a bang, but it doesn't look like that's going to happen."

Mom came over and squeezed my shoulders. "You've done everything you could and I'm so proud of you."

"Thanks."

She sat down next to me. "Now, when are you and Elias getting married?"

Dad choked on his water, almost spitting it out.

"What makes you think we're getting married?"

"Aren't you?"

I held up my left hand and wiggled my naked ring finger. "Not that I'm aware of. Annika is the one planning the quickie wedding, not me."

"Not yet."

"Mom, slow down. I'm not totally sure where this is going."

"But you are back together?"

Dad grumbled.

I glanced at him but he didn't elaborate on what his grunt meant. "Yes, we're back together. And that's good for now. We have plenty of time to figure out what the future holds. In case you haven't noticed, we've been a little preoccupied with the farm."

She patted my hand. "See? Things aren't all bad."

"You're really glad I'm back together with Elias? Elias Stoneheart?"

"His last name leaves something to be desired, but you can always hyphenate."

I laughed. "I wasn't referring to his last name."

"I know. Honey, you two were so young and you were faced with circumstances that would be hard for most adults."

"Neither of us knew how to cope with it."

"Of course you didn't."

"He was going to propose. Did you know that?"

She smiled. "No. But I'm not surprised."

"I wonder what life would have been like if he had."

"It's an interesting thought, but don't let yourself get too lost in what might have been. You can't change the past but you can shape your future."

"The present is a gift," Dad said. He came over to rest his hand on Mom's shoulder. "Even when things aren't going your way."

Mom took his hand and smiled up at him. "Always a gift."

"You two are so cute," I said. "You know that, right?"

There was a knock on the back door and Cole stuck his head inside. "There you are. There's something out here you're going to want to see."

My shoulders slumped. "What, now? Did half the village actually burn down or is there an outbreak of reindeer pox?"

"I don't think that's a thing."

"I know, it's hyperbole. What's going on?"

"Just come out to the village."

I stood and pushed in my chair. "I guess we should head over there anyway. Hopefully a few people will show up for the Christmas Eve bash."

"A few is better than none," Mom said.

I had no idea how she was maintaining her cheerful optimism at a time like this. Everything had gone wrong. We couldn't even celebrate Christmas the way we usually did, not with half the town believing we had a disease outbreak or that we'd already closed down. And what were we going to do without anyone to play Santa?

There wasn't anything I could do about any of it now. So I put on my coat and followed my mom and dad out to the village.

In the waning light of dusk, the Christmas lights glowed, glinting off the snow. I felt a pang of sadness as I walked past wreath-clad doors, cheerful bows, and striped candy canes. I'd always wanted to build a shop that looked like a ginger-bread house, complete with a little gingerbread family out front. It would have made a great addition to Christmas Village.

But soon, this would all be gone.

Before the tears gathering in the corners of my eyes could fall, a sound reached my ears. It sounded like music. Like singing.

Were there people singing in the village?

The sound grew as I got closer to the center of Christmas Village and as the path turned, curving around a giant snow globe, the crowd came into view.

And it was huge.

People were packed in, spilling off to the sides of the path, gathering around the Rustic Noel and the Peppermint Parlor, all the way to Santa's Workshop. All the adults, and even some of the older children, held candles, the warm light flickering off happy faces.

And every one of them were singing.

Cole stood with Alice, holding Maddie in his arms. Annika and Levi were there with little Thomas, along with Annika's parents and her brothers. Levi's brothers, and their wives and kids were there, too, although there was a healthy distance between the Baileys and Havens. Doris Tilburn, the baker, stood with Norman Stanley, the fire chief, and his wife. I saw Jack Cordero, the town sheriff, with his wife

Naomi, and Olive Hembree who worked at the hardware store.

So many familiar faces. It looked like the entire town, and then some, were here.

Their song, *Santa Claus is Coming to Town*, filled the air, and it was all I could do not to burst into tears.

"How?" I asked no one in particular.

Mom and Dad drew me between them and held me tight. They didn't say a word, or answer my question. Maybe we were all too awestruck to speak.

Right as the song ended, Burl Sanderson came out, dressed as Santa Claus in his deep red suit and shiny black boots. He let out a hearty ho, ho, ho, and the crowd erupted with cheers and applause.

"I thought he wasn't coming," I said.

"It looks like he changed his mind," Dad said.

Mom leaned closer. "Or someone changed it for him."

The crowd parted in the center and Elias Stoneheart, my Grinchy Scrooge himself, came out, dressed in the worst—hence, the best—ugly Christmas sweater I'd ever seen.

He even had a Santa hat on his head.

"What's going on?" I asked as he approached.

Mom and Dad stepped away, as if to give us a moment of privacy. Santa stirred up the crowd and got them singing a new song—*Walking in a Winter Wonderland*.

Elias touched my face and leaned down to place a soft kiss on my lips. "Merry Christmas, Belle."

"Merry Christmas."

"Do you like it?"

"Did you do all this?" I asked, gesturing to the crowd.

The corner of his mouth lifted. "I might have had some-thing to do with it."

"I thought you left to go take care of work stuff."

"Oh, I did. But I came back this morning and set to work on damage control."

"How did you convince everyone to be here?" I asked. "I thought the whole town was afraid of a disease outbreak or something."

"They were. But Cole and I spread the word that Damien Barrett was an evil suit out to cancel Christmas by buying the Cook Family Farm and shutting down Christmas Village. That got the town nice and riled up."

"And it's actually true."

"I guess not all rumors are false. Although I did leave out the part where I'm the Grinch. Or is it Scrooge?"

"Neither in this outfit." I ran my hands up his chest. "This sweater is horrible. I love it so much."

"I'm taking it off as soon as possible."

I laughed. "Thank you. This is the best Christmas present I could have hoped for."

"This isn't your present."

"It's not?"

He shook his head. "I have something even better. I was going to wait until morning so I could put it under the tree, but I think I need to give it to you now."

My heart started to race. Was he going to—

He fished an envelope out of his back pocket and held it out.

I tried not to let the disappointment show. Of course he wasn't about to propose. We'd only just gotten back together.

"Go ahead. Open it."

I took the envelope and popped the seal. Inside was a cute card with a little Christmas tree on the front. Inside was a folded piece of paper. I took it out and unfolded it.

"What is this?" I asked. It looked like a contract.

"It's the private loan your dad took out. I paid it off."

My mouth dropped open. "You did what?"

"I couldn't let Nigel get his hands on this place. I'm paying off the second mortgage, too. And the credit cards."

"All the debt is gone?"

"All except the first mortgage, but your interest rate on that is very good and the payment is relatively low. You shouldn't have any problem keeping up with it."

I met his eyes. "How?"

He gave me a sheepish smile. "As Alice would say, I'm cheap. I had a lot of savings. I'll have to sell my condo to cover some of it, but like I said, it was meant to be an investment."

"I can't believe you did this. You saved the farm. You saved Christmas Village."

"You were right about this place." He glanced around at the crowd, now singing *Away in a Manger*. "It matters. It means something. And I wanted to save it for you."

"But all your money? You can't spend all your money bailing us out."

"Actually, I can. Although to be fair, it didn't all go to the farm. Alice needs help paying for Maddie's physical therapy, so I took care of that, too."

"Does your boss know yet? What's he going to do?"

He shrugged. "Doesn't matter. I quit yesterday."

"You quit your job?"

The corners of his mouth lifted. "Do you still love me now that I'm broke and unemployed?"

I threw my arms around his neck and kissed him. "I love you so much."

He put his arms around me and held me close. "I love you, too. I always have and I always will."

Our lips came together and I was vaguely aware of more applause and cheering. And that it was for us.

I laughed, my heart as light as a snowflake.

The sun had fully set and the only lights were from the candles and decorations. The crowd shifted, gathering around an open space for our annual Christmas Eve ritual. Marigold stepped forward and began the first verse of *Silent Night* and with soft, reverent voices, the rest of us joined her.

Dad and Mom stepped forward into the clearing and turned on the lights surrounding our nativity scene.

Elias held me close as we sang in front of the iconic manger scene. My dad had built it before I was born and every year, for as long as I could remember, we lit it up on Christmas Eve and sang the classic Christmas carol.

This year, it meant more than ever. Tears gathered in my eyes and slid down my cheeks. But they weren't tears of sadness or grief. They were tears of gratitude, happiness, and awe. They were tears of love.

Love for my community, for my family, and most of all, love for this man.

It was truly the best Christmas Eve ever.

37

ELIAS

*C*hristmas morning dawned feeling like a new beginning. Notably, I didn't wake up in a bad mood, determined to hunker down by myself and wait out the holiday alone. In fact, I got up early and put the gifts I'd bought under the tree, then made coffee and got started on breakfast, all while humming the Christmas carols we'd sung last night.

Something was definitely wrong with me.

Or maybe something was finally right.

Isabelle got up and we enjoyed our coffee in front of the Christmas tree with a cozy fire crackling in the wood stove. I'd bought her a few token presents—a new tool belt, some Christmas socks, and an ornament for her tree that I thought she'd like. She'd bought me several new flannel shirts, another pair of Carhartt pants, and a stocking cap.

A bright red stocking cap.

It was ridiculous. And I loved it.

We left the wrapping paper and ribbon strewn around the floor and nestled together on the couch.

Isabelle leaned into me and took a deep, contented breath. "This is so nice."

"It is. But we should probably get up and get moving."

"Why? Dinner isn't until later."

"About that. There's been a change of plans."

She leaned away. "What do you mean? I thought we were having dinner with my parents tonight."

"We'll still see your parents, but I arranged something else."

"More surprises?"

"Just a little one, and it's for my aunt and uncle. We're bringing dinner with us and surprising them with it. Cole, Alice, and Maddie are coming, too."

"That's so sweet. They're going to love that."

I hoped so. It was the least I could do.

Plus, I had one more Christmas gift for Isabelle.

THAT AFTERNOON, Isabelle and I drove over to my aunt and uncle's house. They had a cheerful wreath on their door and lights around the windows.

Isabelle had talked me into wearing the ugly Christmas sweater again and she had one of her own. Although, on her, it was cute rather than ugly. She'd worn her hair down and put on a pair of the Christmas socks I'd given her.

She was adorable. And mine.

We parked out front and went up to the door. I knocked and Hattie answered. Her face broke into a wide smile.

"Elias. What are you doing here? Isabelle, hello. It's so lovely to see you."

"Merry Christmas," I said.

"Merry Christmas." She looked between me and Isabelle. "I'm sorry, come in out of the cold."

"I will, but we have a few things to bring inside. Do you mind leaving the door open?"

Her eyebrows drew together. "Sure. Do you need help?"

"No, we've got it."

Isabelle and I went back to the car and started unloading the food. On our way back for our second trip, the rest of the party arrived. Isabelle's parents pulled up, followed by Cole, with Alice and Maddie.

"I hope you don't mind more company," I said as I came in with another load of food. "We didn't want you to have to cook, so we took care of it at Russell and Faye's house."

Hattie touched her hands to her cheeks. "Oh my goodness. Look at all this."

Cole came in, carrying Maddie, with Alice behind him. She helped Maddie with her crutches as Cole set her down.

"Hi, Mrs. Hattie," Maddie said. "Hattie, Maddie. Our names sound like a poem."

"Well hi, sweetheart," Hattie said. "Merry Christmas."

"Merry Christmas. I got a `merica doll. She has crutches like me."

"Isn't that wonderful."

Dale came out from the bedroom, dressed in a worn reindeer sweater. I had a feeling he'd been wearing it every Christmas since I was a kid.

"I didn't know we had guests coming."

"Neither did I," Hattie said. "But they brought dinner."

My aunt and uncle stood next to each other, watching with bewilderment as the activity unfolded. Faye and Russell came in, laden with more food. Russell carried the turkey in a big roasting pan and Faye had a casserole dish. They said a friendly hello before making another trip out to their car for more food. Isabelle came back with pies while Cole and I brought in a few more bags.

Faye took charge in the kitchen, shooing out everyone except her husband. Maddie sat on the couch with my aunt, showing her the doll she'd gotten for Christmas. Alice and Cole sat next to them, their hands clasped.

I moved closer to the tree. It wasn't an ugly tree, like my first Christmas in Tilikum. This one was full, with straight branches and a perfect Christmas tree shape. Many of the ornaments were familiar from my years living here. The garden gnome, the copper heart, the ice cream cone, the little boy on a sled, and the cow that moved its legs up and down if you pulled the tail. There were multicolored glass balls reflecting the lights and red bows tied on some of the branches.

Toward the top, just below the star, was a faded squirrel with a little red hat. The ornament I'd made at school, my first Christmas in Tilikum.

Isabelle sidled up next to me and tucked herself beneath my arm. "Their tree is so pretty. The ornaments look like they tell a story."

"They do."

She was absolutely right, they did tell a story. There was a hockey stick from the time I'd attempted to play ice hockey and a trumpet from my ill-fated year playing in the school band. There were ornaments from the national parks we'd visited over summer breaks and a little handsaw that looked like the one we always used to cut down our Christmas tree. A few I'd made with Hattie when she'd insisted we do crafts together. Others went back in time, from before I'd lived with them. Some looked newer, as they'd added to their collection each year.

"I remember when we made those." Isabelle pointed to the squirrel ornament. "I don't think my mom kept mine."

"I don't know why Hattie kept that one. It's looking pretty sad."

"It's cute. I like that you gave yours a red hat."

The squirrel might have made me feel disconcerted, but somehow I knew they were no longer the heralds of memories and lessons I didn't want to face. I squeezed Isabelle tight and kissed her hair. Life was a journey and I certainly hadn't arrived. But I'd come a long way in facing my demons and realizing what was important.

I had it all, right here.

Uncle Dale handed out glasses of champagne while Isabelle's parents finished arranging the food so we could all dish up.

"I hate to bring this up on Christmas, but do I need to start looking for a new job?" Alice asked.

"I was going to talk to you about that but I wasn't sure if you wanted to talk about work today. You still have a job at DataStream. I made sure of it."

"That's a relief," she said. "I guess. I don't know if I want to keep working there."

"There is an alternative."

Her eyebrows lifted. "What?"

"You could come work for me. Granted, I'm broke and starting from nothing. But I'm pretty sure a few of our clients will come over—enough to get started."

"You're starting your own company?"

I nodded. "And it's going to be based here, in Tilikum. Of course, if you don't want to move here, I understand, but—"

"I'll take it," she said before I could finish.

"I didn't even get to the job description."

"I don't care. I'm in."

I offered my hand. She took it and we shook.

"Mommy, what are you doing?"

She sat and angled herself toward her daughter. "Mommy just got a new job. And that means we're going to move here, to Tilikum. How does that sound?"

Maddie threw her arms in the air. "Yes! Yes, Mommy, yes! Can you marry Cole now?"

Alice's eyes widened. "Oh, honey, that's not— I mean, I don't know if— I didn't—"

"Actually..." Cole stood and pulled something out of his pocket. "I was waiting for the right moment. I guess that's now."

Everyone gasped as Cole lowered himself to one knee in front of Alice. He faced her but also took Maddie's hand in his.

"Alice, I know this is fast, but I love you and I want to spend the rest of my life with you." He turned to Maddie. "Maddie, if it's okay with you, I want to ask your Mommy to marry me."

"Say yes, Mommy," Maddie whisper-yelled.

"Alice, will you marry me?"

"Yes," Alice said, choked up with tears. "Yes, I'll marry you."

I knew I was going to lose her to the farm guy.

Not that I was really going to lose her. And the fact that I was stealing her away from DataStream was like a Christmas bonus.

Cole stood, pulling Alice to her feet, and wrapped her in a tight hug. Then he picked up Maddie and hugged both of them. The rest of us clapped.

Isabelle swiped beneath her eyes and sniffed. "Now that was some Christmas magic."

I couldn't even argue. It really was.

Dinner was served and we all dished up buffet style in the kitchen. After putting the leaf in the dining table, they had just enough room for us all to squeeze in together. The food was delicious and the conversation lively. Before long, we were all stuffed—all except Maddie, who still wanted cookies.

The consensus was to wait for dessert. Hattie turned on a Christmas movie—her favorite, *It's a Wonderful Life*. Everyone settled in to watch, except me and Isabelle. I nudged her toward the back door and took her outside onto the patio. It was cold, with snow flurries whirling through the air, but I wanted a moment of privacy.

"I'm so glad you arranged all this," she said. "It's been the best Christmas I've had in years. Hattie and Dale look so happy."

"They deserve it. They're good people." I brushed her hair back from her face. "I have one more Christmas present for you."

"Oh Elias, no. You've already done so much and I hardly got you anything."

"There's only one thing I want for Christmas." I pulled the box out of my pocket. "You."

Her lips parted and she stared as I opened the box and lowered myself onto one knee.

She squeaked and clapped a hand over her mouth.

"My sweet Belle, will you marry me?"

With her hand still covering her mouth, she nodded. "Yes."

I took the simple gold band out of the box and slid it on her finger. She held it up and her hand trembled.

"This isn't the same ring, is it?"

I stood. "It is."

"You saved it?"

"I never could seem to get rid of it. Now I know why."

"It's so perfect."

I took her hand and turned it, letting the light glint off the gold. "I thought about buying a new one, with a big diamond. That was what I'd wanted to do back then—make sure you had a big rock by our fifth anniversary. But then I realized this is so you."

"I love it. I love it so much and I love you so much. It's like a Christmas miracle. I can hardly believe it."

I scooped her up in my arms and kissed her. "Believe it."

It was a miracle. Not that I'd kept the ring I'd bought all those years ago. The miracle was that I'd been saved from the path I'd been on—saved from an empty life that led nowhere.

My disdain for Christmas hadn't been about the holiday —not really. It had been about the memories I'd associated with it and the loneliness I'd been denying. I'd hated Christmas because it represented everything I'd wanted and hadn't thought I deserved. Community, family, love.

Now I had all three.

Especially love. I'd always loved Isabelle. For too long, I'd tried to freeze out what I felt—the hurt, the shame, the disappointment. The ice around my heart had kept those buried, but they'd also kept out love. And trying to fill the void with greed and ambition had almost led me to ruin. In the end, it would have killed me.

But Isabelle's love—and her sass—had saved me. And that was the biggest Christmas miracle of all.

EPILOGUE

ELIAS

A tap on my shoulder woke me from sleep and I reluctantly cracked an eye open. Sucking in a breath, I jerked awake. There was a face just inches from mine.

"Wake up, Daddy."

My three-year-old daughter, Natalie, stood by the bed, her eyes wide open, a big smile on her face.

"Baby, you scared me," I whispered, hoping not to wake Isabelle. I glanced at the clock. Four-seventeen. "It's too early."

"It's Chwistmas."

I slipped out of bed and took her hand. "It's not Christmas yet. Didn't we tell you Christmas starts at seven?"

"No."

I led her toward her bedroom and lifted her onto her bed. "I guess you can't tell time yet. But Mommy and Daddy are still sleeping."

"No, you'we not."

"Because you woke Daddy up."

"It's Chwistmas."

I had a feeling logic wasn't going to work on her. Not today. I drew back the covers and climbed in her bed. "It's still nighttime. Let's go back to sleep."

She curled up with me, resting her head on my arm. I kissed her hair and tried not to groan when she pressed her cold toes against my leg. This wasn't the first time I'd wound up in Natalie's room in the early hours, hoping to get a little more sleep—and keep her from waking her mommy. Especially since we had baby number two on the way and sleep was precious these days.

Natalie turned over, bent her legs, straightened them, and rolled over again. I waited for her to settle down, hoping her excitement over Christmas wouldn't keep her awake. She'd be a bear to deal with later if she started her day at four in the morning.

So would I, honestly. But with a three-year-old and a very pregnant wife, I'd have to keep my grumpiness to myself.

Besides, it was Christmas. Even I couldn't be a grump on Christmas day. Not anymore.

Finally, she settled down. Her breathing slowed and she seemed to be asleep. I let my eyes drift closed and my body relax.

When I opened my eyes again, light showed through the gap in the curtains, and Natalie was gone.

How had she slipped out of bed without waking me?

I got up to the scent of coffee wafting from the kitchen. I found my wife and daughter in the living room, sitting in front of the Christmas tree. Natalie had her stocking with its candy and trinkets spread out on the floor in front of her. Isabelle sat in an armchair with her legs propped up on an ottoman, her hands resting on her pregnant belly.

"Morning," she said with a smile. "Merry Christmas."

"Daddy!" Natalie jumped up and ran to me.

I scooped her up in my arms and hugged her tight. "Merry Christmas, stinker. Did you wake up Mommy?"

"Not really," Isabelle said. "She came in but I was already awake. The baby was jamming a foot in my ribs."

"Sorry, I wanted to make sure you got some sleep."

"I did. And that's why I had her open her stocking—so you could get a little more rest."

I ran a hand through my messy hair. "Thanks. I needed it."

The months leading up to Christmas had been busy. Good, but hectic. Christmas Village was going strong and with Isabelle so far along in her pregnancy—our baby boy was due in just two more weeks—she had to take it easy. Cole and Alice helped pick up some of the slack and we'd been able to hire another seasonal worker this year, which helped. With the pressure of the farm's debt gone, we'd been able get it back on track, and added attractions that brought visitors in year-round, not just during the holiday season.

My company, StoneTech, had gone through a growth spurt, adding four large clients in just the last several months. I had a small but brilliant team of engineers and developers, plus Alice, and so far, things were looking great. I was busy, but it was satisfying. I liked being the boss, but not because it made me look important or padded my bank account. In fact, I'd been taking a minimal salary and reinvesting all the profits back into the business and my employees. I liked it because I was in control of my own destiny and I could make sure I did right by the people who worked for me.

I put Natalie down and went into the kitchen to pour myself a cup of coffee, then joined my little family in front of the Christmas tree.

"Pwesents?" Natalie asked, her eyes sparkling with excitement.

She was the perfect mix of me and Isabelle—dark hair and green eyes like me and a sweet little nose, mouth, and chin just like her mom.

"Time for presents." I took a quick sip of coffee and put it down so I could find a package for her to open. "This one says Natalie on it. Who could that be?"

"Me, Daddy! Me!" She jumped up and down with her arms in the air.

I handed her the present and she plopped onto the ground and ripped it open. Wrapping paper flew, the bow somehow ended up on Isabelle's foot, and Natalie hugged a fuzzy brown teddy bear to her chest.

"I name him Bear," she declared.

"Not very creative, is she?" I muttered to Isabelle. "Should we be worried?"

My wife laughed. "She's three."

I shrugged and kept going with the presents, handing them out to both my girls. The pile of discarded boxes, bows, wrapping paper, and ribbon grew. But I kind of liked the chaos, especially now that Natalie was a little older. Her excitement over each present was as sparkling as the first.

She waded through the mess and went around to the back of the tree. When she came out, she had a small box that she'd clearly wrapped herself. It was covered with construction paper and what was probably an entire roll of tape, and she'd drawn little hearts in red marker.

"Pwesent for you, Daddy." She handed me the box.

"Wow, thank you." I picked it up and gently shook it. It barely weighed anything. "I wonder what's inside."

"I made it."

"I can't wait to see what it is." I pulled off the tape as best

I could and opened the box. Inside was a piece of thick paper, folded in half. I carefully took it out and opened it.

It was macaroni art, with hard little noodles cemented to the paper by globs of glue. Shapes and scribbles in red and green marker filled the spaces between the pasta.

I had no idea what it was supposed to be. But I loved it.

"That's me." Natalie pointed to a few pieces of macaroni that might have resembled a small person. "That's you, and that's Mommy."

"What's this?" I touched another macaroni glob.

"A puppy."

"We don't have a puppy."

"Santa's bwinging a puppy!"

Alarmed, I met Isabelle's eyes. Dogs were fine—and maybe we'd get a puppy someday—but we were about to have a baby. She stifled a laugh and shrugged, as if to say she had no idea where Natalie got that idea.

"I don't think Santa brought a puppy this year. But maybe someday. And you did get a teddy bear."

"Bear!" She dove into the wrapping paper pile to rescue her toy from the mess. "His name is Boo-Boo."

"I thought his name was Bear."

"No, Boo-Boo."

"That's a nice name," Isabelle said.

"Better than just Bear," I muttered.

I got out a trash bag and took care of the mess while Natalie climbed onto the chair next to Isabelle and played with her new toys. It was still early, so I settled onto the couch with my coffee—not quite so hot, now, but I was used to that—and watched my daughter play.

So much had changed.

It wasn't so many years ago that I would have been holed up in my high-rise condo on Christmas day, irritated at the very existence of the holiday. Now I found myself contemplating whether I wanted to turn on our Christmas playlist or a holiday movie. Our house was decked out with decorations and later, I'd be donning my latest ugly Christmas sweater—one with a great big, smiling Grinch face.

And I'd never been happier.

Every once in a while, I'd look at Isabelle and my chest would tighten with the knowledge of what could have been —what I'd almost missed. I didn't want to ever take that for granted.

Eventually, it was time to start breakfast. Isabelle had baked blueberry muffins the day before, so I went to the kitchen and got to work on bacon, eggs, and pancakes. Before long, there was a knock at the door, and the rest of our holiday chaos began.

First to arrive were Cole and Alice with Maddie. They'd added two more kids to their family—three-year-old Malcom and one-year-old Tristan. Natalie squealed and almost fell off the chair in her quest to show Maddie her new bear. She practically worshipped the ground Maddie walked on and couldn't wait to give Maddie her present—an unwrapped picture she'd drawn of the two of them having a picnic.

Cole helped Maddie get situated on the couch and Natalie proceeded to climb into her lap. At ten going on thirty, Maddie was infinitely patient with her tiny admirer. She still needed her crutches to walk but she'd worked hard to strengthen her muscles and could do almost everything without any help. She was amazing.

Next came Hattie and Dale, both dressed in their favorite holiday attire and bearing more food for our big Christmas breakfast. Faye and Russell arrived shortly thereafter and I was glad I hadn't bothered to turn on music or a movie. It would have been drowned out by the chorus of voices.

When breakfast was ready, we all made our way to the table. Christmas breakfast had become a tradition for our families. The menu varied but there was always an abundance of food, and most importantly of all, an abundance of good company.

We toasted with the mimosas and glasses of juice Alice had poured, wishing everyone a Merry Christmas.

I didn't even have to grit my teeth when I said it.

We ate, drank, talked, and laughed. Alice and Cole's boys made a mess, especially Tristan. Natalie changed her bear's name four times. Maddie told us about her science fair project, my aunt and uncle shared their plans for a vacation in Hawaii, and Faye and Russell were planning to join them.

I looked across the table at Isabelle and not for the first time, I had the thought that right there, in that woman, was everything I'd ever wanted. And celebrating Christmas with her, and with the family we'd gathered around us, it really didn't get any better than this.

Movement outside the dining room window caught my eye. There was a squirrel out there. It sat up on its hind legs, holding some little treasure in its paws, and seemed to look right at me.

The events of my past and the choices I'd made hadn't all been good, or right. My parents had abandoned me, leaving me angry and hurt. Isabelle and I had suffered a loss that would always leave a little hole in our hearts. And I'd spent years of my life chasing wealth and power, obsessed with greedy ambition.

But thankfully, by some miracle, I'd wound up here. I'd been given a gift—the gift of insight. Before I'd done too much damage to my life—and my soul—I'd been offered a second chance.

I'd spent the last five years trying to live up to that chance. To use my life for something more. To love my wife and my growing family—to put them first.

The squirrel bounded away through the snow to race up a tree. I met Isabelle's eyes and smiled. My wife, my love. She was everything. She'd saved me from a bleak and empty future and showed me that I could be loved.

And it was my job to spend every Christmas, and each day in between, loving her right back.

BONUS EPILOGUE
ISABELLE

*C*hristmas Village wasn't just bustling. It was hopping. The Tilikum High School choir had decided to do some spontaneous caroling, filling the air with music. People packed the walkways and the shops were full. We were almost sold out of pre-cut trees and a steady stream of customers were still coming to cut their own. All this after a snowstorm had dumped several feet of snow just days earlier.

It had already been a great season and it looked as if it would end just as strong.

Life was good.

Busy, but good.

I headed back through the village after checking on the u-cut tree lot. Although my parents had technically retired, Dad still liked to help, and he'd been happily chatting up customers, handing out hot cocoa, and helping people pick the perfect Christmas tree. I'd left him to it. As long as he didn't climb on any roofs, I loved still having him around.

My mom was watching our kids so Elias could do some shopping and I could make the rounds through the village to ensure things were running smoothly. So far, so good. There had been some concern about the pipes in the restrooms, but Cole had handled it already. After stopping to listen to the choir sing, I headed home to check on my little ones.

After our son Noah had been born almost two years ago, we'd essentially swapped houses with my parents—at their insistence. They'd moved into the cottage I'd remodeled, glad to be free of the responsibility of upkeep on the larger farmhouse, and we'd moved into my childhood home. Because I'm me and incapable of sitting still, I set to work updating the old house. I loved that we were able to raise our kids on the farm. And with the changes we'd made, and Elias's help, Cook Family Farm was thriving.

Lights twinkled on the porch and a big wreath hung on the front door. My once Grinchy husband insisted on an increasingly elaborate array of decorations, especially as our kids got older and were able to enjoy them. Natalie had made so many ornaments this year, we'd started hanging them on the houseplants because we were running out of room on the tree. But Elias insisted they all be displayed.

He was such an amazing daddy.

I went inside but the house was quiet. Noah's little snow boots were missing from their spot by the back door, as were the kids' winter coats. Mom must have taken them out to play in the snow.

The path from the back door had been cleared and I could see evidence of my kids everywhere. Footprints meandered through the snow in the yard and a group of small snowmen, complete with pebble eyes and carrot noses, stood in a clump. I found my mom further down, following Noah as he played, oblivious to the cold.

"Back already?" Mom asked. "I didn't think we'd see you until later this afternoon."

"I figured I'd come have lunch with you and the kids."

She smiled and I could see the approval in her eyes. Since having Natalie, I'd learned a lot about balance. I couldn't bury myself in work when I had kids who also needed—and deserved—my attention. It wasn't always easy, but Elias and I were doing our best to make our family a priority.

"Mommy!" Noah exclaimed.

Leaning down, I kissed him. "Hi buddy. Are you having fun?"

He awkwardly picked up a bunch of snow in his mittened hands. "Snow!"

"You do love the snow, don't you?" I glanced around, but didn't see my daughter. "Where's Natalie?"

Mom looked behind her. "She was building a snow castle right over there."

I didn't see her but my mischievous little five-year-old might have been hiding behind the pile of snow that was her castle. I went over to where she'd been creating a makeshift wall, but she wasn't there.

"Natalie?"

No answer.

"She was just there," Mom said, a hint of worry in her voice.

"Don't worry. She probably just wandered off in search of sticks or something. Why don't you take Noah inside and I'll go get her."

The back door opened and Elias poked his head out. I couldn't help but smile at his appearance. We'd seen each other just a few hours ago, but the sight of him still gave me butterflies.

He met my eyes and gave me a subtle smile. "I'm home."

Those simple words spread warmth through me, like a cozy fire on a cold day. He was home, in every sense of the word. And for a man like him, who'd never felt truly at home anywhere, it meant more than that he'd just returned from the store.

"Natalie wandered off," I said. "Want to come find her with me?"

A flicker of worry crossed his features. "Where'd she go?"

"I'm sure she's fine. She wanted to build a snow castle, so she probably went in search of sticks or pinecones or something."

Mom picked up Noah out of the snow. His nose and cheeks were pink but he was as happy as could be. "I'll get him in some dry clothes."

"Thanks, Mom. We'll be back in a few."

Elias came outside and paused to kiss his son's round little cheek. Then he took my hand and we headed down the path to find our daughter.

She wasn't supposed to wander off, but she tended to get lost in her games of pretend and forget where she was. I wasn't too concerned. I didn't want her walking through Christmas Village by herself—too many people—but there was enough space between the house and the village, we'd probably find her well before we got to the throngs of customers.

"Natalie," Elias called. "I don't like it when she does this, especially in the snow. Maybe we need to get a herding dog. Could we train it to keep her near the house?"

"Probably. Or we could just move Horace over here. He's the best guard donkey."

He groaned. "No. Horace needs to stay in his barn."

I just laughed.

The noise of Christmas Village carried through the pine trees as we got closer and still no sign of Natalie. For the first time, I started to get a little worried.

"Natalie," I called. "Where did that girl go? She knows she's not supposed to go to the village alone."

"We should still check the Peppermint Parlor. She might be trying to sweet talk them into giving her a candy cane."

"She does love those big ones they carry."

Picking up our pace, we veered toward the village. My heart sank when I saw the crowd. Obviously that was good for the farm, but I couldn't help but remember the year my friend Annika's son Thomas had gone missing. Fortunately, he'd been found unharmed. But it had been a scary experience and the thought of my own daughter going missing filled me with dread.

Elias squeezed my hand, as if he could sense my thoughts. "We'll probably find her sitting on a bench with a giant piece of candy."

"Probably."

A couple went into the Gingerbread House, our newest village shop. It was every bit as cute as I'd hoped it would be, with white trim that looked like frosting and painted gumdrops, peppermints, and other candies everywhere. Annika had taken it on, selling both her own ornaments and décor as well as that of other local artisans. It was quickly turning into the most popular shop in the village.

But no sign of Natalie.

We didn't find her outside the Peppermint Parlor, nor had anyone inside seen her. My heart started to race as we came out of the shop. Where had she gone?

Horace brayed in the distance.

"Did you hear that?" I asked.

"What?"

"Horace. I think he's telling us something."

His brow furrowed. "He's probably just being an ass."

I heard the donkey's bray again. "No, I really think he's trying to tell us something."

Tugging on Elias's hand, I turned us toward the barn. We picked our way through the crowd and Horace brayed yet again. Something was definitely going on. He didn't usually make so much noise.

When we got to the barn, Horace wasn't in his pen. Had someone let him out? He shouldn't have been out of the barn this time of day.

He brayed again and the noise came from outside where some of our reindeer herd were grazing while village guests watched.

"Who let him out there?" I asked no one in particular.

We went out to the enclosure and sure enough, there was Horace. He stomped one of his front hooves into the dirt and dipped his head.

"What's up, big guy?" I asked. "What are you doing out here?"

"Hi, Mommy!"

On the other side of the enclosure was my daughter. On a reindeer.

I gasped. Elias was already on his way to her. He reached her and helped her down off the reindeer's back.

"Natalie, what are you doing?" I asked.

"Buckwheat gave me a ride," she said, her green eyes bright.

"You're not supposed to ride the reindeer."

Her face fell. "I'm not?"

"No, of course not."

"Why?"

Buckwheat snorted as if to emphasize her question.

"Because it's not safe. They're not meant for riding."

Elias leaned closer and spoke softly in my ear. "Have we ever told her not to ride the reindeer?"

That was an excellent question. Maybe we hadn't.

The things you never thought you'd have to say as a parent.

I crouched down. "I'm glad you're okay, but the reindeer aren't for riding."

Natalie's lip protruded in a pout but she nodded. "Okay, Mommy."

"Good." I stood and picked her up. "And you shouldn't have left the house. You know you aren't supposed to be in the village alone."

"This isn't the village," she said, as if that were the most obvious thing in the world. "I walked the long way."

I looked at Elias. Leave it to our daughter to find the loophole. There was a path that went from our house to the barn without going through the village. Apparently we needed to cover our bases more thoroughly with this kid.

"Don't come to the barn by yourself either. You should have asked grandma first. Got it?"

"Got it," she said.

I passed Natalie to her daddy and we made our way back home. Mom was so relieved to see her, she picked her up and hugged her until Natalie giggled and squirmed, begging to be let down. Noah sat at the table, happily eating a cut up sandwich, and happily for us, it was almost his naptime.

We put together a quick lunch and afterward, Mom left to help Dad charm the customers at the tree lot. Elias put Noah down for his nap and I got Natalie set up in her room for quiet time. When the kids were settled, we came back downstairs and plopped down on the couch in front of the Christmas tree.

Elias put his arm around me and I tucked myself against him. He smelled faintly of wood and the clean scent of his cologne. Closing my eyes, I breathed him in, enjoying his closeness. It felt so good to just be with him, basking in the warm glow of the tree.

"I love you," he murmured and kissed my head.

"I love you too." I nestled in closer. "How was your shopping trip?"

"Good. I got a bunch of stuff for the toy drive—probably too much, but I still feel like I'm making up for lost time. I also found that art easel you wanted to get for Natalie and a few things for the little man, too."

"It will be fun watching him open presents this year."

"That's right, last year he just played with the wrapping paper."

"It was cute, though."

"Yeah it was. I got you something, too."

"Ooh, I'm excited." I paused. "What do you want for Christmas this year? I keep trying to think of something but I'm out of ideas. You're so hard to buy for."

"No, I'm not."

"Yes, you are. You always say you have everything you could ever want."

His arm tightened around me. "I do have everything I could ever want."

"But I'd still like to get you a gift."

He kissed my head again. "There is one thing."

"Tell me."

Shifting, he moved so he could look at me. His striking green eyes were full of feeling and he touched my face. "Another baby."

My heart just about burst with love. "Are you serious?"

The corners of his mouth lifted. "Absolutely. And not just so we can have fun trying, although that part is pretty great."

"Even though we're dealing with an escape artist who rides reindeer and an almost two-year-old who's – actually, he's so easy."

"Maybe Noah is lulling me into a false sense of security, but I think we can do it. More importantly, I want to. I want to have another baby with you."

I leaned closer and pressed my lips to his. "I want to have another baby with you, too."

"Then my Christmas wish came true."

Sliding his hands through my hair, he pulled me in for a kiss—deeper this time. His tongue was velvety against mine and my body lit up. Heat raced through my veins, pooling in my core.

Maybe now would be a good time to start trying.

"Mommy?" Natalie's voice came from the top of the stairs.

With a subtle smile, he pulled away.

"I'll be right there," I called.

His eyes were intense, devouring me, and his voice was a low growl. "Tonight."

I nodded, suddenly breathless. "Tonight."

I could hardly wait.

But mom-life called.

Which was fine. We were in a season of life with small children—and hopefully soon a new baby—so we did our best. If anything, the demands of family life made us cherish our alone time even more, precious as it was.

I got up to get Natalie settled and Elias gave me another scorching look, melting me from the inside.

I loved him so much.

And tonight, I was going to show him.

Elias and I had been through a lot to get to where we were. But every bit of it had been worth it. We loved each other, and our children, fiercely. He'd gone from hating the holidays to living the Christmas spirit all year.

He was mine and I was his, and our family was the best Christmas miracle I could have asked for.

DEAR READER

Dear reader,

I'd been wanting to write a Christmas romance for quite a while when I started planning this book. Like a lot of my books (or maybe most of them), this one started with a *what if* question. What if I wrote something inspired by a classic Christmas story?

A Christmas Carol came to mind and I'm sure you could see where I drew inspiration from Charles Dickens. I also drew on some Grinch vibes, mostly for Elias's character.

There's so much to love about the original A Christmas Carol, and I won't pretend my little holiday romance is anything in comparison. But who doesn't love a grump whose heart is melted by a healthy dose of reality, woven in with Christmas spirit and love? That's what I was aiming for with this story.

I love a grump with a heart of gold and that's exactly what we have in Elias Stoneheart. His obsessions are all too common. Money, power, prestige. So many of us can relate, if we really look at ourselves honestly, even if we're not quite as dramatic about it as he is. But there's a wounded little boy inside that Christmas-hating exterior. And his encounters with his past and present, as well as the glimpse into his future, start to crack the ice around his heart, opening him up to the love he's aways carried for Isabelle.

Isabelle spends a lot of her time and energy trying to outrun her problems by working harder. Obviously hard work has its place but she tends to use it as a way to avoid being vulnerable. She can't keep getting away with that when Elias comes back into her life. Fixing a hole in Horace's fence or shoveling straw won't mend her wounded heart.

Fortunately, she and Elias learn to be vulnerable together. Add in the backdrop of Christmas, and I hope this was a heartwarming and satisfying holiday romance for you.

Thanks for reading!

Claire

ACKNOWLEDGMENTS

Thank you to everyone who helped make this book possible.

Nikki, Alex, and all of Team CK, thank you for everything you do!

To Eliza for fitting this little book into your schedule and cleaning it up. And to Erma for your eagle eyes yet again!

To Lori for this adorable cover. I don't think I can gush about it enough. It's so perfect.

To all my readers for your support and love. You're the best readers in the world!

And to my sweet family, Merry Christmas and may the blessings of the season be upon you now and all the days of your life.

ALSO BY CLAIRE KINGSLEY

For a full and up-to-date listing of Claire Kingsley books visit
www.clairekingsleybooks.com/books/

For comprehensive reading order, visit www.
clairekingsleybooks.com/reading-order/

The Haven Brothers

Small-town romantic suspense with CK's signature endearing
characters and heartwarming happily ever afters. Can be read as
stand-alones.

Obsession Falls (Josiah and Audrey)

The rest of the Haven brothers will be getting their own happily
ever afters!

How the Grump Saved Christmas (Elias and Isabelle)

A stand-alone, small-town Christmas romance.

The Bailey Brothers

Steamy, small-town family series with a dash of suspense. Five
unruly brothers. Epic pranks. A quirky, feuding town. Big HEAs.
Best read in order.

Protecting You (Asher and Grace part 1)

Fighting for Us (Asher and Grace part 2)

Unraveling Him (Evan and Fiona)

Rushing In (Gavin and Skylar)

Chasing Her Fire (Logan and Cara)

Rewriting the Stars (Levi and Annika)

The Miles Family

Sexy, sweet, funny, and heartfelt family series with a dash of
suspense. Messy family. Epic bromance. Super romantic. Best read
in order.

Broken Miles (Roland and Zoe)

Forbidden Miles (Brynn and Chase)

Reckless Miles (Cooper and Amelia)

Hidden Miles (Leo and Hannah)

Gaining Miles: A Miles Family Novella (Ben and Shannon)

Dirty Martini Running Club

Sexy, fun, feel-good romantic comedies with huge... hearts. Can be
read as stand-alones.

Everly Dalton's Dating Disasters (Prequel with Everly, Hazel, and
Nora)

Faking Ms. Right (Everly and Shepherd)

Falling for My Enemy (Hazel and Corban)

Marrying Mr. Wrong (Sophie and Cox)

Flirting with Forever (Nora and Dex)

~

Bluewater Billionaires

Hot romantic comedies. Lady billionaire BFFs and the badass heroes who love them. Can be read as stand-alones.

The Mogul and the Muscle (Cameron and Jude)

The Price of Scandal, Wild Open Hearts, and Crazy for Loving You

More Bluewater Billionaire shared-world romantic comedies by Lucy Score, Kathryn Nolan, and Pippa Grant

~

Bootleg Springs

by Claire Kingsley and Lucy Score

Hot and hilarious small-town romcom series with a dash of mystery and suspense. Best read in order.

Whiskey Chaser (Scarlett and Devlin)

Sidecar Crush (Jameson and Leah Mae)

Moonshine Kiss (Bowie and Cassidy)

Bourbon Bliss (June and George)

Gin Fling (Jonah and Shelby)

Highball Rush (Gibson and I can't tell you)

~

Book Boyfriends

Hot romcoms that will make you laugh and make you swoon. Can be read as stand-alones.

Book Boyfriend (Alex and Mia)

Cocky Roommate (Weston and Kendra)

Hot Single Dad (Caleb and Linnea)

Finding Ivy (William and Ivy)

A unique contemporary romance with a hint of mystery. Stand-alone.

His Heart (Sebastian and Brooke)

A poignant and emotionally intense story about grief, loss, and the transcendent power of love. Stand-alone.

The Always Series

Smoking hot, dirty talking bad boys with some angsty intensity. Can be read as stand-alones.

Always Have (Braxton and Kylie)

Always Will (Selene and Ronan)

Always Ever After (Braxton and Kylie)

The Jetty Beach Series

Sexy small-town romance series with swoony heroes, romantic HEAs, and lots of big feels. Can be read as stand-alones.

Behind His Eyes (Ryan and Nicole)

One Crazy Week (Melissa and Jackson)

Messy Perfect Love (Cody and Clover)

ABOUT THE AUTHOR

Claire Kingsley is an Amazon #1 bestselling author of sexy, heartfelt contemporary romance and romantic comedies. She writes sassy, quirky heroines, swoony heroes who love their women hard, panty-melting sexytimes, romantic happily ever afters, and all the big feels.

She can't imagine life without coffee, her Kindle, and the sexy heroes who inhabit her imagination. She lives in the inland Pacific Northwest with her three kids.

www.clairekingsleybooks.com

Printed in Great Britain
by Amazon